Sisters Without Mercy

Clarence J. Moore

Writers Club Press
San Jose New York Lincoln Shanghai

Sisters Without Mercy

Published by Writers Club Press
an imprint of iUniverse.com, Inc.

For information address:
iUniverse.com, Inc.
620 North 48th Street, Suite 201
Lincoln, NE 68504-3467
www.iuniverse.com

ISBN: 0-595-10072-4

Printed in the United States of America

Dear Reader,

What better way to start off the new millennium then with a book about the military woman? Her fighting ability and her ability to care about home and family.

This type of woman has a love for her fellowman and a love for her man—once she finds the one who is strong enough to stand up to her. A man who is not afraid of his own masculinity.

Sisters Without Mercy is such a book. There is love and warmth and desire. But it also shows what can happen if you try to tear up this woman's home.

Since this is my first book to be published, it has taken a long time and a great deal of rewriting to get it exactly right.

I hope you will enjoy Sisters Without Mercy as much as I did writing it.

Clarence J. Moore

Acknowledgement

My profound thanks to my mother, Jacquelyn C. Moore, who not only believed in my project but also contributed her time and ideas to the story and by doing all of the editing and rewrite. Thanks again, MOM.

For Dr. Michaelson.

Thank you for Reading my First Book. I hope you enjoy it

Clarence J Moore

Sisters, this is Mother Superior. Pull the plug…

Captain Anthony looked over at Dora and spotted the detonator in her hand. He called in a very loud voice, "Lieutenant."

Dora looked up at the window of the Cambridge Building and smiled. She was showing the detonator in her hand to Todd, Sr. She mouthed the word 'bomb'.

Her finger depressed the button for the big explosion just as the door opened and David exited the building.

Dora was screaming "David" as the building came down.

The Colonel came over to her, shaking her head—"you just had to do it your way, didn't you."

Dora started to shake her head…

Chapter One

"Yea, though I walk through the valley of the shadow of death, I shall fear no evil, for Thou art with me..."

The voice of the minister droned on as he recited the Twenty-third Psalm. Family and friends stood with their heads bowed in somber prayer on what had turned out to be one of the sunniest days of the year amid the gloom and darkness of shattered hearts. They had come to say good-bye to a young man who, in the minds of every one present, had the potential to become a great professional football player. He'd had both good looks and brains and he'd earn the glory heaped upon him from his football exploits. Mark Simmons was a young man who seemed destined to achieve all that he and his family had dreamed he would. Another Walter Payton or Jim Brown, or even O. J. in his heyday. He had been a senior in college, and a shining star—both on the field and in the classroom. Mark had been strong enough to stand up to peer pressure and say 'no' to gangs and drugs.

Hope, Mark's beautiful mother, stood gazing at the casket, wondering, for the hundreth time—or was it the thousandth? why anyone had wanted to kill her handsome son? But here he lay in a bronze coffin and she'd not had an opportunity to see or touch his sweet face again. His body had been too badly burned and mutilated. Hope looked up from the coffin to see her daughter coming towards her across the lawn of the cemetery. Dora made her way through the crowd of mourners and curiosity-seekers to get to her mother and younger brother, Charlie. Even at a time like this, Hope noticed how cat-like her daughter moved. She was lithe and graceful with long-legged strides, her head held high, and her carriage very erect. Also watching Dora was Mark's friend. The friend who was with Mark the night he was killed.

* *

Mark and David were having dinner at their favorite restaurant. They were talking about old times and laughing at some of the stunts they had pulled as kids. David was a few years older than Mark, but from the time Mark was a toddler, he and David had always gotten along. David had always been able to keep Mark out of trouble, but tonight, David sensed that Mark had something on his mind other than dinner.

As a rule, Mark was a very light-hearted, carefree person—gregarious and funny. Tonight he seemed—distant. Finally, David asked, "What's up?"

Mark replied, "Nothing."

"Okay! Can you repeat anything that we've been talking about for the past hour?"

Mark smiled, "You know me too well. I just have a lot on my mind. Relax, I'll be fine."

"Mark, you know you can tell me anything, like always."

"I know." He grinned again. "Cool it, man, you're worse than my sister."

The two friends finished their dinner and left the restaurant. They said good-bye and split up—each going to his own car.

David's phone was ringing as he reached his car. He unlocked the door, and just as he leaned in to pick up the receiver, there was a loud boom, a bright light and the earth moved. The force caused David to fall forward, so it was several seconds before he was able to get up. David looked back over his shoulder towards the light and realized that it was coming from the spot where Mark's car had been parked. He ran towards the flames. There was hardly anything left of the car—or of Mark, that he could see.

It was David's unpleasant duty to inform Mark's family of his death. He was also the one who had to write up the report. As a witness to the tragedy, he knew most of the details except, of course, who planted the bomb and why. As he told his boss, with that type of destruction, there was no doubt it was a bomb, and a powerful one, to demolish the car like that. David was also upset with himself for not pushing Mark a little harder to find out what was bothering him. He, Mark, must have known he was in danger.

David is police Sgt. David Aimsley, a homicide detective for the county of Los Angeles. He had seen many killings since becoming a cop, each one a little more senseless than the last, but this one hit home. He never did understand why people insisted upon killing each other, especially when they were young men like Mark. Why would anyone want to kill Mark? Why wouldn't he tell him what was wrong? Since Mark hadn't seen fit to confide in him, he would have to find out the hard way. But that was okay. Solving cases the hard way was how he managed to make detective before he was thirty.

* *

Dora made her way to her mother. She threw her arms around her and her brother Charlie, holding them close, giving them her strength and drawing from theirs. Dora was in the Army, attached to a special service outfit. Even she thought she would not be home in time for the funeral. She never talked about what she did on these special operations, but the number of medals she had been awarded told a story of their own.

Hope heard the minister saying, "ashes to ashes, dust to dust" and it was over. People gathered around to offer their condolences to the family.

Hope and Dora left the graveside arm in arm. Charlie walked in front with head bowed and his hands in his pockets. No one said anything. There was no need. They each could feel what the other was feeling.

David was standing out in front of the house when the limo pulled up. Hope was the first to emerge. She was glad to see David—he had always seemed like a son to her. Dora was not so happy. She wanted to talk to her mother alone. There was much to find out. So many questions to be asked and answered. Dora wasn't sure her mother had any of the answers, but she wouldn't know until she asked her.

David's eyes lit up as Dora got out of the car. This was the one woman that David was determined to call his own. He'd been in love with her all of his life. Dora didn't quite see it his way. Patience where Dora was concerned was a lesson he had learned early in his dealings with her. He'd wait.

Everyone took a seat on the back porch. No one spoke, not knowing what to say. They wondered how they would gather the strength to get on with the rest of their lives, but knew they would, sooner or later.

David picked up Hope's hand and asked, "Is there anything I can do?" Before Hope could answer, Dora spoke up, "What the hell do you mean, is there anything you can do? Of course there's something you can do. You can do your job. You're the hotshot detective. Find the people who killed my brother. That's what you can do—for all of us."

Hope spoke very softly, "Dora, don't." Dora looked at her mother, instantly contrite. Her mom didn't need this, but she wasn't sorry that she blew up at David. "I'm sorry Mom." She turned her back to David, distress outlined in her very stance.

David knew that it wouldn't serve any purpose to try and talk to Dora at this point. He thought it would be better to leave. Dora, never one to take things lightly, would be very interested in how the investigation was going, but right now she wouldn't even listen. David kissed Hope on the cheek, gave her hand a squeeze and said, "I'll call you." He said "good-bye" to the others and left.

Hope, needing to be active, went into the kitchen to prepare a light dinner—thinking all the while that any moment, her handsome son would come walking through the door and she would wake up to find this had all been a bad dream. A very bad dream.

Dora followed her mom into the kitchen. She needed to talk to her. The last thing she wanted to do was make it harder for her mother to deal with Mark's death, so she was very uncertain as to how to approach the subject.

She heard a noise coming from the back of the house and went to take a look. Her brother Charlie was throwing a basketball threw the hoop—the same hoop that Mark had put up for him. He seemed to be in another world while making basket after basket. Dora was thinking how well he seemed to be handling all that had happened when her mother made a noise. She turned in time to see her mother slip to the floor with her face in her hands, sobbing. She kept saying over and over again, "They killed my baby; they killed my baby."

Dora ran to her mother and sat down on the floor beside her, gathered her in her arms and held her, kissing her and trying to comfort her as best she could. Dora told her mother that whoever was responsible for Mark's death would pay. She made that promise to her mother and to herself with tears streaming from her eyes.

Dora rose early the next morning. She couldn't sleep anyway, and there was a great deal to be done. Finding the person or persons who killed her brother was her number one priority. She'd start her investigation by going through her brother's room. She was not surprised at some of what she found. Some of the stuff Dora had learned since being in the Army would have made her brother blush. Dora found many items that brought back pleasant memories from when they were kids. She was shocked to find all of the letters she had written to her family saved in a box as if they were very special to him. She had always thought that he really didn't care for her being a member of the armed forces, but finding these letters hidden here in his room showed that he was very proud of her. Finding these mementos made her even more determined to find out who killed him and why.

In a locked drawer, which Dora dealt with very easily, she found a file on a U.S. Senator by the name of Thomas Jackson. As Dora read the file, she thought the top of her head would explode. Some of the stuff written in the report made no sense to her, but what she did understand made her wonder if the contents in the report was reason enough for someone to kill her brother.

Reading the file, Dora learned that her brother wasn't just a kid in college trying to make a name for himself. He had been hiding a lot that no one would have ever believed. Mark was an undercover FBI agent. He belonged to a special task force known only to a chosen few.

The file contained information about some of the largest drug and arms deals that had taken place in the last two years. Dora also found a small appointment book listing dates and times. On the inside cover was a series of numbers. She put the little book in her pants pocket and continued to look around the room trying to find anything that would shed some light on what had happened.

Dora sat at her brother's desk and stared at his picture. She asked herself, "What was this kid into? Why would someone in college be an FBI agent? Why undercover and what did a U.S. Senator have to do with the picture?" None of this made any sense yet, but she knew if anyone could figure it out, she could. Dora heard her mother calling. She put the folder away and went to see what she wanted. She would come back later to continue her search. But first, she must see to her mother.

Hope was standing at the back door looking out at the big tree that had withstood so many, many storms over the years when Dora found her. "What's up, Mom?"

"Nothing. I just wondered where you were? I was standing here looking at the old tree out there and wondering why people can't be like that old tree—able to withstand whatever nature throws its way."

Dora hugged her and asked if she would like to go for a walk with her?

"I don't think so, darling. Why don't you go?"

Dora said, "OK, but I think I'll go for a run instead. You sure you wouldn't like to come for a walk? Fresh air will do us both a lot of good."

"No. You go for your run, darling. I'll be fine."

Dora set out at a very fast pace. One that few people could have maintained. She was running against the people who killed her brother, and also running against herself. She had to think. She needed to gather her thoughts—figure out what her next move should be and do it fast. Dora only had a sixty-day leave. She needed to have, at least, a basic understanding of the mystery surrounding her brother's death.

Dora had run about six miles when she noticed a car following her, and it didn't look like they were interested in how she looked from behind. She knew she looked as good from behind as she did in front, because 'fine' was not the word to describe the way this woman looked. Dora was tall for a woman—just a tad under 6ft. She was medium-brown with a reddish-brown urchin hair cut, which emphasized her almond-shaped brown eyes. Because she was in the Army, she was in great shape—nicely rounded in all the right places. She ran another mile and still the car paced her. She decided to take a path that was coming up on her right to see what their next move would be. The car kept on going down the street and she did not see it any more that day.

Dora finished her run and decided to treat herself to a dip in the hot tub. Sitting in the tub, letting the swirling water beat on taut muscles; she tried to recall conversations that she and her brother had had from time to time. What he had hoped to do with his life? She could still hear him saying that he "would someday make a difference in the world." He had wanted to be a builder like his father, but Mark wanted to build things that were different. Thinking about that also reminded her of how her brother was always building things with secret ways to get into them. Once again she recalled the series of numbers that she had found in his room. Could it be a code of some sort? Dora couldn't help thinking—hoping—that the numbers may well hold the key to some of the answers she was seeking.

Dora heard her little brother coming out to the hot tub, although describing Charlie as 'little' was a misnomer. Charlie, at sixteen, was well on his way to being six feet and more. Charlie had dreams of being another Michael Jordan or Magic Johnson. But she was glad he had come out on the porch where the hot tub was located. Dora had not had an opportunity to talk to him privately since her arrival. Charlie took a seat beside the hot tub.

"Hi! Sis, enjoying the water?" Dora responded that the hot tub was great, especially after her long run. Then he asked her if she liked the way the tub was built?

She said, "Yeah! Sure! It's great! Is there something special about it I should know?"

Charlie grinned and said, "Sure, I helped Mark build it." That remark started Dora thinking.

"Charlie, is there anything else around here that Mark may have built?"

"Yeah!" said Charlie, "but I haven't seen it. I do know, or at least I think, there is a secret passageway in Mark's room that leads to other rooms in the house, but I've been unable to find it."

"Bingo!"

Charlie told her that Mark had found a set of blueprints left by their dad who had built the house originally. According to the blueprints, the dimensions of some of the rooms were off. Since dad was the builder, Mark said it was done on purpose. This house had been very special to their Dad. According to Charlie, Mark had told him about it, but had never shown him how to get into that part of the house. All he knew for sure was that Mark had made some changes, but didn't know what or where.

"Dad left a lot of building material in the shed out back and Mark used it to do whatever it was he did."

"Mark also told me that I would never be able to figure out what had been done. I guess he was right because you never heard him hammering or anything. There was never any noise but I'm sure it exists."

Brother and sister sat with their own thoughts for a minute, thinking about their tall handsome brother. Dora also thought about her beloved dad who had died five years ago in an accident at a building site.

This secret place, if there was such a place, belonged to their brother and only their brother. "Charlie, do you think Mom knows anything about the section of the house Mark was working on?"

"Nah! I don't think so. I'm pretty sure I'm the only one he ever told." Charlie wanted to know why she was so interested in the room? What could be so important about it? Dora shrugged her shoulders and said, "Nothing special. I would just like to see what Mark had built." She told Charlie to forget it and to run along so she could think.

Dora got out of the hot tub, donned shorts and tank top and went into the house non stop for Mark's room. Once inside, she started looking around—trying to find an entrance to another room—a room that was supposed to be there. As she looked around, it was hard for her to believe that another room existed, but she knew her brother, if he said there was a room, then you could bet your fanny it was there.

She ran her fingers around the wall, knocking as she went to see if the sound would change, but nothing happened. She went into the closet and did the same thing in there, still nothing.

When Dora came out of the closet, she sat down at Mark's desk trying to remember what her brother had said about "the things he would build some day."

Looking across the room, she saw an old bell with a long rope attached. It looked like a replica of the one that hung in the Munster's house. Dora remembered how crazy he was about that TV series. Her brother used to talk about that bell on the Munster's and how he just loved the sound it made when the rope was pulled. He had also said that he would one-day have a door that would open by pulling on a rope just like the one hanging here.

Being very sure of herself, she marched across the room to the bell and pulled on the rope. Nothing happened. She pulled again. This time the wall inside the closet began to move. When it stopped she was looking at a downward staircase. Dora stared at it in disbelief, yet happy because she had found the secret opening.

Dora went to the staircase and felt along the inner wall for a light switch. Once she located it and flicked it on, she started down the stairs. When she reached the third step, the door began to close. She had mixed emotions about this—finding the way out might be as hard as finding the way in.

Dora continued on to the bottom of the stairs. She found herself in a room with doors to the left and the right. One of the doors seemed to be a safe with a numbered keypad. Dora was willing to bet that the numbers she had found in the files would open this door. She pulled the little book out of her pocket that she had retrieved when she dressed. And she was right, they were indeed the code to the door of the vault.

There was no way she could have been prepared for what she found on the other side of that door. The room was filled with weapons that would have put the base armory to shame. She took a quick glance at the weapons and knew she would have been happy with any one of them. In fact, she was thinking, "Which one would be my T.O. weapon?" A T.O. or 'Turn Out' weapon is one that is issued to a particular person in the military but remains in an armory until checked out by that person. In this vault were guns that she knew about and others she had only heard about. Mark could have taken on the entire State of California with the firepower he had in this room.

Dora went into the outer room and started going through the desk. There were more files, papers and computer disks. And—there was a letter addressed to her from her brother. Dora looked at the envelope.

Turned it over a couple of times. Then slowly—very slowly, slit open the envelope. She pulled the letter out and began to read:

Hi Sis,

"If you are reading this letter, I must be dead or hurt. And knowing you better than you know me, I knew you would find this place before anyone else did.

"You see, a lot of the missions you were sent on were set up by my agency. I knew every move you made and a few you shouldn't have. No one else in the family knows what you do for a living. I want you to know that I have always been proud to have you as a sister. I wish I could have told you all that I was aware of, where you were concerned.

"Sis, I joined the FBI as part of an experiment. The agency wanted to see if there was a way for younger people to be fully functional in the field and still go on with their everyday lives the same as the older agents. A man came to see me at school and asked if I would like to try out for a very elite kind of unit. I told him I was not joining the marines. He laughed and said it wasn't them. I began asking questions and he stopped me, saying I would be told what I needed to know when the time came. He said good bye and that he would be in touch. His name is John Hammond.

"One night, this same man came to the house with a few answers. He began by saying he was a scout for a pro team and that he had seen me play football. He wanted to know if I would try out for the team? I was ecstatic. You can imagine how I felt. I was told other players had been asked to try out also. I told him that I didn't care if there were a hundred. I was going to give him all I had and then some.

"I was told that a car would pick me up the next day and that I should explain that I would be gone a week or so. I really didn't think Mom would let me go without an argument, but she was as excited as I was. She didn't quite understand why I had to stay a week or two. But John explained that the camp was run and controlled by a lady and her husband and that there would be total supervision for the week—or weeks, if selected. Mom said, "it was cool." The next day the limo came to pick me

up and there were six other guys who were also trying out for the team, just as mom and I had been told. The driver was a man I had seen at the Country Club when I use to caddie there during the summer. If you look in the file, you will find pictures of him and a few others. I was never able to get a picture of the main guy. Anyway, when the ride began to last longer then we thought it should, we questioned the driver. When we asked where he was taking us? The driver replied, "We're almost there. Everything will be explained to you then."

"Actually, it was almost three hours before we pulled into this camp that was totally enclosed. The gate closed behind us and we went down this long winding road that seemed to go on forever. We eventually reached our final destination, which was this big house and standing out in front was John Hammond and another couple.

"John greeted us and welcomed us to what he said was the first day of the rest of our lives. We were taken inside and directed to our rooms, told that dinner was at six and he left us to settle in.

"At dinner we tried to ask questions, but we were told that all questions would be answered very soon and to finish eating. When dinner was over, we were taken into the parlor where we seated ourselves on two couches that were placed in front of this huge fireplace.

John Hammond stood up and said, "Okay gentlemen, you will now learn why you were chosen for this project. But first, I have someone here I want you to meet, actually two people."

A door opened at the end of the room that I don't think any of us had noticed, and two gentlemen entered. John introduced them as U. S. Senator Thomas Jackson and the director of the FBI, Laurence Parker. The Senator was the first to speak. He began with an apology for the cloak and dagger act. He said it was necessary to keep everything tight and secure. The Senator told us that there had been people watching us for about a year. Of all those who had been scrutinized, it had been decided that we were the best for a program which the government was about to launch. The Senator said that we could leave anytime we wanted to, but if we stayed we had to take an oath to uphold the law and not reveal any of the information we were about to see and/or hear. We were told we all had top-secret clearances. That our backgrounds had been checked and double-checked. We had also been chosen for our physical and scholastic abilities. This unit would be much like the armed forces except that there would be no uniforms after our training nor would there be anyone to hold our hands on assignments. We would be trained how to do our jobs and told where and when to do them.

"Sis, let me tell you, looking around that room at the guys, I could tell that no one was going to turn down the opportunity for the job. We still didn't understand, but whatever it was, it had to be good. I certainly wasn't going anywhere and as I said neither was anyone else. When the Senator asked if anyone wanted a ride home, not a person moved. The only part that was left out was—there really was no way out. We were in—period. Since none of us made a move, he took this to mean that no one wanted to leave and we were asked to stand and take an oath. He said, "Gentlemen, the oath you are about to take will allow us to inform you of details surrounding why you were chosen and what is expected of you. The nice thing about it is you will still have the right to cry 'uncle' and go home. The reason you have to take the oath is because you will learn things that are top secret and you will be prosecuted if you reveal anything you see or hear or the identity of any person seen here. The penalty for these revelations will be severe." What he omitted was 'till death us do part'. We then repeated an oath that was very similar to the oath taken by members of the armed services with a few extras thrown in. The oath was a reminder that if you didn't want to play, you would be in big trouble, especially if you let your mouth run away with you. We signed some papers. And the Senator began to talk.

"Men, we have a very grave problem in this country. There are people here from other nations that would destroy all that we believe in, and they really don't care how it's done or who gets hurt. Consequently, our schools have become havens for people pushing drugs, guns and any other illegal

paraphernalia. I am sure you all know someone in your schools or your work place that fits this description. The bad thing about this is many of them do not realize the damage they are doing. These parasites feel they are doing what is needed to make ends meet. The truth of the matter is they are doing exactly what certain people in the world want them to do: strategically rendering our country helpless. Every move is planned. They ensure that there are always vast quantities of drugs, guns, etc. available to the pushers. They want the persons they are using to push the contraband, to succeed. These people hand-pick their operatives as carefully as we picked you. Many times the persons they pick have no money to start an operation so he or she will front for the person that does."

He stopped talking at this point and looked each of us in the eye, one by one, letting us digest all that he had said. He continued by saying, "Many of you or all of you are wondering, what does this have to do with you? You are probably wondering how you can help in the fight that is facing our nation? From where I' m sitting, you people are the only solution to resolving this problem." At this time, he stopped talking to give the floor to the FBI Director. The Senator smiled and quipped, "Can you imagine how this would look to the Congress—me stepping down to let someone else talk." Everyone had a good laugh.

After saying thank you to Senator Jackson, Director Parker said, "Ask not what your country can do for you, ask what you can do for your country". These were the words said by the late President John F. Kennedy in his inauguration address. Every American has either read them or, if alive and in front of television on January 20, 1961, heard them spoken. They know and understand the meaning of that statement. Another well-known phrase is 'We the people, for the people, and by the people.' The problem with words, are they are only as good and as strong as the people who support and defend them." Parker said, "We have our military, you may say. And we also have our civil servants, laws, and the churches. To this I say you are 100% per cent correct, but who can trust all of the people in these organizations. The one thing you all have in common is your training. You are all in the top one per cent of your ROTC training. When this plan was first conceived it was thought to use true combat soldiers. We thought about it a little more and decided that this unit would be so special, that it would be better not to use already trained soldiers but to train an elite group such as yourselves to fight the type of warfare that you will be engaged in. The training you will receive from this day forward will take you above and beyond. The training you received prior to this day was in preparation to become a member of this unit."

He waited for a few seconds, looking at each of us, and then his expression changed. He said, "Mr. King, you have been making snide remarks about one thing or another since your arrival, why don't you enlighten us.' Jesse King, one of the six guys who came with me in the limo, was feeling a little small at having been singled out. He also knew that Parker was right.

Parker said, "Mr. King, please, standup and let everyone in on how you feel about what has been said or done to bring you to this place."

Jesse stood and began stammering. "Well sir, I don't mean to be rude. I guess I feel that this can't be true. After all, this is the USA. I'm just not sure that it is as serious as you say."

Parker walked over to Jesse and very softly said, "What happened to your real family when you were about fifteen years old? Tell everyone here the reason you lived with foster parents." Jesse stared back at Parker, all the while wondering why this man was singling him out, but he answered the question. He took a deep breath and with long sigh, Jesse told us the story.

"When I was fifteen, my parents gave me a birthday party. There was a kid there that I didn't invite because he was trouble, with a capital 'T'. He showed up anyway and my father couldn't see any harm in his being there, so he let him stay. About an hour after his arrival, we noticed that everyone was acting a little strange. Even the kid began acting unnatural. Those of us who were out in the backyard couldn't see what was going on inside. And it was too late to do anything if we had known.

"From then on everything seemed to happen at once. A fire erupted in the basement and the gas heater exploded taking most of one section of the house.

"The explosion carried that half of the house—two houses down the street along with my whole family, killing them all."

Parker looked at him and said, "Jesse, I'm sorry, but there is a reason for making you go through that agony again. Tell us what the findings were and the reason for the explosion.'"

Jesse said, "The boy that wasn't invited was giving drugs to my friends, that was why they were acting so peculiar. He also punctured the gas line and started the fire. He was trying to make a name for himself and become part of a mob. This was the reason he killed all of my family. The boy was tried as an adult and sent away for thirty years. The man who gave the boy the drugs and told him what to do was sent away for life. It was later learned that it was a hit on my dad to prevent him from running for governor. He would have made too many changes in the State. There were people who did not want my dad to be governor. The only way to make sure he didn't win the election was to kill him."

Parker looked at Jesse and asked, "How do you feel about all that happened to you, to your family? Especially, after what you have heard here today and given a moment to think about your feelings." Jesse stood there shaking his head, saying nothing. Parker said, "I can't hear you." Jesse looked at him and said, "I'm pissed. That's what I am. They used young kids and drugs to do what they themselves were too chicken to do." Jesse turned to the rest of us and apologized.

Parker looked at us and said, "Recruits, if you don't like what I just did, that's fine. I hope that you're also angry about what happened to Jesse's family. It's not going to go away. It will also not get any better until 'we the people'—meaning you—do something about it."

"Men, it is time to stop feeling sorry and change it. I reiterate, this is not a game and I will remind you once again, anyone who wants to leave may do so now." No one made a move. Parker had made his point by using

Jesse's tragic life to remove any doubts. It was clear, this was no joke, nor could it ever be mistaken for one.

Parker told us to retire for the evening. We would receive further instructions in the A.M. At that time, there would be no turning back. He told us to think long and hard by morning and either be packed to leave or dressed to go into training. He hoped we would all decide to stay. He said we would find boots and utilities in our rooms and that we were not to wear any other clothes until it was time to leave."

* *

Dora felt her family would be looking for her pretty soon, so she replaced everything as she had found it. She didn't know if anyone else knew about this room. The people who killed her brother might know. She didn't understand what was going on, but she knew it was big and she did not want to be caught with her 'pants down' so to speak. After securing the safe, Dora started up the stairs and was relieved to find that the third step from the top also opened the door to the closet. Once inside the closet, Dora spied a peephole through which she could check out the bedroom before entering it. She also made sure she had put everything back in its proper place in the bedroom, before going to look for her family.

Dora didn't hear any movement in the house and she wondered where everyone was. She heard the television in the parlor as she descended the stairs and figured her mom must be in there watching it. As she walked in, she wondered what she would tell her if she asked where she had been for so long and what had she been doing. Upon entering the room, she found it wouldn't be necessary, the television was doing all the watching, her mom was sound asleep.

There was no sign of her young brother. She hoped he was out with his friends doing 'boy type' things. Dora bent over and kissed her mother on the cheek. She was rewarded with a smile. One that said, "I am happy to see you daughter and I love you."

Hope had been doing a lot of thinking these past few days. She had lost her husband and now her oldest son. She still missed her husband terribly, but time had helped her cope along with being busy with three children. She still had two children and Charlie would be around for a while. She had to get on with her life. Yes, I still have two very lovely children and I am very grateful to the Almighty.

At the same time, Hope knew she would never forget her son, nor did she want to, but she had to put his death aside or she would die of grief. She asked Dora what she thought of visiting her aunt in Detroit.

Dora said, "I would love to, but there's a lot to be straightened out before my leave is up. But I do think it would be a good for you and Charlie to get away for a while. Her mother didn't want to leave her alone in the house, so she started to object. Dora wouldn't hear of it.

"Look Mom," she said, "You don't want the task of going through Mark's things, so while you're gone, I'll take care of it." Hope thought about it and said, "You're right. I haven't gone near his room since his death. I've tried, but I've been unable to do so. I just hate to leave you all alone."

"It would be better for all of us if I do it, OK?" Her mom knew she was right.

"Okay, you take care of it and Charlie and I will get out of your hair while you do it." With that settled, they went to bed.

Dora needed to put together a plan. This idea of her mom's to visit Aunt Hesper was heaven sent. With Charlie and her mom out of the house, she would be able to dig around Mark's hideaway without worrying about being found out. With this thought in mind, Dora dropped into a deep and dreamless sleep.

Dora woke to the smell of bacon, eggs and hot coffee. This was a sure sign she was home. Her mom loved to cook and breakfast was just the start. She adhered to the rule that you start off the day with a good meal under your belt. If you didn't stop her, Hope would cook all day. Her mom was always saying "I know they don't feed you enough at that camp of yours. If they did, you wouldn't be so skinny." And she would go on like that all day.

Dora was headed for the kitchen when the phone rang. She picked it up and before she could say hello, a voice said, "Stay out of it and go back to camp or end up like your brother." Dora looked at the receiver and very slowly hung the phone up. Her mom came in and asked, "Who was on the phone?" Dora said, "Oh, it was a wrong number." She linked her arm with her mother's and walking into the kitchen said, "How about some of that down-home cooking I've been smelling."

Dora hit her brother on the back of the head with a light tap.

"What's up Sport?" And she sat down to eat. Hope started piling food on the table like there was no tomorrow, or even the rest of today. Charlie leaned closed to her ear and asked Dora "If she'd had any luck." She looked at him and said, "No, nothing." Her mom hollered, "Hey you two, what's going on? No whispering at my table." Dora smiled and thought "Yeah! I'm Home."

Charlie wasn't too happy about leaving his sister home alone while he and his mother visited his aunt. But he knew his mother wasn't going to leave him behind, so he would have to go.

Dora was thinking about the phone call and was wondering how anyone could know she was looking around. She was thinking that maybe, just maybe, the house was bugged. As casually as she could, she asked her mother if any work had been done to the house? Hope didn't understand the question, so she looked at her daughter very puzzled and asked, "What do you mean?"

Dora said, "Oh, I was just wondering if you've had anyone from a company to come in and fix anything."

Her mom said, "No." But Charlie jumped in and said, "Yes there was. The phone company was doing some work on the lines about two weeks ago." According to Charlie a man came to the house and said they were tracking down a problem in the neighborhood and he would like to check a couple of the phones in the house and also the inner lines. Dora could tell that her mother knew nothing about this.

Charlie was home alone and he neglected to mention it to his mother later. This also meant that Mark had known nothing about it either. Dora could see that her mom was wondering—why such a question? Dora told her mom that she had found a pair of crimps in her room, the kind used by phone installers that was why she had asked. She was looking at her mother and trying to feed her face at the same time.

She was also trying to change the subject in a round about way, and her mother let her do it. The problem was Dora forgot that her mom was the lady who had taught them to think things out. And though she didn't say so, Hope knew there was more to the question than she was being led to believe. Another nice thing about her mom, she knew when to let something drop. This way her children didn't have to dance around the truth and end up telling her a lie. Hope knew that sooner or later, she would be told all.

Breakfast over, Hope went to pack and Dora began to look around for a clue as to whether or not the house was bugged.

Charlie was worried though. He came to his sister and asked, "Did I do something wrong by letting those men in and not telling anyone." She just looked at him and gave him another soft tap.

"No, Sport, you didn't do anything wrong. After all you're the man of the house when no one else is here. Now that Mark is gone, you're the only man of the house. I told you why I asked."

Charlie smiled knowingly and said, "They didn't go anywhere near your room." Dora started laughing, this kid was no dummy. He was going to be quite a man some day.

They heard their mom coming down the stairs. She was carrying one suitcase and she sent Charlie to get the other. They left for the bus station, which was five miles from the house. Once again, Dora noticed the same car was following her. It had been doing so since leaving the driveway of her home. She mentally took down the plate number and left it at that for the present. Dora pulled into the bus station. She and Charlie grabbed the bags while her mother went in to purchase the tickets to take them to LAX. The bags were checked and Dora stayed with her folks until the bus left the station.

When she came out of the little station, she couldn't help but laugh. Nothing much had changed in this small town of Semi Valley. Once outside she checked out the area to see if the car and its driver were still around, but she didn't see it.

As she approached her car, Dora noticed a blue wire laying on the ground near her front tire. It didn't look like it had been laying there long, so she decided to leave the car there and call the only person she could call at this point, police detective David Aimsley.

He was very happy to hear from her and was there in a matter of minutes. Upon his arrival, Dora asked if he could have the bomb squad check out her car. She explained about the car that had been following her and its sudden disappearance while she was in the station. David thought she was crazy but did as she requested, and called in the bomb squad.

While they waited, David asked what she had been doing with herself and what were her plans. Dora didn't feel like indulging in small talk, but what could she do, she had called him. David was non-stop with questions until the bomb squad units turned into the station. One unit carried the bomb dog, the other was a disposal unit. They were told about the wire and went to work. It didn't take them long, with the dog, to find the bombs—one on the gas tank and one on the engine. The squad disarmed them and left the scene.

David was at a loss for words. Dora was not telling him what he needed to know, so he continued to ask questions. Unknown to David, Dora had been questioned by experts. By the best available and all they were ever able to get out of her was name, rank and social security number. What David was trying to do was a piece of cake compared to the instructors at Ft. Campbell. They had done all they could do to make her say 'uncle' and go home. They hadn't been able to break this woman and neither would he? David finally gave up. He knew he was fighting a losing battle. Dora surprised him with, "Would you like to take me to dinner, tonight?" This was so unexpected David was caught totally off guard. He smiled like a little boy and said, "Yes. What time do you want me to pick you up?" Dora said, "About eight thirty and I'll let you know where I want to eat at that time." An officer came over and said he had all the prints he could lift and she could go.

"Okay. See you later, David."

Chapter Two

Once the officers had told her she could leave, Dora headed for her car and home. She was in a hurry to get back to the files and tapes she had found in the secret room. Dora remembered seeing something about the Country Club when she was reading the report. She wasn't too sure about its worth as a clue, but it was early days yet and it could be significant as the investigation continued.

Dora made a bee line for Mark's room. She opened the secret passage and went down the stairs to the vault. Opened it and pulled out the box that held the papers she had been reading the day before. Scanning the papers, she found the part she was looking for and she was right, the chauffeur was connected in some way to the Club. Dora found the place where she had left off yesterday and began reading.

"OK Sis," he said, "at this point, you are wondering—What in the world is my brother talking about? I would be, too. But I left a series of tapes for you to listen to; each tape is sequentially marked."

Dora looked around for a tape player and found a complete system in a cabinet. She put in tape number one. It was strange hearing her brother's voice. Hearing it brought tears to her eyes. She listened closely to all Mark had to say.

"Dora, if you ever believed anything in your life, please take what I'm going to say to heart." Then she could hear him laughing a little. He was saying, "Taping is much better than writing and it will be easier on your eyes."

"As I was saying, the next day we came down to breakfast early, and I do mean early. The sun had not come up when we were called to 'rise and shine.' At breakfast,

I took a head count around the table and everyone was present. We had all decided to stay. The only persons missing were the Senator, the Director and the driver.

"All of the us were dressed in camouflage uniforms and boots; John too, was dressed like the rest of us." John gazed around the table and congratulated us on our decision to stay. He went on to explain that we would be in class most of the morning "where you will be provided further explanation as to why you are here. This afternoon, we will open the floor to questions. Give you an opportunity to get whatever you have to say, off your chest." After breakfast, we went into the sitting room and John began where he left off the day before.

"Yesterday, we told you to feel free to leave and you still can do so, but if you stay from this point on, you will not be given that option. We are going to discuss things that cannot leave this room and will not be discussed with anyone outside of this room."

At that point, he turned and looked each man in the eye. This was it. We go or stay. I guess you could say, Sis, this was the last train to Black Rock, but there were no ticket holders. Satisfied, John began speaking again.

"You people were told that you were hand-picked for this job. We will now explain a little of what will be expected of you." John started to walk back and forth as he talked. It was strange; he seemed to grow taller and straighter. Maybe it was the uniform.

"The government has decided to fund this program even though not many people will know who you are, only that it exists. Yesterday, we told you that our country was being systematically taken advantage of and slowly being destroyed. Your role in this venture is to stop the devastation. Take back our city streets. You will let the world know that the USA will not put up with anymore abuse. We are fighting back. Dealers will fear for their lives every time they try to sell drugs or weapons. We will go after

anybody and everybody in order to get the job done. We are going to get back the respect we once had; and you people, are going to do this—with our help and guidance, of course."

"If you are wondering how you are supposed to do such a job, I will explain further.

"You'll all remember, that 007 had a license to kill. Well men, you now have that same license. You will be allowed to do whatever is necessary to complete the job. We are going to make you the most elite team of non-military people in the world. The nice thing about your training is—you will be allowed to continue your schooling and the jobs you have. We don't want to change your way of life, just add to it. Officers of the FBI are not all in the office. There are many that work other jobs, but when called upon, they also uphold the law in their official capacity. This is what you will do, but you will go one step further, you will have 'license to kill'. This is a very dangerous job and if you are not up to it, you could be the next to die."

Again, John looked each of us in the eye. Measuring how his words thus far were affecting us.

He spoke again. "I would like for you to take a good look at each other because you will have to depend on each other for survival, once you leave here for good."

"How long this training will take is up to you. We planned to have it all completed in six months. You'll return to your homes in five days, but you will return here the following weekend and every weekend until school closes. All of you will spend your summer vacation here. For those of you who work, we will arrange a 'leave of absence' for you. This job could have been done by the military, and we almost went that route, but we decided to put people to work who already deal with the mess, day in and day out. If this unit lives up to expectations here in California, we plan to enlarge the group by recruiting young people such as yourselves all over the nation. Then 'Operation Clean Up Our Nation' will stretch across the country."

"All of you will come to know the laws as if you were lawyers. This will be very important when dealing with local authorities. If you're ever caught by them for any reason, you will not be with them long. You will not fall under their jurisdiction nor will their local laws pertain to you; 007 you're not, but you will be the next best thing to him."

Dora was feeling very proud of her brother and wishing she could tell him so. He wanted a better country and from the looks of things, he might have paid the ultimate price—his life. A further look around the room, Dora noticed there were four monitors on a shelf. She turned them all on and found that they showed the inner and outer perimeters of the house. This she liked, from this room she could check comings and goings. Noting the clock on one of the monitors, Dora realized it was almost time for her date with David. She hated stopping the tapes, but did so. Again returning everything to the vault just as she had found it, Dora went to her room to dress.

She didn't have much time, so she hurried. Since she did the inviting, Dora decided that the least she could do, was to dress in something slinky and feminine.

Dora grabbed a pair of lined black silk tight slacks, topped it with a beautiful hand spun silk white blouse that tied on the side, high heel black strappy shoes, matching black purse, pearl earrings, and a single rope of pearls that had been given to her on her 21st birthday. Being in the Army, Dora didn't use much makeup other than lipstick, but tonight she decided a little eye makeup wouldn't go amiss along with a squirt of her favorite perfume 'Red Door'.

Fifteen minutes later, she heard a car pull up. It was David. She went to the door and was out before he could ring the bell. He was trying to open the car door for her at the same time she was reaching for it. They both smiled and Dora backed off.

"I'm sorry. There's not much chivalry where I come from, but I promise I will try very hard to behave tonight."

David looked at her and said, "Deal! I would really like to show you how much of a gentleman I am." David got into the car, turned to Dora and said, "Well lovely lady, where would you like to go?" Dora asked him if he had a membership in the Country Club? "But of course," David replied.

"Then that is where I would like to go, kind sir." David smiled and started the car. He turned right at the end of the driveway and headed west to the Country Club. It wasn't a very long drive, but the countryside was beautiful to see as they made their way up and down the mountain roads en route to Malibu. Dora used to think that God was angry when He made California, because of the many hills and mountains. At the same time, He must have felt a pity because He created the greenest hills and some of the most beautiful beaches to be found anywhere on earth.

The bomb incident had left David very perplexed. He was dying to ask questions, but was too afraid of ruining the evening. He stayed with small talk, about everything and anything that he thought wouldn't spoil the mood. He hoped that Dora would open up and let him in on what was going on.

They went through the gate and up the driveway to the Club. At the entrance, a valet was waiting and helped Dora out of the car. As they crossed the areaway of the parking lot, Dora saw a car that looked very much like the one that had been following her. Dora asked David if there was another entrance to the Club off the parking lot in the direction she wanted to go. He said there was, so they walked in the direction of the car. She needed to see the license plate to be certain it was the same car. Once they were close enough, she made a positive ID on the numbers.

Dora turned to David and asked if he would run a plate for her without asking questions. David looked at her for a moment, and then said, "Yes, wait until we get inside and I'll call the station." David made sure Dora was comfortably seated, took down the numbers Dora gave him and went off to make his call. He returned with a grim look on his face. He looked so upset when he sat down that Dora reached for his hand.

This was something that seemed to go unnoticed by David. Normally, he would kill to be touched by Dora. He sat there looking at her for almost a full minute and finally, he asked her the question he had been wanting to ask since he'd picked her up at her house—"Are you ready to tell me what is going on?" Dora let his hand go and said, "I don't know what you are talking about." She was sorry she had asked him to check out the plate. "As far as the plate goes, I was thinking I had seen the car before and I remembered the number. Now," she said, "suppose you tell me—what is your problem?"

David kept looking at her, saying nothing for a long while. The silence more threatening, than if he had yelled at her. Very softly, David said, "There's been another murder. One of Mark's closest friends was shot down while running in the park." Dora looked at David in disbelief, stunned. David continued, "The kid was dead when they found him. Would you mind taking a cab home? I have to go check out the crime scene." She said, "Of course, I'll be fine." David turned to leave when Dora had a thought.

"David, the young man, what was his name?" David replied, "King. Jesse King. So when you feel like letting me in on what you know, I have two ears and an open mind."

David left her at the table, tipped the headwaiter, asking him to make sure Dora got a cab. He went on out the door and Dora got up and began looking around the club. There was a private party-taking place out on the back lawn complete with big band and a huge Texas Bar-B-Q you could smell a mile away.

It was a birthday party for the daughter of the club's founder. Tom Walker was old money with very old ways, originally from Texas. This was a man who could make a city disappear if he felt like it and no one would ever know where it originally stood. When his daughter was in the Peace Corps, she was sent to Morocco on assignment. While there, the local government put her in prison for wearing a low-cut blouse. They wouldn't let her go even with the U.S. trying to negotiate her release. Walker was so upset with the Moroccan government and with the U.S. that he called on the services of an old friend. In less than forty-eight hours, the two mounted a twelve-man team of mercenaries who entered Morocco to free the daughter. The rest, as they say, is history. U.S. officials ended up with egg on their political faces. Tom earned the reputation as a man you didn't want to cross. He didn't care where the hellhole was, he had people who would go anywhere and take care of the problem. "Have gun, will travel."

Dora was looking for the chauffeur Mark had mentioned in his letter. If she could find that man, she would have a place to begin her investigation into the murder of her brother Mark and possibly, Jesse's, too.

Someone spoke to her from behind. She turned and saw it was the waiter offering her a glass of Champagne. Thanking him, she accepted the drink. Dora, with drink in hand strolled out to the patio and started mingling with the guests. She was hoping to find either the men who were driving the car or the chauffeur.

To her way of thinking, it was impossible for everyone to know every person that was at this party, she'd just be one more guest walking around. Dora was wandering across the lawn towards the fountain when she spied the guy that was driving the car. She continued her stroll and when she reached the spot where he was standing, she stopped and looked around. "Nice party, isn't it?" He said, "Yes it is. I don't think I know you. I've seen every angel that has come to the Club tonight, and you are, by far, the queen of them all. There is no way I would have forgotten you." Dora thanked him for the compliment. "I'm a friend of Frances Walker. We go way back." She was not telling a lie, Dora did know Frances from school. The fellow asked her if she would like a refill, she said, "No not yet, but thanks for asking."

Dora noticed another man coming towards them and she thought this might be the other guy she was looking for. The man was less than three feet from her when she felt something hard pressing into her back. She didn't have to be a rocket scientist to know what it was, so she chilled, waiting for them to make the next move. The guy walking towards her, came closer and told her not to make a sound "just turn around and start walking towards the golf course." Dora was not very happy about this, but kept her cool. She knew that these guys were for real. She still had no idea why they were trying to kill her.

They were out of sight and hearing distance of the people at the party. Dora knew that she would have to make her move soon or die. These guys were going to take her out. There was no doubt of that. Hoping to get them to talk a little, she asked, "Why do you want to kill me?" The first fellow she met that evening, told her. "You like to put your nose where it doesn't belong. Most people would have gotten the message with the bomb, which you somehow escaped. But no, you had to continue buttin' in. Well, we are going to help you stay out of something that is no business of yours." Dora said, "I guess my brother should have done the same."

One of guys grabbed her by the arm and forcefully turned her around. Bad move. This was the worst mistake he could have made. Using the momentum of the turn she broke his nose with the first punch. She threw a crushing roundhouse blow to the larynx of the second guy which killed him, but not before he got off a shot—killing his partner on impact. Looking at both bodies lying there on the ground, Dora knew that it was time to move—to get out of there. Things were about to get funky and she still had to find out why. She checked her back as she made her way through the garden and then out of the club. She reached the cabstand without incident and got into a taxi.

During the drive home, Dora's thoughts were on her brother's report. She knew it was imperative that she finish reading it and listening to the tapes. That was the only way she was going to know what to do and to whom.

There were a lot of strange occurrences that night. David was called out to the scene of an accident that involved a car. The same one he had called in about for Dora at the Club. The police dispatcher gave him a call because he thought it was strange that the same car David had run a check on—turned up three hours later with two dead men in it. The car had a "fight" with a lamppost and the lamppost won. Or so it would seem.

The coroner made a preliminary exam at the scene. His tentative report was that the two men looked as if they had been fighting in the car and the driver was shot in the scuffle. A bullet was found in the door on the driver's side and the gun was still in the passenger's hand. He, the coroner, also felt that the passenger had been killed upon impact by a blow to the throat. David saw all of this, but was certain that all was not as it seemed. For now, he would accept it. He would however, continue investigating. That was what he was good at, investigating crimes. He was also very certain that Dora, somehow, had something to do with the mess he was looking at tonight. There was more to this woman then he or anyone really knows. David was hoping that he was wrong about her, because he would hate to have to arrest her. One thing about David that all his friends in the department knew and that was he would arrest his own mother. If he didn't, the sheriff would. The sheriff was a very unhappy man and he just loved to make other people feel as bad as he always did. This guy could eat a whole pizza, a couple hamburgers, a large order of fries and look around for the dessert wagon. The sheriff was as big as a house and he hated everybody.

Dora put on a pot of coffee as soon as she got home. She knew it was going to be a long night. She also knew that time was running out, for two reasons. First, someone was trying to kill her and secondly, her leave status. The sixty-days were running out fast. What was causing her even more anxiety was she did not know who would be the next to die—or if she would be able to stop whoever was doing the killing.

Grabbing a bag of Ding Dongs and the pot of coffee she had made, Dora headed for the secret room.

Dora started the tape at the place she had left off just a few hours ago. She stopped a moment and mused to herself—could it only have been just a few hours ago?

Her brother was saying:

"Sis, you are the only person who would understand the silence that fell over the room at the phrase 'license to kill'. I, for one, wasn't sure I wanted such a license. What a thing to have and you're not at war. Parker told us, "I know what you're thinking and feeling right now. It will pass once you have all the facts and figures. There won't be one of you who will not want to do the job. Now gentlemen, the floor is open for questions. Who would like to be first?" Jesse was the first to raise his hand. "How do we get paid?"

Parker laughed, "Good question. You'll all be provided with Swiss bank accounts. The reason for that is—we don't want people trying to figure out who you are or know about the amount of money you earn. All of you have been on the payroll since the limo picked you up."

Next person to ask a question was Evan Kindle. He wanted to know if we would be given a permit to carry weapons?

Parker replied, "Yes. You will be issued an international permit the same as all our other agents."

Curtis Hall was next. He wanted to know if the fact that we were all language major's helped with the decision as to who would be chosen for the job.

"It was one of the considerations, but not the only one," said Parker. "Having people who speak more than one language means they can travel to other countries with little or no help."

Next guy to ask a question was Eric Rojas. "Sir, what if we have family in the country where we are sent?"

"Parker's reply to that was the agency would ensure that we didn't end up in any country where we had family. One of the reasons for that is—in case the family is involved in what we were sent there to do. They want to make sure we do a thorough job. Secondly, if they are involved, they might figure you are there to stop them from doing business. And a third and

fourth reason is—we wouldn't want to intentionally place you in danger; and to use an old cliché—put you between a rock and a hard place."

We were told that we would start our training in the morning. Continuing each day until it was time to leave for our homes.

It was the next morning when we were routed, but it was also the middle of the night. They had us up at 0300 hours. Breakfast was served a half hour later. We were told it would be the last meal we would eat in the house and to remember our bed. It would be the last time we would see it for a week. Just as we were about to leave, we heard what sounded like cannon fire. We were all wondering what kind of place was this that shot off cannons in the middle of the night? There was a mobile unit waiting for us outside. It was time to mount up. We climbed up into the back of a five-ton truck.

The base camp we were taken to looked like a fort. Once there, we were issued all the equipment we would need. We were turned over to a Marine 1st Sergeant by the name of Cummings. Around the base, he's called 'Top Raman' Cummings because he's always eating Raman noodles.

The Sergeant had us sit in a circle around him. He said, "I am now your mother and your father and I own you. You will do whatever I say do without comment and immediately. You will be the best I have ever trained. These are my orders and I always follow orders. You people don't have any idea of what you are capable of but you will be among the must highly trained men in the world. Is there anyone here? that doesn't believe what I'm saying?" Not one of us moved. This guy was as big as a tank and upsetting him did not seem like the thing to do.

"We will begin with weapons training today. The first weapon, you will learn about is the Gluck 9 with extended clip. You are going to learn to take this weapon down to parade rest and back to attention in a hundred and twenty seconds. Any longer then that—you're dead."

Top gave us the command to get on our feet and follow him. We went to a truck parked a little way from us and Top opened the back door. Sis that truck was loaded from back to front with arms. The truck was a rolling armory. We were issued weapons without ammo, told to have a seat in a big tent that had tables and bench type seats. Here, we were taught how to break down the guns, clean them and reassemble them. This went on all day and by nightfall, I could see gun parts with my eyes closed. Which led to the next part of the training. We were blindfolded, and the break down and reassembling started all over again. Top dry-fired each weapon to see if it had been reassembled correctly. Top said he was happy with our progress and that we could take a break. My hands hurt, but it felt good to master the weapon, even if it had taken all day. When Top said we would continue early in the morning, we knew that meant '0 dark 30'. We were beat, and yet, happy to be there.

The next days of training were hard and we were very glad that we were in good shape to begin with otherwise we wouldn't have made it. This man was a machine and he treated us as such. From early morning until late at night we trained. At week's end, not one of us looked the same as we did when we arrived. There was a certain sureness about us that was different and we loved it.

We were sent home and, as promised, picked up again by the limo the following week. The weekend training sessions continued until summer vacation. Mom kept asking if I had made the team and I kept telling her we wouldn't find out until sometime in the summer.

"Sis, by the end of summer, we were a unit that could be sent anywhere and do anything asked of us."

My first assignment was in a school. This fellow had been spotted selling drugs to kids. Once they were hooked, he was teaching them how to steal, sell the drugs and finally he got them into selling guns. The kids would do whatever he said do in order to feed their habits and keep their pockets full.

We picked him up, put a bag over his head and took him to a place outside of town. We didn't let him see our faces. The guy was scared to death but he was more afraid of his supplier because he wouldn't give him up. He said, "You'll have to kill me. I ain't saying nothing." We told him that he was out of business. If we picked him up again, he was a dead man. We took him back to town and let him go. To tell you the truth, I was glad to let him go. I was afraid they might want him dead and I wasn't sure I was ready for that as yet.

"We kept going after small time people in hopes one would give us some information we could use. Most of them gave us information we already had. We did manage to clean up some street trash.

"Then came a break in the case, I thought. I was driving in downtown LA one night and I saw one of the people we had talked to going into one of the office buildings. It seemed strange to see a fellow like this in such a place. He was carrying a brief case and moving fast. I watched from a distance and once he had gone into the building, I followed him. I couldn't find out what office he went into but the elevator had stopped on the eighth floor. I did a little checking and found out that the offices of Cambridge Shipping, Inc. were housed on the eighth floor. Now, I didn't believe for a moment that a dirt bag like this guy had any legitimate business in this place, it could only be dirty. I called the others and when they showed up, we went to work.

"We found out that the company was transporting video tapes overseas and this dirt bag was making the movies. You got it. Child porno. Some of it was worse than you can imagine. We also learned that he was into slavery of all types. If a person was willing to pay the price, this company would deliver anything they wanted anywhere in the world. We also found the place where they had been keeping children locked up until they were needed. He had these kids in a building without light and very little food. They were made to perform any act this clown wanted to make his 'movies'. Most were runaways, but some were kidnapped off the streets. All of them had been reported missing at one time or another. Sis, after seeing the building where the kids had been held prisoners, that's when I knew I could kill.

"We made our report and were told to pick him up, but when we got there, he was dead. Someone had put an ice pick in the back of his neck. Months of work gone, and we had nothing.

"The next few weeks we started leaning hard on folks and in a way, it started to pay off. A source had given us information that would have put us in touch with one of the headmen, but he was killed before we could pick him up. My friend, Jesse, began thinking that someone on the inside was responsible for the murders. We talked it over and decided we had better keep our suspicions to ourselves. Nathan Price was another of our operatives. He informed us that there was a coded message at his post office box that told us to purchase a case of Mack 10's from some people in LA. When we went to pick up the guns, there was a welcoming committee waiting for us. Luckily, we picked up on the trap and were able to pull off a counter attack. After this attack, we knew for sure someone on the inside was trying to take us out. Who and why? were the big questions. There was no trace of us in any system, which meant we had to look within the unit and at the handful of people we had dealt with from the beginning. We decided we could trust no one.

"We continued our attacks on the 'trash' wherever we found it. We did notice that the streets were a little cleaner. People were feeling safer. The junkies were getting uptight—the street was drying up. They didn't know why. They did know that people were afraid.

"One day, word came that one of our guys had taken his own life. We were told that he had gone to Las Vegas with some money with which he was suppose to purchase a large shipment of arms. The story was he played cards with the money and lost all of it. He left a note saying he was sorry. He just couldn't face what he had done. He also wrote that he would rather be dead.

"Sis, we checked all around and could not find the so-called club where he had supposedly lost the money. At this point, I figured we were all marked for death and we needed to find a way to protect each other. That was when I began making tapes, keeping records of everything and gathering as many pictures as I could. I didn't know if it would help, but it certainly wouldn't hurt. To date, I have not been able to find out who's

at the top and chances are I won't because you are going over my records. I don't know what you can do, but please, be careful."

* *

Dora was really upset by the time she had finished the report. Someone had gone to a great deal of trouble to set up a special team to eliminate a growing problem. Then capitalizing on the fact that the job was done, decided the players had to be removed. That meant the team had to be eliminated permanently. Not a bad plan either, they just should have used someone else's brother. If it was the last thing she ever did, the people responsible for murdering her brother would regret doing so until the day they died. Dora looked up at the picture of her brother and said, "Yeah Bro! You're right, I will find out the 'who' and the 'why'. This time it will be different." With these words she went to the rack on the wall and took down a 9-millimeter colt and four clips of ammo.

Dora went upstairs to find it was daylight. She had spent the whole night listening to the tapes and reading the reports. She took a shower and lay down. It wasn't long before she fell asleep, her antennae posted for anything and anybody.

She woke up just past 1500 hours (after 3 PM) and the sleep had helped. Dora had a plan. She also would need help. She placed a phone call and in response to the voice on the other end, she simply said, "Walk like an Egyptian, 1.7" and hung up. This was the way she called for help. It also told her team what time she would call back on the secure phone that her team carried with them at all times.

She hadn't finished checking the phones in the house and thought she had better get to it right away. Using a micro detector that was also part of the secure phone she carried, she found the first of the 'bugs'. They were on all the phones in the house and in a number of other places. She decided to leave them there.

The front door bell rang and she went to open it. It was David and he didn't look a bit happy. She invited him in and offered him coffee, which he accepted.

They seated themselves on the back porch and David started right in with the questions. His first words were, "You won't have to worry anymore about the two men who were driving the car whose plate you asked me to check out. They were both killed last night in their car. Dora, I need to ask you a couple of questions. I need to know what you know about what's happening around here. I can't help but feel that there is a lot you're not telling me. I need you to understand that I am a good cop and I believe in what I do." He grabbed her hand and lifted it to his lips.

"Please Dora, if you know anything, anything at all that can help me, please tell me. You also need to know that your brother wouldn't trust me either and look where he ended up." Dora withdrew her hand, startled at his comment.

" What do you mean, Mark didn't trust you? Did my brother come to you for help or with information and you didn't listen?"

"No, that wasn't the way it was. He just asked questions, the type of questions you have been asking. I will do all I can to help you, but you have to let me in."

Dora stared at him. "Look, David," said Dora, "I don't know what you're talking about. I came home to a funeral. My brother and I haven't talked to each other in months. I have no idea why he was killed nor do I know anything about the death of those men."

David was beginning to get a little angry with Dora. He stared at her. He started a sentence, changed his mind and said, "I find it hard to believe that an ordinary person would have picked up on those men following them, or be able to fathom that a bomb might be attached to their car just from the fact that a piece of wire was lying on the ground next to the tire. No, Kid," he said, "you're more than meets the eye. And I must tell you this, if I find out you're involved, I will arrest you. I'm reaching out to you with all my heart. You know I have loved you forever. Why won't you let me help you?" Dora was getting just a little angry herself.

"David, there is nothing to tell you. Look, I'm beginning to get a splitting headache, would you mind leaving now." David gazed at the face of the woman he loved. She had asked him to leave. What else could he do? Actually, in a way, I just threatened her, he thought. So he left, not because he wanted to, he had to.

As soon as David had driven out of the driveway, she went down to the secret room because she had found during her sweep for bugs, that this was the only 'safe' room in the house. Dora made the call to her friend and teammate on the secured phone. Elizabeth was one of best explosive experts she knew and she had a feeling that big 'blow outs' or 'blow ups' were going to be needed. She had just started to explain the situation when she heard another voice on the line. It was Delores, another of her teammates who had queued in on a three-way link up.

Dora brought them up-to-date on everything that had transpired since the day she came home for her brother's funeral.

"I don't have anything concrete, just a gut feeling—and you know my gut is usually right." Without preamble, the girls said they would see her in 72 hours; to fax what she had and they would find out as much as they could before they got there. Dora hooked the computer to her phone's portable modem and faxed all the documents including the information from the computer. She signed off and went upstairs to get dressed.

It was getting dark and Dora had decided that she wanted to have a look around the Country Club's office. She was pretty sure there was a lead there, if only she could find it. Someone had gone to a lot of trouble to hide the fact that those guys, who had been tailing her, were killed on the golf course and not in an automobile accident. Yeah! There had to be something.

Knowing she would have to leave by night and not use her car, she dressed all in black and went out the back window. She crept to the garage where her brother kept his motorcycle, pushed it across the lawn, out the back gate. She went along a path until she thought it was safe to start it and headed out to the Club.

The man sitting outside of her front driveway never heard a thing. As far as he knew, she was still in the house.

The bike was in tiptop condition as only Mark's bike would be. It felt good to let all those 'horses' loose. It had been a while since she'd felt so much power under her. The bike roared along the highway making her forget for a little while, why she was on it and where she was going.

Dora pulled on to a back road that led to the Club. She rolled the bike to within one hundred yards of the building, parked it and went the rest of the way on foot. She made her way around the building and was about to step into the open when someone struck a match.

Dora stepped back into the bushes to wait until the person finished smoking and went back inside. She knew that this might be her only opportunity to find anything at the Club. If she were seen here again, someone would figure something's up.

She went up to the window and looking in decided there were too many people about to chance going in now, so she went back down the road to wait.

The last car left the parking area just after midnight. She waited another fifteen minutes before going back to the Club. Again, she took a careful look around. The only person she saw was the night watchman. He was 'kicking back' near the front door. She noted that there was electronic surveillance equipment. She was prepared for that, but not for the dog that was lying on the floor beside him. The watchman was playing the radio very loud. Dora hoped the music would drown out any sound she might make while searching the office. Thank God for "Rent-a-Cops." She used the special equipment she had with her to open the window. She climbed in, closed the window behind her and tipped to the door of the office. She listened for minute then used pepper spray on the bottom of the door in case the dog decided to take a little walk and start sniffing around. One whiff of the spray and he would be worthless for the rest of the night.

In the desk, Dora found only ordinary business papers—accounts due and accounts paid in full.

There didn't seem to be anything that was out of place, but she kept on reading, hoping to find something that would help.

After finding nothing worthwhile in the desk, Dora looked behind the picture frames on the wall for a safe. Nothing. She then decided to use the electronic locator she had with her. 'Bingo'. She found a wall safe behind a panel, also another alarm system, which she easily dismantled. Once opened, the contents of the safe provided all kinds of information. Enough to point out that something very large and very profitable was going on. Much too large for a common Country Club; most Clubs barely make enough money to pay the help.

Dora began photographing everything she found and replacing it very carefully.

She was certain that when the intelligence officer on her team finished reviewing all the facts she had gathered, they would know why Mark was killed and maybe, who killed him.

Dora replaced everything, making sure that the safe was closed as before and the panel back in place with out breaking the connection to override the alarm. She left the same way she came in. Unfortunately, Dora didn't know that there was a 24-hour loop-to-loop video recorder linked to a camera behind a fixture that she had not detected. The good thing was—the tapes probably wouldn't be reviewed—unless they had reason to do so.

Dora made her way back to the bike and was soon happily, on her way home. She returned the same way she had left, very quietly. She thanked her training for being able to pull this off. The guy was still sitting out front in his car unaware that she had left and returned.

Once in the house she began making noises as if she had just woke up and was raiding the refrigerator. Taking a shower, Dora wasn't sure if she wanted to develop the film or sleep. Sleep won out. She decided to wait for Christine, the fourth member of her team. She hadn't spoken to her, but she was sure either Liz or Delores had and that she would be coming with them. Besides, Chris was the better person to develop the film. It could only be done once.

She was also the intelligence officer and would be able to decipher what it all meant—"I hope."

Chapter Three

Dora awakened in the morning feeling great. For the last couple of days she had been playing it safe, staying home, keeping an eye on the monitors. Very low key. But today, a few of her teammates would be arriving and she was raring to go.

Christine pulled into the driveway first. Elizabeth and Delores pulled up right behind her. They all hugged each other and went inside the house. Dora, making small talk about their trip, indicated the 'bugs' as she took them around the house. Once the girls had settled in, Dora decided it was time to introduce them to the secret room.

Christine was the first to ask, "What the hell is going on?" She went on to tell Dora that the information she had been faxed indicated that Mark had found out something that had to do with shipments in and out of the USA. Millions of dollars were changing hands. Also from the information, she gleaned that someone was using Mark and his unit as moles.

Delores jumped in the conversation. "You see, what was happening, Mark and the other agents were being sent all over the world to create as much unrest as possible. At the same time, guaranteeing those people that the bosses were in control and that they could get whatever they wanted whenever they wanted it. The folks in those countries were ensured safe passage of whatever it was they were shipping in and out of the U. S. There are people making a boat load of bucks and we figure your brother had also figured out what they were doing. The only thing he didn't know was who and how. There must be a shipping company up to its bridge in this whole mess."

Dora stopped her there. She said, "I did a little recon while waiting for you guys to arrive." She told them about the Country Club. "I took photos of everything that was in the safe at the Club."

Chris groaned and said, "Oh God!" Everyone broke out laughing. The last time Dora had attempted to take photos, she had forgotten to load the camera. Her buddies were never going to let her live it down. Dora didn't say another word. She handed the film to Chris and showed her to the dark room. Chris processed the film and hung it up to dry.

The girls trooped up the stairs and they all went to the kitchen to help prepare their dinner. When it was ready, they sat around the table and talked about old times, the places they had been, and the good times they'd had in those places.

Elizabeth asked Dora if she remembered the two guys they went to see in France.

Dora laughed. "Oh yeah, I'll never forget them. They acted as though they were scared to death of us," she told the others. "They were friends of my brother's who were going to school there. He asked me to look them up. I thought we would be welcome since we were from home and could go out and have a little fun. Those two were a trip. They started talking about a lot of stuff that made no sense—at all. For some unknown reason, those guys acted as if they were totally afraid of us, so much so they were ready to run to the hills. We never saw them anymore after that night. And of course, I left two days later, if you remember."

Chris said, "Yeah! That was when you received word of Mark's death."

Elizabeth spoke up then. "You know I was there for three more days after you left Dora, and I didn't see them again either. They left town without saying good-bye. Just checked out of school and 'boogied.'"

Christine laughed and said, "You two would scare the devil herself out of hell."

"Now that's a new one, since when did the devil become a woman?" asked Elizabeth.

Dora grinned and remarked, "Didn't you know, since women were given jump wings."

They cleaned up the kitchen and went back down to the room they were now calling the command center.

Chris looked through the photos and began comparing them to the information Mark had left. After about an hour, she came up for air with a smile on her face.

"You guys won't believe what's going on here."

Everyone gathered around to hear what she had to say. Chris would never be considered beautiful. But she did have striking features. Light brown complexion, light green eyes, red hair, freckles which she hated, and like Dora, tall at 5ft. 10in.; and 140 lbs of a good solid muscular body. She had graduated from the University of Pennsylvania Magna cum laude from the Wharton School of Business. She has a fantastic analytical mind. One, which could fathom the most muddiest of evidence.

"Look guys," said Chris, "this business started in Viet Nam. It doesn't say who they are except that they've been doing it for years. They are also the people who send us on assignment."

Now it was making sense to Dora. She understood what Mark meant by "sending her places to do a job."

"We, and other units like ours, are being used and have been used for years to further the ambitions of others. We go in for God and country and the fat cats, who are only in it for the money, keep getting fatter."

Chris stared at one of the photographs, whistled softly, and looked up at her buddies. "You know those two guys we were talking about. They weren't afraid of you, they were running for their lives. According to these records, there are only two of them left and that's because the bad guys have been unable to find them.

From what I can tell, the small timers they were sent to remove was just a smoke screen until they caught up with the one doing the porn and holding the kids. At this point they became a threat to the organization. Your brother and his team were for real, but they weren't suppose to be."

"The one name that keeps showing up in this report is a code name, Invincible One. We need to find this guy. It seems he's the one in the know about every shipment—where it's going, how much, and when the shipment is suppose to arrive and by what method of transport."

Dora was wondering to herself where to start looking for this guy when Chris looked up from the records she was still reading, "Maybe the man we're looking for is the chauffeur. It would certainly be a good cover."

Dora agreed, "But where would we find him. I've been looking without success. "

Chris and the others agreed it would be a good cover. We would be looking for a paid employee, not for a rich man with servants to attend his every want. Where to start? Which was a question that they never got an opportunity to answer because at that moment, looking at the monitor, the girls saw four men making their way to the front door. All had guns down at their sides and were looking all around as they got closer to the house.

"Wonder who they're looking for?" said Delores.

"I don't know," replied Elizabeth. Looking around at her compadres, Liz said,

"Ladies, shall we go say 'hello' to these bozos?"

The girls checked their weapons and went upstairs to deal with their visitors.

The men split up once they had gained entrance to the house, two went upstairs to check the bedrooms while the other two checked out the rooms on the ground floor. The girls split up also, Elizabeth and Delores went up the back stairs. Elizabeth was the first to encounter one of the men. She was standing just inside the small powder room when he opened the door. All he saw was a reflection in the mirror and fired. He killed the mirror.

"Bad luck," mumbled Elizabeth and hit him with so many rights, he was begging for a left, which she gave him. Down he went and he stayed down.

Hearing the ruckus, the second guy came running to join in the fun. Delores shot him in his tracks. All he heard was the whisper and 'thunk' of the bullet as it slammed into him.

Meanwhile, the two hoodlums upstairs, hearing the struggle down stairs assumed their buddies had taken care of whoever was found down there. They continued their search through the bedrooms. Christine and Dora waited for them in Dora's bedroom. The war started as soon as they stepped into the room. Dora hit one and Christine the other. The guy who was fighting Christine was pretty good. Christine was very good in martial arts and was kicking this guy's face to pieces.

The other fellow, still had his gun in his hand, but decided he didn't need it for Dora. He threw the gun aside and pulled a knife out of his boot.

He started tossing the knife from one hand to the other. Smiling, he said, "I'm going to cut you in half while you watch. The two guys you killed were friends of mine."

Dora smiled, too. "Good, you'll be joining them soon." She went to work.

When it was all over, amid the broken chairs and other debris, three guys were dead and the fourth unconscious. Dora called the cops. She wasn't in the least surprised to see David walk through the front door. He stopped as he came into the house, amazed at the destruction he encountered. He glanced at Dora, noting that she seemed to be all right. He walked over to scan the faces of the corpses and the fourth fellow whom paramedics were having a tough time trying to revive. He glanced at Dora again, shook his head and looked back at the dead men.

He found it almost impossible to believe that Dora, alone, had killed three men and beaten a fourth so badly that he probably would never revive.

Dora wasn't about to enlighten him. Her friends had gone below to wait.

David waded right in with the questions and was getting nowhere.

"Look these guys broke into the house and I had to defend myself," Dora told him. "What would you have done?"

David raised his voice at this comeback question. "I understand self-defense, but you have killed five men by my count, since you came home. Of this I'm sure. So don't talk to me about self-defense unless you are ready to tell me what the hell is going on."

Dora refused to say anymore. David started to read her her rights.

"Are you crazy? You are arresting me?" asked Dora.

"Yes, for your own good. I have got to find out what is going on around here and since you won't tell me, maybe a little time in jail will help you to understand that you can't take the law into your own hands."

Dora knew that there was no reasoning with this man. She also knew that she didn't want to hurt him, so she went to jail.

David put Dora in an area set aside for persons being held in protective custody. This way, she wouldn't end up with an arrest record in case she was telling the truth. The bottom line was, this man really loved her and would do most anything for her short of breaking the law.

Night had come and gone and Dora had not closed her eyes. Sleep was elusive in this place of confinement. Dora kept hoping that David would change his mind and release her before she would have to do something on her own to get out of there.

She heard the door opening and turned to see the big man himself enter. Big, as in huge and just as ugly. The great Herman Johnson, sheriff of the county. Everyone said that he hated everybody, but he hated himself more. He came in, pulled out a chair and sat down.

"Did you sleep well?" he asked.

"I've slept better," Dora replied.

"Would you like to go home?" Before Dora could answer that question, the sheriff interrupted, "Let's cut to the chase, shall we? You need to start telling us the truth. David believes you know more than you're telling as to why people are suddenly getting killed around here and quite frankly, little lady, I am very unhappy about it."

Dora was a little more than unhappy with this man. He had just called her 'little lady', a name she found demeaning at best, and a misnomer at worst, because first, she was anything but little; and secondly, she couldn't stand condescending men.

Reaching deep inside herself, Dora called on all her training to remain calm and in control.

"Sir," said Dora, "I don't understand what it is you want from me. I came home to my brother's funeral. As for those men who broke into my home, what else could I do? I was home alone and only trying to protect myself."

The sheriff guffawed at that. "Protect yourself. Lady, with what you did to those guys, you could protect the President of the United States. I've seen less killing in a war zone."

Dora had to laugh herself. The sheriff laughed so hard that he was turning red in the face. Dora thought he would burst his enormous gut.

He was about to say something else when the door opened and a very small, but beautiful lady stood in the doorway, in uniform. She looked like a picture.

Her name was Carrie. Lt. Colonel Carolyn Marshall, team leader and the last person Dora expected to see—here. Carrie stood five foot three, had long blond hair which you couldn't see because of the way she had it tucked up under her hat, and piercing blue eyes that could look right through you. Her hair was the envy of every woman who had ever seen it and she had the brains and the body to go with it. No dumb blonde was this lady. She had more missions under her belt than any woman in the service and was just as dangerous as she was beautiful.

When the sheriff got over his shock at seeing such a beautiful woman, he bellowed, "What is the meaning of this and who are you?"

The colonel advanced into the room and stopped directly in front of the sheriff. She introduced herself. "As for my reason for being here, you have one of my people locked up and this sir, you will correct immediately."

By the time the colonel had finished talking, she was staring this clown down like a dog.

"I understand you are holding her in protective custody, is that right?" The sheriff said, "Yeah! That's right." He was very unsure as to how to deal with this woman who stood in front of him and who was very much in control of the situation.

"Well sir, you will either charge her or release her. You will not treat her like a common criminal."

Dora could almost feel the rage building in this man, but she held her peace. She wanted to be released.

The old boy stood his ground. Saying, "Dear lady, you have no jurisdiction here, and that is that." Carrie let him have it after that very macho statement.

She began, "Do you have any idea who you're dealing with? Sheriff, I will take you to places 'where no man has ever been before' and that's just for starters. You, and no one else in this hick town will hold this soldier or anyone else under my command without having to deal with me, and man, I can tell you, that's the last thing you want to do. I've been known to pull buildings down around people like you, so I say to you again, either charge her or let her go. You have one hour to make up your mind, or I will be back." With that remark, Carrie walked over to Dora and shook her hand as if to say good-bye but placed something in it at the same time. Dora closed her hand around the small object and Carrie turned towards the door. She looked around the room, then at the sheriff. "This is a nice jail, I do hope its still here an hour from now. With that last aside, she marched out the door.

The sheriff, who was still in shock, followed close behind as if he couldn't believe the whirlwind that had just blown through.

After the sheriff left, Dora opened her hand to find a piece of C-4 explosive. Just enough to open any lock in the place, also, a small electrode to set it off. She wasn't too happy about this. Breaking out of jail was not to be taken lightly. She would have to think about this. She couldn't believe the Colonel actually wanted her to do this. That's something we do in an enemy's jail, but not in the good ol' USA.

She was still mulling it over when the Sheriff and David came back into the lockup and started in with the questions again.

Dora had no more to add to what she had all ready said. David said, "I still don't believe you are capable of doing what you said you did."

"Look David, those guys tried to kill me. If you really want to find out what is going on, why don't you question the fellow that's still alive?"

With that, the Sheriff started laughing, "Oh, we forgot to tell you, he's no longer with us." At the look Dora gave him, the Sheriff said, "That's right, he died about an hour ago. Now we are holding you for four dead men not three. What kind of woman could do that much damage in so short of time? That is the question somebody is going to answer before you go anywhere and I don't give a damn about your boss and her threats. I mean, what is she saying? She acts as if she is going to take you out of here, with or without my consent."

David, looking at Dora, knew that what the Sheriff was saying was just what might happen and he didn't want to see such a thing take place in this jail with the woman he loved. He was doing his job, but this was one time, he wished he could walk away. He knew that this feeling he had was because of the love he had for Dora and he had better find a way to fix all of this and fast.

David was certain that they had learned all they were going to from Dora. To clear up this mess, he would have to do some of the best detective work he had ever done in his life. He was determined that he was not going to lose her before he ever had a chance to win her.

While he was thinking that over, an officer came in and stated that the judge had just called and said to release the prisoner if we had nothing to hold her on and as far as he, the judge was concerned, we didn't.

The Sheriff almost had apoplexy over that. He said, "Okay Missy, you're free to go, for now. This time your boss won't have to break you out. But I'll being seeing you again and that's a promise." This was said in such a sarcastic tone of voice, that Dora, being the devil she is at times, looked him dead in the eye and threw him the C-4 as she went through the door, saying, "I guess I won't be needing this."

As he was choking on whatever he was trying to say, Dora patted him on his big belly. "Bye now!"

Once out on the street, Dora took a deep breath, then another. Her next breath was more of a shudder when she saw who was waiting for her. Before her stood the only man alive—that she knew of—that she feared. His name was Captain Raymond Anthony, U.S. Army Airborne. This man was her instructor and Sansei at Fort Campbell.

Around the base, he had another name—P. W. Perfect Weapon. This man could kill you and literally not touch you. The story was that he'd made a deal with the devil. He had been raised by an order of monks that ordinarily, never considered taking in an outsider, but Anthony was the exception. At the age of six, he was being trained to kill and dismember people in ways that only the gods and fallen angels could have devised.

This particular group of monks was like none other in the world. If you have ever heard of the term 'devil's advocate', then you would find that these guys were the real McCoy. Anthony lived with them until he was seventeen. As part of his graduation, he received the one gift to which he had been working since his arrival at the monastery—the markings that would identify him for rest of his life as a disciple of this particular monastery's teachings—a three-line tattoo on the side of his face. It started at the hairline on the right side of his face and ended at a dot on his cheek. It meant he couldn't be stopped—even in death.

Dora had every right to fear this man. She had seen too many people try to stop him and fail miserably. The captain came over to Dora and shook her hand. "Well, Lieutenant, I hear you've been having a bit of a problem with the local yokels." Saying this, he came as close to a smile as she'd ever seen on him. Dora laughed and asked, "How did you know and why have you come?"

"The colonel called me and I flew in to see if I could help."

Knowing how this man operated, Dora knew that the colonel was not joking when she'd told the sheriff that she wouldn't be in jail longer than one hour. This guy was like the colonel's personal pit bull. He would have pulled the walls of the jail down to get Dora out—brick by brick if necessary. Dora asked if he had a place to stay? "You're welcomed to stay at my place." But the Captain said, "No, I'll head on back to Campbell unless you feel I'm needed here."

"I don't think so, but thanks for coming." Taking this as a dismissal, he did an about face and was gone.

Dora hailed a cruising taxi to take her home. She spent most of the ride in deep thought, trying to map out her next move. She had high hopes that the team may have come up with something new to work with by the time she got home.

She looked up in time to catch the driver of the taxi watching her in his rear view mirror. She thought, "I've seen him before, but where and in what capacity?" He kept watching her, but trying to make like he wasn't. Dora was beginning to get annoyed. Looking at him, she asked, "Do you see something you like?"

His eyes got big and he apologized. "I'm sorry for staring, but I had almost forgotten how beautiful you are."

Dora leaned over the back of the seat. "Do I know you?" she asked.

"Yeah!" he responded. "We met in France. I was a friend of Mark's."

Then Dora remembered who he was. This was one of the kids who had disappeared so fast. He was the one person who might know who was doing the killing. The cabby was speaking again.

"I've had to hide to stay alive. The same men who killed the others are looking for me. They may even know that I'm back in the States. The one thing I've learned to do well, is how to be somebody else and be elsewhere when the need arises. They are having a hard time trying to find me and I don't think they have found Mike yet, either."

Dora was trying to remember his name, but couldn't, so she asked him.

He laughed, "I guess I didn't make a very good impression the last time we met."

My name is Curtis. Curtis Hall, and I know all about you. Mark told me that if I could make it to you still breathing, I would probably stay that way."

Dora took a good look at this young man, decided she liked what she saw and asked the $64,000 question.

"Okay Curtis, what do you know and how can you help?"

Curtis began talking. A lot of what he said she already knew. But he did say a few things that she didn't know.

"Everyone is under the impression that the big scores are in guns and porno. The truth is its—drugs and power." Dora was thinking he could be right, but there was no evidence of any kind to support such a belief in the information Mark had left behind. Dora asked some questions of her own.

"Do you know any of the people involved?" Curtis said he knew a few, but nothing he could prove. He went on to say that he had tracked some of them down, but no leads to the boss of the operation.

Dora's next question was to ask if he could provide any names and pictures. Curtis said he could. That driving a cab had been more beneficial than he had thought it would be. "I wired the cab. And I have been able to tape some very prominent people running off at the mouth about one thing and another. Most of the time I don't pay to much attention. But one day this guy got in the cab and made a call on his cellular phone. Being the genius I am, I switched my system to the same FM frequency of the cellular and overheard this guy talking about some things that he shouldn't have known. He did very little talking but listened for quite a while. Of course, he didn't know he was dealing with a super spook in the driver's seat. I had him three ways to Sunday."

Curtis knew from the look he was getting from Dora in the mirror that she was annoyed at his bragging. She said, "In all your greatness, do you have any information that will help me find these people?"

Curtis shook his head, looking penitent. "I guess I'm making a fool of myself once again. I'm sorry. It's just that everything is so messed up. Everywhere I look I see bad guys with guns pointed my way."

By now they were nearing the house and Dora wanted to keep his identity secure.

The car with the two men in it was still parked down the street. She told him not to get out of the cab, but she needed the information he had. He asked her if she had access to Marks' computer. She answered in the affirmative and Curtis said he would transmit all he had in an encrypted message using the cellular phone and fax modem he had in his cab. She told him to return ASAP if he encountered any problems. For now, at least, she thought his cover was safe.

At the front of house she got out of the cab and handed him some money. He thanked her in a loud voice so the men in the car could hear. Then pulled off.

Once inside the house the girls all but mobbed her. They started right in with questions. What happened? How did you get out? Dora was a little concerned about the bugs in the house, but the girls just laughed at her.

Delores said, "Relax. We put devices on the bugs that translate everything said into a different language each day. When and if they figure out what language we're using and react to it, we change the unit and they have to start all over again. Today we're using Latin. Furthermore, with these devices on, they cannot record. The only sound they will hear is a loud squeal."

Dora took the team down to the command center. She told them all that had transpired and about running into Mark's friend. It was then that the computer started to ring and the information from Curtis started to come through. Christine looked at the readout and then up at Dora and said it's encrypted. Dora laughed, "Yeah, I know. Its from the kid, he's not as dumb as he looks."

Once the transmission was completed, Christine went to work on it.

Delores told Dora to have a seat. They needed to bring her up to date. "We have a surprise for you. We've been doing a little calling on our own. The rest of the team will be in tonight. We even have some of our brothers standing by if we need them." Dora asked when had they put out the word? because she was wondering how the colonel had gotten wind of what was going on. And finding Capt. Anthony outside the jail was mind-boggling. She couldn't believe he was just going to break her out of jail. Delores said she hadn't gotten in touch with the colonel, but someone had, I wonder who? The question went unanswered. Watching the monitors, the girls saw two cars pull up in the driveway. Eight figures emerged. The sisters without mercy had arrived. The team was now intact.

The team came in with duffel bags and an assortment of paraphernalia as if they were a bunch of girls coming to a pajama party. The truth is, this was a clean-up crew. A military field day outing, which would result in the destruction of the enemy as soon as they were told who was to be destroyed and where to find them.

The girls put their gear up and they all went down to the command center.

Christine spent the next half hour bringing them up to date. When she finished, the 'sisters' wanted to know what they were to do in the mean time. Did Christine have a plan?

She said, "Yes. After I finished transcribing the info Curtis sent in, I think I found a starting place for us. This is what we know. Guns and porno are being sold all over the world, right! What we didn't understand was why anyone would go to this much trouble for this type of business. There's nothing new about it. So we dig a little deeper and 'voila' we find its all a smoke screen. Behind door number three, we find drugs in quantities like no one has ever seen before."

One of the girls, the youngest on the team, whom they called Lil' Bits, mused, "If it's drugs, why would anyone go through the pain of putting together a unit of FBI agents and then systematically start killing them off? That doesn't make sense."

Christine said, "Good question. One that I can't answer at the moment, but I'm getting there. However, first things, first. Dora, you said Mark said something about a camp where they were trained?"

"That's right. He said it was over a three-hour drive."

"Okay. Looking at the map, there are two bases in the area that are about three hours away. One is Camp Pendleton and the other is El Toro. What do you think?"

Another of the sisters, Jodi by name, offered her opinion. "I see what you mean. What better place to train an elite group and not having people asking questions.

You're one hundred per cent correct. These guys could be trained, using advanced techniques and fire power, and no one would ask why?"

They all sat around and thought about what they had just learned. Could it be true? Mark and company were told that what they were about to embark on was a true effort to clean up the streets. To rid the U.S. of drugs and other scum bags. When in truth, someone was out to rule the world in drug trafficking. To own every drug pusher and junkie on earth. To dry up the world of drugs so that the only drug deals would be those that are totally controlled by one organization. The whole operation was being financed through arms and porno deals.

Christine spoke again. "What I don't understand is the slavery ring that seems to be going on. According to these documents, the sale of young boys and girls and women is good, very good indeed. You know, I think, that what we have here is a group of people who want to control every illegal way to make money and they are on a roll. If allowed to continue, this group, whoever they are, will own it all and there won't be anyone to stop them. The one thing they didn't count on was their plan backfiring as far as the agents were concerned."

Regina spoke up for the first time saying, "There's one more thing they didn't plan on," she paused for effect—then said, "us." Regina was tuning the computer to one of the very special toys that would allow them to access the nearest satellite that could photograph the area around the Country Club and both camps. The nice thing about the satellite, it could be moved all over the state to find the camp they were looking for. Regina told the team it would take about an hour to get it into position. Dora said, "Right! I don't know about the rest of you, but I'm hungry. How about some food." They all agreed and left Regina to do whatever she had to do with the satellite and went upstairs to prepare dinner.

The phone rang as they trooped into the kitchen. It was Hope calling to see how Dora was getting along. Dora told her she had almost finished with Mark's room.

"What do you want me to do with Mark's things?"

"Just box them up and I'll give them to the Salvation Army or something. Hold on a moment Dora, Charlie wants to speak to you."

"Hi Sis, I remembered something else that Mark told me once. He said if for any reason he wasn't here to take care of us there was a place he had never told anyone about and it seemed very important to him at the time." Dora interrupted him, afraid that someone could be listening in on Charlie's side.

"Look sweetheart, why don't you save it until I see you, okay." Charlie understood immediately, that he should keep what he knows to himself. "Okay, here's Mom again."

Dora talked to her mom a few more minutes and hung up. She was wondering as she made her way to the kitchen, what it was that Charlie thought so important that she should know. She realized that her brother understood a lot more than he let on.

Once in the kitchen, she joined in the feast. They were enjoying the meal and feeling good that they were altogether and about to do some serious damage to a bunch of scum bags.

Sandra, who was looking out of the window, noted the changing of the guard.

"Oh, oh, what have we here?" The girls gathered around her.

"What's up?" asked Lil' Bits.

Sandra pointed to where there were usually two men, now there were five or six. This increase in surveillance manpower was of some concern. Why so many to watch the house? And why now? Although it wasn't entirely unexpected, but what would be their next move?

The last time that many men had come to the house, it was to take them out. They knew that there were more than four girls in the house now. Oh, well, it didn't matter. Whatever those guys had in mind, the 'sisters' would deal with it when it happened.

Regina went back down to the command center to see if the satellite was in position for the first shot.

"We'll only get one shot before the tracking station notices that the satellite has been moved. Hopefully, they won't worry much about it because it's a common practice between the Soviets and the U.S. It's easier this way then for everyone to fill the skies with satellites. They'll pull it back on course, that's why we'll only get one shot."

Regina called everyone over and pointed to an image on the screen that looked like a military five ton truck, but was in the wrong place. Dora saw what she meant and printed the picture and everything around for miles. Then she started a sweep for body heat. She found only one person moving, very fast, as if he was on a motorcycle. Next, Regina did a sweep for ordinance and found a place filled with it.

Dora was still thinking about the person on the motorbike. Why would anyone be at the club this time of night riding a motorcycle?

Then something very strange happened, a chopper landed and from the heat censors, they could tell it was full of ordinance. Why would a gun ship be landing at a resort?

Regina moved the satellite over the camps and started scanning the areas. Once again she found a chopper where it had no business being. After confirmation that they had hit pay dirt, she made copies of everything and signed off. They decided to call it a night. There was no need to post a watch. They just climbed into their sleeping bags in the command center. Even if those guys outside decided to force an entry, they would never find them in the command center. Also, Regina had set up an infrared system that would alert them if anyone were to gain entry.

CHAPTER FOUR

The team slept without incidence and awoke early in the morning. They firmed up plans to visit one of the sites. They would, first, have to shake the bloodhounds. With six of them, that wasn't going to be easy.

Regina was the one to come up with an idea. She went upstairs to the bedroom and opened the curtains. She then dropped her robe and began to dress in front of the window. As she knew they would, the slimeballs outside took their attention from the front of the house to watch her. All but two of the team left by the back door. The two were left just in case there were unwanted visitors and they didn't want Regina to be found alone.

When they were a couple of blocks away, Dora knocked on the door of a friend of her mother's. She asked if she could borrow the Bronco, explaining that her car wouldn't start. Her mom's friend gladly handed over the keys and the girls climbed in and headed out to the first site on the list. They were all laughing about how easy it was to fool some men and what better person to do it than Regina, who had the body of a goddess and the skin of a newborn baby. Those guys out front must have thought they had died and gone to heaven. Whenever they needed a decoy, Regina was always the one they sent in. Not that anyone of them couldn't do the same, all of them could have stopped a runaway train with their looks. But Regina had a sense of the dramatic. She had dreams of becoming an overnight sensation as an actress. They were still laughing about old times when Dora spun the wheel and pulled over to the side of the road.

"This is the back entrance to the Club," she told them. From the outside it looked like an estate. The girls sat awhile, checking for any unusual activity before they went onto the grounds. When they were pretty sure the coast was clear, they climbed the wall and made their way toward the main house through the woods.

They were about three miles in when they spotted the chopper that they had picked up on the sensors the night before. There were also bunkers and a couple of buildings.

Lil' Bits reconned the area and reported back with the news that the place was deserted.

"There is no car in the garage nor is there any sign that anyone is living here. Very peculiar, don't you think?"

Dora, still looking around, spoke up. "There's a lot of peculiar things about this whole caper. Let's go."

The team made their way to the house where Tracy, lock picker extraordinaire, unlocked the door and they all went in. They carefully checked all of the rooms before relaxing—satisfied that no one was in the house. They looked through everything, leaving things as they found them. This came from years of working together and knowing their jobs. Armed with cameras, they photographed everything as they went along.

Finished with the house, the team started looking around outside. They wandered into one of bunkers. It was filled with all types of military ordinance, which made Elizabeth's day.

"Ladies, I've just died and gone to heaven. I could take on a third world country with all the armament in this place."

They all burst into laughter. "Girl you are sick," said Lil' Bits. The rest agreed.

They knew that Liz was never happier than when she was blowing up things. And she was good. Very good at her job. There was none better then she when it came to bringing down buildings, bridges or mountains with precision—including people.

They decided to take what they needed back to the house. Mark had secreted a lot of weapons in the basement of his home, but nothing like they'd found in the bunker. Some of the weapons in this arsenal would be hard to come by.

The girls loaded their loot into the bronco, locked the bunker back as they found it, than went to look at the chopper.

Tracy, checking it out, gave a soft whistle, "Can you believe this, the keys have been left in the switch. You know, we can steal this chopper and fly it down to Pendleton."

No one answered her; everyone was watching Dora who was gazing down at the ground.

"Look girls, this road shows signs of a lot of vehicular movement and what ever it was—it was heavily loaded."

Liz, looking around said, "What about the chopper?"

"It'll keep," said Dora. "Just put a mini camera and tracking device on it."

There was no sign of unloading until Liz noticed that all of the greenery in the area was newly planted, deliberately so.

"Let's take a walk, shall we," said Liz.

They walked through the maze of beautiful greenery and came upon the largest spread of marijuana plants they had ever seen.

Lil' Bits gasped, "Look at that—it goes on for miles."

Someone had spent a lot of time and money on making this place look like an overgrown wood. The only problem was, this lot alone was not enough to supply the amount of drugs being shipped in and out of the states. More photos were taken and the 'sisters' returned to the Bronco. They believed they had found a starting place and—start they would.

The problem now was to reenter the house without those bozos out in front seeing them. Another diversion was needed. The team dropped the Bronco off and started the hump back to the house, lugging all the gear they had removed from the bunker at the Club.

Liz called Regina and asked her to come up with something and did she ever.

The guys outside of the house were a new bunch, but the departing voyeurs had told them about the show they could expect, so they were watching for any movement at the windows. Sandra and Regina treated them to a sight they never expected to see. The two girls undressed down to their bikinis, removed their bras and pulled out a number of clothes, holding them in front of each other as if they were trying to decide what to put on. While all eyes were glued to the window, the others made it into the house undetected. Sandra and Regina figured they had done enough for now and each chose an outfit and donned it.

Dora, along with the girls who had gone out on the scout, brought the housebound team up to date on what they had discovered and showed them the arsenal they had brought back with them. Regina, Sandra and Jodi started laughing. The girls looked at them. Knowing they hadn't said anything funny, Dora said, "Okay guys, what gives?"

Regina spoke up, "After you left, we decided to listen to the tapes again."

"Yeah", said Jodi. "And guess what we found out."

"There is another way out of this very special room," Regina picked up from Jodi.

"I would have loved to have known your brother, he was undoubtedly, a genius," continued Regina.

Liz started asking questions. "Have you checked it out yet?

"Not all the way. We decided to wait until you returned before going any further," said Regina.

"Yeah!" Chimed in Sandra. "We found an area down there where your brother has set up a place for making his own ammo and evidently did some gunsmith work, too."

Jodi wanted us to quit wasting time and check it all out.

Dora looked at Regina and told her to "lead the way."

Regina headed to the back of the vault and moved one of the Colt. 44s that were hanging there and another door opened. Leading the way, she hit a light switch. The door closed behind them.

"We continued on for another fifty meters and came face to face with a shooting range. One that could handle small arms and some of the larger weapons."

Sandra took the lead this time and led the group at a slight right angle past the area where Mark made his ammo.

"This is as far as we explored. From this point on it will be new territory," said Regina.

The 'sisters' continued along the corridor which opened out into a larger area. The girls couldn't believe what they saw. Mark had stashed a Hum V fully loaded with two sixty-caliber guns and a rocket launcher in this underground chamber. Lola looked all around and then back at Dora.

"Was your brother of this world? That kid had a serious problem. He was ready for World War III."

Lydia found cases of grenades, rockets and all kinds of ammo. The girls looked at each other and started laughing.

"I don't believe we just hauled all of that stuff from the bunker and all of this was waiting for us right here. This is unbelievable," said Lydia.

Everyone laughed again. Liz said, "I'm going to have a good time with somebody's cakes and cookies.

"Hey, we've gotten this far, let's find our way out of here," quipped Christine.

"Not necessary. It's all on the tapes," said Regina.

They returned to the main room. Deciding it was time to eat, they went up to the kitchen. While the 'sisters' were sitting around the table talking over the day's events, the telephone rang. It was David and he was terribly upset.

"Dora, someone took a shot at my car and I'm sure that the lady who was riding with me was mistaken for you because she is just about your height and weight. Now I know something is afoot, more than you're willing to let on, but if you don't start confiding in me soon, there are going to be more dead bodies. Do you hear me, Dora, what the hell is going on?" David was fairly yelling by now.

"What do you want from me, David? There is nothing to tell, but if I find out anything, I promise, you'll be the first to know. Now, good night, and please stop blaming me for people getting—uh, dead."

After hanging up the phone, Dora looked at her team. "Girls, we're going to have step things up a bit before someone else gets killed."

They all agreed. "Let's clean up this mess and get a good night's sleep," said Regina. With that in mind, they finished up and retired to their sleeping bags in the command center.

Christine was the first one up in the morning. She wanted to develop the film taken at the Club and the marijuana farm. While the negatives were drying, she decided to read more of the documents Mark had left. Suddenly, she sat up very straight. Dora, who was walking in the door at the moment, noticed her stance.

"What is it? Did you find something?"

"Yes. And you won't believe what it is. We need to take a trip to the harbor down at Long Beach. There are a few yachts we need to check out. It looks like they are set up like a destroyer screen and are used to escort the ships that are transporting whatever it is these people are shipping illegally."

"Furthermore, the main office for the shipping lines is right here and these people own all kinds of ships—and according to this information, all of the ships are being used to move the dope. These people, whoever they are, are in 100% control of any imports or exports to most countries. If that isn't enough, they own most of the shipping lines. These folks also have ships under their control that do not carry their names.

Dora, standing beside Regina, was thinking about the taxi driver. The kid might be able to shed some light on some of this. When the rest of the team trooped in, Dora and Regina brought them up to date with what they had just learned. She told the 'sisters' that she thought she had better talk to the kid before they went up to Long Beach.

The phone rang as Dora was going up to take a shower. It was her brother Charlie.

"Hey Sis, I'm sorry to call back so soon, but I have something to tell you that is very important. I'm using a friend's phone, so it's okay to talk."

Dora asked for the number and told Charlie she would call him right back.

After going to a secure phone, Dora called Charlie asking, "What's up Bro?"

The information Charlie had for Dora was that there was another way out of the house other than the front and back doors. Dora told Charlie that she had already found it. And he was right, it was perfect for getting in and out without being seen.

Then Charlie told her something she didn't know. "Mark had a girlfriend, but she hasn't been around since before Mark's death. I haven't seen her anywhere since all this happened." He gave Dora what little information he knew about the girl and hung up.

Dora finished her shower and went down to apprised the team of what she had learned from Charlie.

They now had to figure out exactly where the exit was and the mechanics of how it worked.

Christine was having a ball deciphering all the new information they had gathered. The others were cleaning and arming their weapons, readying them for action for whenever the time came and they knew it was coming very fast.

Tracy decided to go for a run. She donned a pink see-through tank top with a pair of darker pink minute mini shorts. One of the girls told her she was going to get arrested in that outfit.

Tracy laughed. "I plan to. I'm going to give those clowns something to write home about."

Dora needed to get out of the house. Using Tracy as a decoy, she wanted to get to the motorcycle without being seen.

When Tracy ran past the men, she stumbled and began to hop like she was hurt.

All the guys went to help her and Dora was out of house like a shot. She rolled the bike out of the side gate and took off to find Curtis. She did a lot of dodging and turning to make sure she wasn't being followed. Comfortable at last, she called the taxi company and asked to have his cab pick her up in front of the skating rink.

When the taxi pulled up, she stepped out of the building and into the cab.

Curtis was happy to see her. He'd had mixed emotions about responding to the call, but some instinct had told him it must be Dora.

Upon entering the cab, Dora took out her phone to scan it for bugs. Satisfied, she began telling Curtis what they had learned when he started laughing. A big belly laugh. Dora looked at him in the rear view mirror.

"Did I say something funny?" she asked. Curtis, looking in the rear view mirror saw the look on her face and figured he had better let her in on the fun.

He started by saying, "Mark told me that you were the one person he could trust and that you would leave no stone unturned to find the truth. I see he was right. You are better than I thought you would be and I feel better about life now."

Dora ignored the accolade and started in with the questions. Curtis was answering them as best he could when he noticed he was being tailed.

It was the same car he had seen before and he knew they were after them.

He wasn't sure they knew who he was, but Dora was another story. He floored the pedal in the cab. They were heading north on 101 and he was trying to think where he could get off and lose these guys when he heard the first shot and glass breaking.

That cinched it. They were definitely after them. There were a few exits near Carpenteria that were dead ends, but there was one that he thought would be a good place to take on these guys. There was another shot—this one hit the hood of the car.

Dora shouted, "We need to get off this road."

"Yeah! We are. Just ahead." Curtis took the exit on two wheels, made a left and headed into the fuel depot. There was only one way in and one way out. A great place for an ambush. As he went through the gate, there was a huge tanker parked on the left. He pulled in behind it and stopped. Dora was checking her weapons. Curtis couldn't help himself, he had to laugh again. This is definitely Mark's sister. She had two nine millimeters with extended clips.

Dora said, "Let's split up and we can hit them from two sides."

They bailed out of the car. Curtis ran to the east end of the yard. Dora went closer to the front gate.

She didn't have long to wait. The car came barreling through the gate and headed straight to the back of the yard. Dora closed the gate so they couldn't make a run for it without doing some damage to their car, which, in all probability, would stop them or at least slow them down.

Curtis opened fire on the sedan. Dora joined in. It was getting rough for the would-be assassins. They were trying to get out of the car. One was down and another hit. Curtis rushed the car and fired at the guy who had been hit. This time he stayed down. The driver was trying to turn the car towards Dora to run her down. Dora emptied a magazine into the car. The driver, evidently hit by the hail of bullets thrown his way, lost control and plowed into one of the tankers. Both vehicles exploded into flames. The others trapped in the car were screaming as the flames engulfed them.

Dora and Curtis got back into the taxi and headed for the freeway. Luckily, they didn't meet up with any of the local law.

They continued on to Santa Barbara to check out the boats they were interested in. En route, Dora asked Curtis if he could run the plate on that sedan using his modem in the taxi. He said he could, so she gave him the numbers. The read out came back that a Matt Harrison had rented the vehicle. Dora whistled softly to herself as she read the sheet. The name didn't mean anything to Curtis, but she knew this guy was a CIA hit man. Now why had they sicced this man on her?

This whole business was getting very confusing. Just when she thought she had an idea of what was going on, something else showed up that made very little sense.

Arriving at the docks, it didn't take long to find the boats on their list. There were some of the best kept boats that could be found anywhere—tied up at this dock. All of them were low in the water, which meant they were carrying more weight than the other boats. Dora and Curtis decided to park and wait. Maybe something would develop that would shed some light on the situation.

Just after sundown, a couple of cars pulled up and discharged a few well-dressed men and one woman. Neither of them recognized any of these people.

Dora's cell phone started ringing. It was Jodi calling to say that David was looking for her and she should give him a call. She did. David was beside himself.

"Where are you? Why can't I find you? What are you doing?"

Dora replied by saying, "The last time I checked, you were neither my father nor my mother and to ask me questions like that, you would have to be one or the other."

David told her that there were more bodies and it looked like some more of her handy work.

Dora went off. "What makes you think that every dead body you come across is tied to me in some way? I don't believe you truly think that I'm capable of all these acts of murder."

"All I know is, there were no bodies until you showed up and now there is no room at the morgue for them. I've asked you to level with me. Let me help you."

David was angry. Of this, Dora had no doubts.

"David, I am not listening to anymore of your hysterics. Goodbye." With that, Dora put away her phone.

While Dora was on the phone with David, Curtis had donned an old raggedy coat, scuffed up shoes, and sallied up to the cars to place bugs on each of them. Dressed as he was, anyone would think he was looking for bottles or cans. Anything that he could sell for a couple of bucks.

When he returned to the taxi, he tuned in the radio to pick up the conversation from each car then set the recorders to ensure he got all of it. He couldn't monitor both of them at the same time.

Dora took pictures of the clowns as they returned to their automobiles. Once the cars had left, the taxi followed along listening in to some very interesting conversation. Curtis really had this cab loaded. Dora was beginning to feel very close to this kid. He reminded her of her brother. He was smart and a survivor.

"What's the distance on monitoring the cars, Curtis,"

"Don't worry, the relay I'm using works up to 150 miles."

"Okay. How about taking me back to my bike? And you can transmit all the info to the house. All right?"

"Yeah! I'll do it later."

Dora had Curtis drop her about a block from where her bike was park. She walked the rest of the way, dropping into a couple shops en route to the parking lot.

She kick-started the bike and headed home. She went right on by the men without giving them a look—going in through the back door.

The mail had come and there was a letter from Charlie except it looked like Mark's handwriting. Upon closer inspection of the postmark, Dora found that it was mailed the day before he died and from three thousand miles away. How could this be? Mark was nowhere near Washington, D.C. on the date it was mailed.

The letter was from Mark, addressed to Charlie, but it was for her.

Chapter Five

Mark's letter began with the salutation, "*Hi, Sis,*" Then he went on to say:

"I hope you're doing well. I also hope you are making more progress than I did in figuring out this caper. I knew they would get to me, so I put a few things of my own in motion, just in case. You need to know, that you may have to bring down some pretty important people in high places when you start to play your hand. Those same people will want you dead. If necessary, they will kill everyone in the house to get to you. This letter was not mailed by me, but by my girl friend who I sent away so she would be safe.

"You will find I have left you enough information and a lot more to do what has to be done. If you are as smart as I think you are, you will know this all ready. (smile)

"What you don't know is, there's a three-mile tunnel that runs underground from the house. You will also find transportation at the end of the tunnel. I also left everything you'll need to pull off what you must.

"One thing you must do is get Mom and Charlie as far out of harms way as possible because they will use them to get to you just as they did me.

"And Sis, see if you can find a way to help whoever is left of my team. The CIA and the FBI cannot be trusted. There are people in both agencies that have a big stake in all of this and will kill anybody that gets in their way.

"You need to start looking at people who are doing better than they should. I left some information about various bank accounts and fake company names that if you dig deep enough, you will find that they are owned by the same people or their dead relatives."

The letter continued, but Dora stopped reading when her 'sisters' came into the room. She told them all that had transpired since she had left the house that morning.

"We're going to wait for the info from Curtis," Dora informed them, "then we'll be moving out."

"It's about time," said Elizabeth. "I've made some very special ammo for this glorious occasion. It doesn't just kill, it vaporizes people."

She had hollowed out the head of each bullet and filled it with magnesium and recovered the head with liquid lead.

"Phew! I love it. That ought to slow 'em down a bit. We are about to get very busy, so let's finish up," said Dora.

Jodi took over computer duty. She read everything that came in, but so far there was nothing earth shattering. All the info so far was about parties the women hoped to attend. There was some talk of business but nothing out of the ordinary. The evening was uneventful.

Dora kept thinking about Mark's girl. She had to find her and make sure she was safe. She looked for pictures of her in photo albums, but there was nothing. Mark had cleaned them out. Her brother seemed to have thought of everything and she, Dora, was going to have to think like him if she was to find her.

They all retired for the evening. Dora, however, could not sleep. She was getting an itch behind her ear like she always got just before going on an assignment. First thing in the morning, she would talk to David. He wanted to help so much, let's find out what he knows about Mark's girl. They would also need to find the way in and out of the underground passage. From here on out, that is the way they would leave and enter the house.

When morning came, neither she nor the girls had gotten much sleep. They had taken turns on watch. There was still lots of talk about big parties. There was one mentioned 'where everyone who was anyone would be there.'

The 'sisters' were finishing up their breakfast when there was a knock at the front door. Dora went to answer it and found David standing there looking as if he could eat nails and anything else that came his way.

He started right in on Dora. "I thought you said that you were nowhere near the shootings yesterday. Now, before you answer, I want you to know if you lie, I will throw you in jail so fast, you won't know your head from a hole in the wall." With that said, he threw a video tape on the table.

"I pulled this out of the camera at the fuel dump and I better get some answers—and quick."

Dora looked at him for a second, then very calmly said, "What are you talking about officer? If your question is—did some men try to kill me since I've been home? The answer is yes. Have I defended myself? The answer is also yes. So tell me dear officer, what would you have had me do? Let them kill me like they did my brother. I don't think so. What you should be saying is, 'I'll find the people who killed your brother, Dora', but you haven't at any time mentioned Mark's name. But that's all right. I will avenge his death. Me. With or without your help."

David broke in saying, "You know I can't do anything like that."

Dora gave him a deadly look and said, "I suggest you get to stepping in a hurry then, because things are about to get funky."

David's mouth was hanging open. He could not believe what she just said.

Looking at her, he said, "Who are you and how did you get so efficient at killing?" In a very low voice, he said, "I saw less action during the LA riots."

The rest of the girls could hear everything that was being said and did not know what to think. Was this guy going to haul Dora away again? This time he had proof. They were looking at each other when they heard David say, "Look I'm not going to arrest you, but you have got to stop taking the law into your own hands."

The look Dora gave him, said 'back off'. She wasn't going to drop it. The words that came from her lips made David shiver. How could one so beautiful sound so cold. He didn't know if the devil could have sounded any colder. Dora told him "blood for blood." He knew it was time to go. He wasn't going to learn anything further. As he was about to leave, Dora asked him if he knew Mark's girlfriend. David replied that he did, but he hadn't seen her since Mark's death.

"Do you know where she lives?"

"Not around here. She's Hispanic and I'm not sure where she stays." Looking at her, David asked, "Dora, what has she got to do with all of this?"

"Nothing, as far as I know. I've never met her and would like to before I return to base."

David asked if he could use the telephone, he would check to see if anyone had seen her lately. He also asked for a glass of water, though he really needed something stronger. Much, much stronger.

En route to get the water, Dora detoured to Mark's room to talk with her 'sisters'.

The girls asked, "What are we going to do?" Liz coming up from the command center said, "I know exactly what we are going to do and where we're going to do it."

"What ya got there?" Everybody was talking at once.

"This just came in over the wire. There is a very large shipment of drugs being flown in this afternoon. The plane will land at Burbank at 1500 hours. From there it will be moved by truck to a warehouse at the end of the runway and there it will stay until Customs clears it. Now here's the kicker, from there it will go South to Mexico where there won't be any questions asked because the guys on duty in Customs are in on it and will just clear the shipment."

"Are you suggesting that we pay them a little visit," asked Lola.

"You bet your booty, I am. I do believe we have a little something special that will do the trick. If we drop a canister in the truck, I'm pretty sure we can make them dump the drugs. Remember what we did to the poppy fields in Turkey?" The girls answered in the affirmative.

"Well, we can do the same here. Make them lose all of the shipment and the money in one feeding—so to speak. We can make the canister out of some of the stuff left by Mark. Everything we need is downstairs. It won't take much to fabricate it" Elizabeth looked at her teammates, "Well, what do you guys think?"

Dora said, "Fine. We had better leave by the underground and return the same way."

The 'sisters' decided that there was no need for all of them to go. Four would be enough. Dora figured she had better not go; she still had David to contend with.

Dora returned to the living room with the glass of water that David had asked her for while her 'sisters' prepared to go to war.

The girls who were going on this assignment packed their ditty bags with ammo and weapons and started out for the Hum V. About a mile along the passage, the team came to the room where all of the chemicals were stored. They made up the canister and continued along the passage to the unit. Once in the unit, they followed the instructions Mark left for getting out of there. They drove another two miles to a large rock, which turned out to be a door. They drove through and the door closed behind them. They found themselves surrounded by a thicket of trees, which was great because that meant that no one could see them leave. They turned left per instructions and about three hundred yards further on, the road came out of the trees and onto an old dirt road formerly used when there was mining in the area. It hadn't been used for anything since. Checking the map, they saw that this road would take them to a service road that led to route 101. From there they headed south to route 405, then on to Burbank.

Back at the house, Dora was trying to figure out how to get rid of David. She needed to find Mark's girl friend, make sure she was safe, and find out what she knows, if anything, about all that had taken place before Mark was killed and since.

David had popped the tape in the VCR while he was waiting for Dora to return to the den with his water and was getting mad all over again. He began another diatribe on the rights and wrongs of what she had done. Dora waltzed over and turned the tape off. She removed it from the VCR and placed it in its box. Laid the box back on the TV and was just about to tell him off again, when Delores, who had been watching on the monitor, decided that enough was enough. It was time to get rid of this fella—and now.

She walked into the room and stopped, "Oh, I'm sorry. I didn't know you had company. Umh! From the looks of him, I'd say g-r-r-e-at company, too."

Dora smiled and introduced Delores as a cousin who was visiting for a few days.

David was standing there with his mouth open wondering how so much beauty could be in one family. He quickly returned the compliment when he regained his composure.

Dora informed Delores that David has a video tape that he feels implicates her in a shooting, and is trying to get some answers.

Delores said, "Ooh, I just love cops and bad guys. Is this the tape?" Dora said it was and Delores picked it up. Dora wondered what she was up to. Delores was slipping a small electrode into the box with the tape then she put it back on the television.

"Are you going to arrest my dear cousin?"

"Not right now. I haven't finish looking at the entire tape yet. But I have seen enough that I'm sure once my chief sees it, we will be back for her. Maybe you can convince her to tell me what is going on, so I can help."

"I doubt it. Once 'Cous' makes up her mind, you may as well forget it."

David turned back to Dora, "You know, I really do understand your wanting to find your brother's killers. I want to find them, too. But I don't want you getting in the way. I'm going to say this just once more. You cannot take the law into your own hands." With that he picked up the tape and went to the door.

"Oh yes! No one has seen Carmen Delgada in days."

David left the house convinced that he would be back to arrest Dora. Unfortunately, for him, the electrode that Dolores had put in the box had erased the entire contents of the tape.

Regina, who was watching on the monitor, activated a magnetic field. David was going to be very, very angry when he attempted to show that tape to his boss.

In the meantime, as the team drove toward the Burbank Airport they were devising a plan to get on the field. They decided that the best thing to do was to park the unit and leave one member with it. The others would walk to the field, find the changing room and the rest would be easy—they hoped.

Jodi was the first to find what she needed—the uniform worn by the sweeper driver. She donned it and went out onto the field and started up one of the big sweeper machines. She checked out the frequency of the radio, gave Lydia the info and she drove around close to the gate and waited. Lydia was to call that there was an accident in the parking lot and to go clean up the glass. The call came in and she was given clearance to go out the gate with the machine. When she got to the gate the guard on duty waved her through. He told her that he knew about the accident and that she had been requested to clean up the glass. Once through the gate, Jodi headed for the Hum V.

Lydia loaded what was needed into the cab of the sweeper. As soon as they received word that the other two members of the team were in place, Jodi and Lydia headed back to the field. They saw Christine, who had dressed in camouflage fatigues, holding a clipboard in her hand. She indicated the direction she wanted them to take. Christine and Liz jumped on one of the field units and headed down the airfield. Lydia and Jodi followed close behind. When Christine was almost to the hangar where the truck loaded with drugs was being kept, Jodi pulled the sweeper along aside. Christine told them to start working in the area and to work their way around behind the building. The plan was that Christine and Lydia were going to get into an argument over where else they could park the choppers since the truck was evidently parked in the wrong hangar. They were working it when the guards came out of the hangar and one of them asked, "What's the problem?"

He was put in his place very quickly. First, he had forgotten to salute an officer; secondly, Christine demanded to know by whose authority had he parked the truck in this particular hangar.

"This hangar is for three inbound choppers and somebody is going to answer for this mistake."

The marine on duty told Christine that he was only the watch, not the one in charge. He went on to say that the truck was already parked there when he reported for duty. All he knew was that it was a military tractor-trailer and he could do nothing unless given orders to do so.

The marine's partner on the watch came up and snapped to attention, asking for permission to speak. Permission was granted. The Sergeant was very understanding and asked what he could do to correct the situation. He was unsure of just what, but he was willing to do whatever was necessary. He said he would contact HQ to see if he could get permission to move the rig. Jodi was now on the other side of the hangar and had gone inside to plant the chemical bomb.

The best thing about this particular device and the chemical within—is it would not kill anyone, but it would make anyone who came within ten feet of the drugs extremely nauseous. The chemical eats through the plastic that the drugs are wrapped in rendering the drugs useless which means they couldn't be sold.

Chris saw Jodi working her way back around the hangar on the sweeper.

"Never mind Sergeant, I'll handle it myself." With that she dismissed both men and headed back towards the gate. She felt good knowing that this shipment would never hit the street. They regrouped and left the area. Jodi was laughing as she said goodbye to millions of dollars in drugs. She was thinking how upset some people would be in a very short time.

Once back on the road, Chris signed onto the laptop to let Dora know 'mission accomplished.'

* * * * * * * * * * * * * * * * * * * *

Meanwhile, Sandra, who had been playing around with the computer, found what she thought might be very important. She told Dora that she heard the folks in the limo talking about a power plant that was located somewhere near Camp Pendleton that was only used for emergencies. "I've been able to access the blueprints through a main frame in San Clemente, and it seems it is only used by the hospitals. It's an old nuclear plant, but they keep this one up and running, just in case."

Regina was about to comment further when the vault opened and Christine and the girls walked in.

" It was a piece of cake," said Christine with a big smile on her face.

Down at headquarters, David found himself in a little hot water with the DA. Upon returning to HQ he decided to finish viewing the tape so that he would have some answers before he had the meeting with the DA. Of course the tape was blank.

In a way, he was glad the tape had been erased. He really didn't want to bring Dora into this if he didn't have to, even though he knew this entire mess centered around her. He knew he had seen her on the tape. Still, he had nothing, and the men killed at her house were still considered to be self-defense.

The DA's first question was "could anyone tell him why, all of a sudden, his town had turned into a war zone?" No one could answer that. David left the office feeling as if he had left part of his behind on the hot seat. He was in trouble, he knew, but right now, there was nothing he could do about it.

* *

Nightfall found Regina busy reprogramming the anti bug devices. She had been scanning them as she did everyday and found that the guys outside were close to figuring out how to break the codes. This was expected, if the guys knew their business. It was also the reason, she changed them whenever necessary. Time was the enemy of those fellows on the outside because it took time to adjust their system to counteract whatever she was doing. So far, they had not been able to keep up with the changes.

The following day found the big tractor trailer on the move—and surprise, surprise, Jodi had not only planted the gas canister, but she had also planted a bug.

She told her 'sisters' that even though they knew where the truck was headed, they had no idea of its final destination. She was very proud of herself. No one else had thought of it. As she said, "We will be able to track that bad boy wherever it goes."

The information gathered by the team was that the truck would be heading for Mexico. The bug indicated that the truck was indeed headed south. The plan was to take the truck into Mexico, have the drugs 'stepped' on a few times, then bring the cut drugs back into the USA to sell for five times the original price. They would love to see the faces of the people when they opened up that truck.

One of the girls asked if it was possible to lose the truck?

Regina said, "It's possible, but we can find it again by moving a satellite around.

Sandra came into the room, "Hey, I think I've found a way into the plant, but we'll need a boat. There is a very large duct under water at the base of the plant.

Some of us can set off shore and fish our hearts out while the rest of you can swim in and find out what's going on."

Dora was thinking. Where could they find a boat? The girls were talking but she wasn't really listening. She was remembering something that she had heard on Mark's tapes. On one of the documents, she had come to an underlined passage, which stated, "If you ever need to go to sea, look up the Gypsy." The only problem was she didn't know where to look.

Dora made a few phone calls, but no one seemed to know anything or anybody named Gypsy. She went back to re-read Mark's files to see if she could find out who this person was. She looked up from her reading to her brother's picture. "What are you trying to tell me? Why was the name Gypsy so important? What did this person have to do with going to sea? Until now, things had made sense, but this was off the map.

The phone rang and as she had expected, it was David. He was livid. "I don't know how you did it. But I know what I saw. The tape is blank now and you've made me look like a fool. What are you trying to do to me?"

"David, I didn't touch the tape. How can you blame me for whatever you're talking about?" She was looking at the pictures on the wall as she was talking to David. A couple of them had boats in the pictures, but none were called Gypsy.

She interrupted David's tirade to ask him if he knew a friend of Mark's named Gypsy. He said, "No. And if I did, I wouldn't tell you because she might end up dead." There was absolute silence on the line after that statement. The girls, listening in on the conversation, were bursting their sides. This guy is going to bust a gut if he didn't chill out.

In the mean time, Lola, who was holding some pictures in her hand that she had taken out of one of Mark's folder's was gesticulating wildly at Dora. She mouthed, "Hang up. Tell him you'll call back later." Dora told David she'd call him later and hung up the phone.

Everyone gathered around Lola to see what she was so excited about. She was pointing at a picture of a boat. The name on the aft end was Gitano. That is Spanish for Gypsy. "It's not a person, it's a boat," she bellowed. Dora ran over to the pictures on the wall and saw the same boat in one of the pictures. She started smiling, Mark was on it to the max. That's why he had said to look up Gypsy. He thought she would remember her Spanish and if she didn't, he knew there would be people around her who would.

The questions that came to mind now—were; one, where is the boat? and two, who would she find on it?

One of the girls started calling around to different harbormasters to see if any of them could tell her where the boat was anchored. The third call was a winner. The boat was tied up at that very moment in Ventura.

Dora was wondering why her brother thought she would need to go to sea and would it bring her any closer to finding out who killed her brother and why?

Would the owner of this boat have any information for her and could this person be trusted? She knew none of these questions would be answered sitting here. She would just have to follow Mark's lead. There were so many questions and not one concrete answer. The days were going by. Time was running out. They would soon have to return to their unit. There would be an assignment waiting for them, she was sure. All this would be very cold by the time they would be able to return.

As a matter of fact, Dora wasn't too happy about having her 'sisters' put their lives on hold for all of their sixty-day leave. She was kind of down. She was looking very thoughtful like when Regina came up to her and asked, "What's up kid? Why are you looking so down in the mouth? We'll get to the bottom of this mess."

Dora looked up at friend. "I know, but I'm taking up so much of your time. It isn't fair." The others heard what she said and came over to her.

"Look Lady, don't go there!" said Lil' Bits. "We are here for you, just as you would be for any one of us. Now, that's the end of that kind of talk. You got it."

No response. I said, "You got it. Do you understand?" All of the girls were looking at Dora, shaking their heads in agreement as she looked each one in the eye. This was something that no one could take from them, the family feeling among the Airborne.

Dora said, "Okay, I got it."

It was decision time. Who would be going on the boat and making the swim to check out the plant?

Lydia was looking over the blueprints of the plant and started to whistle.

"Look here, guys. This duct we have to go through is wired and has a fan with very large blades. It looks like its set up to keep everything but water out. Like if a fish or whatever swims through, it would be their last swim. Now how are we to get through without setting that thing in motion?"

Dora looked at her and said, "I don't know, girl, but you had better figure it out since you'll be the first one going through, being that you're the first volunteer."

Lydia grinned, "Somehow I knew you were going to say that."

Lil' Bits, Dee Dee, and Jodi also wanted to go. They liked to recon, plus they all thought it would be better if Dora remained at the house. She could keep David off guard until they had to make their move. Dora told them that she would go and meet the person who owned the boat and make arrangements for the charter. Regina was on her feet at once. "I'm your shadow." They both headed for the motorcycles and went out through the underground. Once they reached the road, they let the hogs go, smiling at each other as they did so.

Elizabeth was monitoring the limos. All was quiet, pretty normal, and then the cell phone rang. The news made the guy in the limo blow his stack. He was yelling, "What the hell do you mean the shipment has been destroyed." He followed this indictment with some very choice words, none of them very nice. The guy on the other end of the phone sounded as if he would rather be any place else other than talking to this man, who was still unnamed.

Liz put it on the speaker so that everyone could hear. They all began laughing.

Liz was trying to shut them up. She needed a name. She wanted to know who this guy was so she could call his next of kin. If he continued as he was doing, he was going to have a heart attack. He told the fellow, that he didn't' care what it took, but he was to trace that shipment from the time it was cut to where it stopped in Mexico.

"I want to know the name of everyone who touched that goddamn truck.

And when you find the person who did this, I want you to Fed Ex his goddamn head to me. Now—what part of that order didn't you understand?"

Another man took over the phone at the other end. In a very calm voice, he said, "we'll find the person responsible, that is a guarantee."

The head man in the limo, who still remained nameless, said "OK, show me how invincible you are, send me their heads. Do you understand?"

Silence. The message was understood loud and clear. The line went dead.

Elizabeth rewound the tape to listen to it again.

"...show me how invincible you are." She looked thoughtful and said, "There's that 'invincible' name again. We need to find this guy and maybe everything will begin to come together. Yeah, he may even be the one that killed Mark."

Tracy spoke up, "You know, we need to find that limo so that we can put a lipstick camera inside. That way, we can at least see their faces."

"That's no problem," said Christine.

Sandra spoke up then, "We can track them but that won't tell us where they are."

Christine started laughing, "Normally you would be right, but not in this case. When we placed the bug, I scanned it later to see if they had anything on board to check and counter our device. Doing so, I planted a new invention called Lo Jack.

This great tracking device will tell us where they are as long as they are in range of the Lo Jack systems. Christina worked her magic and found they were in Malibu, parked somewhere at the lower end of Highway 1. Tracy and Sandra wanted to go on this one. They went upstairs and changed into short pants and halter-tops and headed for the Hum V. They put in all the equipment they would need and headed out for Malibu. They were hoping these guys had stopped to eat. They would be there for a while if they had.

Once they reached Highway One, it didn't take long to find the limo. It was parked at a very nice seafood restaurant. The girls drove on pass and parked a couple of blocks away. Tracy decided that she would make the first move. She would first have to ascertain if he was alone, then she would go into her act. The driver saw her as she crossed the street and it was obvious that he was enjoying the view.

She sidled up to the car with pure wonder in her eyes. "Wow! This is some limousine. You know I've never seen the inside of one of these. What's it look like?

Does it actually have a TV inside and a bar like I see in the movies?" By this time, Tracy was all but gushing all over the driver. She was hoping the driver would offer a guided tour, which was exactly what he did.

Tracy gushed some more. "Are you sure it will be all right? I don't want to get you into trouble with your boss." The driver said, "No, it's okay." He motioned her to step back so he could open the door for her to get in. Tracy used every trick she knew to hold his attention. She didn't sit on the seat and swing her legs around. She crawled across the seat on her knees giving the driver a better view of what he had been looking at anyway. The look on his face was that of a cat that had just ate a cage filled with canaries. Once she had seated herself, Tracy plagued him with questions about the car: "How long had he been driving the limo? What was its length? Was it very hard to handle?" Tracy was leaning forward showing a lot cleavage. Then she leaned back on the plush seat and stretched out her long luscious legs. The driver's eyes were almost popping out of his head. He didn't seem to hear any of her questions or if he did, he didn't answer any of them. All he could do was look at her.

He couldn't believe this woman had walked into his life. Just like that. His problem now was how to keep her in it.

Tracy was looking all around the limo trying to find the best place to hide the lipstick camera. It had to be in a place where no one would find it, but at the same time see all the parties in the car.

The driver climbed into the limo beside Tracy. This was not part of her master plan. He offered her a drink and introduced himself. "My name's Todd. What's yours?"

"Jackie."

"Well Jackie, how does one go about taking you out on a date?"

"That's simple", she replied, "you just ask. Although I must warn you, I won't be in town very long. I'm visiting my aunt. In Malibu."

Sandra, figuring that she had given Tracy enough time to get settled, headed for the limo. Tracy seeing her headed for them, told Todd, "Oh look! Here comes my girl friend. I'll have to go now."

Todd got out of the limo looking very disappointed and not at all happy to see Sandra. But his hang-dog look gave Tracy the opportunity to stash the camera on a speaker in the corner of the car. She climbed out of the car saying, "Maria, I see you found me. Let me introduce you to my new friend. Todd this is Maria. Maria meet Todd." The two acknowledged each other.

"Todd drives this fabulous car. You ought to see the inside."

Sandra grinning at Todd and Tracy said. "It is beautiful, but we got to go, girl. We're going to be late getting home." Todd stopped Tracy with, "Look, I'd like to see you again. Let me give you my telephone number."

He gave her his card. Tracy murmured thanks, and she and Sandra took off down the road to their unit. A good thing, too. The meeting in the restaurant had come to an end. They were all in agreement. The person who destroyed the shipment must be found. The group emerged from the restaurant and got into their respective cars. Although four of them had arrived at the restaurant in the limousine, only one returned to it as they departed.

The girls were back in the Hum V checking on the camera. The pictures were coming through without any problems, but the man was not someone that they recognized. Just knowing it was operational was enough for now.

Sandra also called the house to ask if there was some way to run the plates on the limo to see who owned it.

Chapter Six

While the other two members of the team were hightailing it for Highway 1 looking for the limo, Dora and Regina arrived at the pier. They found the berth and the boat was anchored there. Using their field glasses, they looked all around to see if anyone was moving about on board. It was very quiet, so they decided to wait for a while, maybe they would get lucky.

The phone rang while they were waiting. Dora was told that Curtis needed to see her ASAP. It was a code red message. This meant the kid was in trouble or had found out something that required immediate attention. Dora told him to meet her at the pier if he could, or tell her where he was and she would come get him. The message was relayed to Curtis and he said he was about an hour away, but the pier was fine. He would be coming from LA. That was okay. Dora would be waiting.

Regina, watching through the glasses, pointed to the boat. "There's someone on that tug. The person is washing dishes like he lives on board."

She sat the glasses on a small tripod and hooked them to a mini camera with a four-inch screen. Now they could watch the boat without holding the glasses or being obvious. All they had to do now was wait. With any luck, they would soon find out who the person is.

Time passed and before long, Curtis arrived at the pier. Dora noticed as she went over to talk to him, that he wasn't looking very well. He asked her to get in and he began his story.

"I had a fare to LAX and they were talking about you." He paused, "Look, I don't know how to tell you this except to blurt it right out. There's a contract out on you and your family. The people involved have decided, that they have no way of knowing how much Mark has told his family and the best thing to do is take you all out. They also want his girl friend dead, but to date they haven't been able to find her. They are offering a quarter of a million dollars to any one who can provide information leading to you, the family, and Mark's girl. If the person or persons who find you want to complete the job, they will be paid three million for your deaths."

Dora was stunned that she commanded such a large sum of money. But Curtis had a bit more to relate. "My fare didn't know they were being taped and photographed. They feel that the girl is the most dangerous because she was always with Mark. And, her disappearance makes them pretty sure she knows everything."

Dora told Curtis he had better beat it and to be careful. Just as she was getting out of the cab, Curtis handed her photos of the clowns who were doing the talking. She took them without looking at them. "See ya," she said.

She went back to the bikes and told Regina all that had been said. "We've got to find that girl before they do." Regina was grinning like the proverbial Cheshire.

"What's up with you, lady?"

"I don't think you need worry about the girl."

"Oh! Why not?"

"If my hunch is right, the guy doing the housework on the boat is a girl. I think she has camouflaged her appearance and judging from what you've just told me, she has good reason to do so."

They waited until dark and there were few people about. Once they were sure no one else was on board, Dora made her way to the boat. Calling softly, "Hello." "Hello on the Gitano." A voice came back in a low tone, "Who's there?" The girl was standing in the shadows. "My name is Dora, I am a friend. You knew my brother, Mark."

The girl stepped out of the shadows holding a pistol aimed directly at Dora.

Dora said, "Be cool kid, I'm telling you the truth. I am Mark's sister and I've come to help you." The girl wasn't buying.

"I don't know what you mean and what makes you think I need help?"

Dora was very uncomfortable with this inexperienced girl holding a gun on her.

It was one thing if the person was a professional, but a frightened person—that was something else altogether.

Dora continued to talk softly trying to calm the young girl. "Look, I know what you have been going through, but you're not alone any longer. Has Mark ever talked about me or showed you my picture?" Still the girl said nothing.

"Your name is Carmen, right?" The girl wasn't dropping her guard.

"I don't know any Mark." Regina knew what Dora was going through standing there with a scared kid holding a gun on her. She slipped off the pier into the water and swam around to the port side of the boat and climbed aboard. Moving like a cat she came over the top of the cabin. Before the girl could react, she was flat on the deck and disarmed. Dora went over and pulled the cap off her head and watched as her long jet black hair fell down around her shoulders. She was terrified. She kept saying, "Please don't kill me." Over and over again. Dora took the girl in her arms. "Don't worry, you're safe now, you're safe." The girl was crying uncontrollably. Dora kept talking to her in very calm and soft voice. It finally got through to Carmen that she was being told the truth.

The three girls went below to talk. Under careful questioning from Dora, they found out that she knew absolutely nothing about what was going on. Mark had kept all things secret and she was being hunted for no reason. Dora got to thinking about her family and knew she was, literally, between a rock and a hard place. She would have to fight these people on their own turf, and at the same time, keep her family and Carmen safe. As the British would say, "We're batting a sticky wicket."

Carmen was sure no one knew about the boat. She had sailed it from Catalina Island where Mark had purchased it for her. It was registered in her name. Mark was the only who had seen it, but he had never sailed on it. She said that was why she decided to stay on it instead of going home. A few days before Mark was killed, he told me to hide and he didn't want to know where. That if anything happened to him, that I shouldn't go home. In fact, he said to stay wherever I was hiding until "my sister finds you."

"He never told me why, but from the tone of his voice and the look on his face, I knew it was serious." Dora asked if she would mind taking them to San Clemente to a place off shore that they needed to check out. Carmen said, "Okay, when."

"We'll be back. I think you're safe here for the time being, so stay put."

"Okay. I'll stay put." Feeling quite at ease now that she had met Dora, Carmen told the girls, as they readied to leave, "Mark called me his Gypsy woman." Dora smiled at her and she and Regina left the boat.

On the way home, Dora was wrestling with the problem of how to keep her family safe. There had to be a way and she had better find it, and quick.

* *

Sandra and Tracy had made it home without incident and were eating when Dora and Regina returned. They both started talking at once. Sandra said, "Me first."

"Be my guest," replied Tracy.

"We've got to go shopping because we're running out of everything. The 'mess' is about empty." Dora told them to go ahead, but they had better shop out of town. "No need to advertise how many people were in the house."

Elizabeth suggested that they go to the Commissary at Port Hueneme. "Take one of the cars because they have base stickers on them. If you are followed, they won't be able to get on the base. When you depart, leave by a gate on the far side of the base."

Jodie chimed in, "It might be better if you came back through the underground.

Leave the car there. That way if we need another vehicle, we'll have it." Everyone thought that was a good idea.

Regina had been tossing the events of the day around in her mind and decided that she had better go to Detroit to ensure nothing happened to Dora's family. She informed the others of her plan. Everybody agreed. In fact, two of the other girls felt that they should go along. Now the only problem was to convince her mom to allow them to stay with her. Dora was thinking it was time to inform her mom of all that had transpired. She had a right to know. Dora also knew if she didn't tell her, she would fight them tooth and nail.

Elizabeth asked, "Do you really think they will kill your mother and young brother?"

Dora replied, "We've killed for our country for nothing, and these people are willing to pay three million dollars, what do you think?" There was no need to say more. They all knew that there were people who would kill their own mother for that kind of money.

"Liz, is the chopper still at the resort?"

"Yeah! It goes and comes, but it's there at the present time. Why do you ask Dora?

"Because I'm going to Pendleton. Someone there is going to give me some answers."

"Oh! There's someone at the front door." They were looking at him on the monitor. He was dressed in a UPS uniform and holding a package in front of him.

Dora went to the door to get the package. It was from her mom in Detroit. She was wondering why her mom would be sending her a package when the phone rang. She said "Hello." It was her brother on the other end.

"Hi Sis. I was just calling to thank you for the gift." Gift. What gift? At this point her mind went into overdrive.

"Charlie, did Mom send me a package today."

"No, I don't think so, I'll ask her." Dora told him to forget it, just listen carefully and do exactly what I say.

"Okay, shoot."

Dora in a very calm voice asked, "Charlie, where is the package now?"

"Sitting on the floor by the door, why?"

"Charlie, I want you to stay away from it and get Mom on the phone."

Charlie started to say 'but' and Dora cut him off. "Charlie, just do it."

"OK" and went for his Mom. Her mother came on the phone and asked, "What is the matter?" Without preamble, Dora said, "Mom you have a package by the door that I did not send. Mom, I need you to call the police and tell them you have received a package that they need to come look at. Tell them it might be a bomb." Dora heard her mom take a deep breath. "What are you talking about? Why would anyone send a bomb to me?"

"Please Mom, just do as I ask. Don't ask questions right now."

"Does this have anything to do with Mark's death, yes or no?"

"I hope not, but I also received a package today that has your name as sender. Did you send me anything?" Dora was having a rough time. She felt she ought to be there to take care of her mother and brother. Why, in God's name couldn't she be in two places at the same time? Regina came into the room, hearing part of the conversation. Dora signaled that the package might be hot.

Regina also sensed that her mom was giving her a hard time. She went to make a phone call of her own. When she returned, she told Dora to tell her mother to get everybody out of the house, that help was on the way. Dora, not understanding, excused herself and asked Regina what she was talking about?

"I sent two of our 'sisters' over to the house, Kim and Ruthie. They both live in Detroit and are only about ten minutes from your aunt's house. Ruthie is one of the best when it comes to explosives. Between Elizabeth on this end and Ruthie on that end, they should be able to disarm them both. Just get your family out of there. "

Dora went back to the phone and asked her mother to please go outside and wait until her friends arrived. Her mom said there was car with two girls pulling up now. The girls jumped out of the car and ran up to the house just as Charlie opened the door. Dora waited for what seemed like hours before she heard Kim's voice in the room.

Kim took the phone from Dora's mother, "Yo ladies, I hear you're having some fun in your hometown. Nice of you to invite us. Ruthie is making sure everybody is out of the house and checking the package." Elizabeth took the phone from Dora and told Kim that the box was filled with C-4 and the top had a small detonator attached to it. Kim relayed the message. Ruthie saw that she was right and disarmed it.

Ruthie came to the phone and said, "Piece of cake. Let me talk to Dora."

"I'm here."

"Kim and I are taking your family including the dog with us. Your aunt isn't here, but we'll stop at the library and pick her up. And if I were you, I would return the 'favor' to whoever sent the nice gift. An eye for an eye, you know. It's time you started earning your keep." Dora laughed. Her buddies didn't know that there were a few layed out 'favors' already on slabs at the morgue. Dora wanted to know if they had been briefed as to what had happened so far.

"Affirmative. We'll handle this end. Take care of your butts, will ya?"

"Thanks guys. You know you don't have to buy into this, whatever it is."

"Yes we do." Ruthie proceeded to issue a few choice statements of her own.

Dora knew it was her way of saying, "You mess with one, you mess with all."

She thanked them and broke the connection. She immediately called United Parcel Service to find out where the packages originated. She was told it was a drop-off and was paid for in cash.

The girls that were going on the boat were putting their gear together. Dora was thinking about the bomb. She decided that it should be returned to at least one of their 'friends'.

Dora picked up the box and went out the front door and got into her car. She knew the guys would follow her. She drove to a spot in front of a frontage road she knew very well. There was a cover of trees along the road and she stopped the car and got out. She started to walk along the road, than she cut through the trees heading out toward the beach. When she was sure they were too far away to get back to their car before she did, she took off at a run. She ran down the beach a ways than began to back track until she was standing by their car. She was walking towards her car when the guys came out of the woods. She opened her door and turned to them, "Thank your boss for the nice present, but I'm returning it." With that said, she pushed the button on a hand-held detonator causing the total destruction of the car.

Dora returned home with a smile on her face that could light a candle. The look of disbelief on the faces of those two men was well worth the drive. That, she said to herself, was fun.

The boat party had already left for San Clemente. They had found another way into the plant by cutting a hole in the side of a drain, thus, bypassing the fan that was going to give them a problem.

Once on the boat, the 'sisters' had about an hour ride, so they put on their suits and kicked back to enjoy the water.

Jodie was handy with an underwater torch, so she would be the one to cut the hole in the pipe they would use to gain entrance to the plant.

Lil' Bits would cover from the boat in case they needed additional help. Destiny and Lydia would handle whatever they encountered on the inside. The only thing any of them knew for certain was there was a lot of computer activity going on in a place that was only suppose to be a backup power plant.

* * * * * * * * * * * * * * * * * * * *

David was standing outside Dora's house looking like thunder when she pulled up in the driveway. He barely let her get out of the car before he began yelling at her.

"Now tell me you didn't just blow up that car," he said, with a grim look on his face. "I have a car that has been blown to smithereens and it has your name written all over it."

"Why David, I'm glad to see you, too, but you don't have to make up stories like that to see me. Just call and ask. I would love to go out with you anytime you say."

Once again she had disarmed him, said the unexpected. He couldn't even say all he had planned to say. How could he love this woman so much and yet think she was capable of the things he was accusing her of. Just as he was about to say something he shouldn't, a car came tearing down the street at high speed, shots rang out like the 4th of July. Dora hit the dirt and with the reflexes of cat, had her 9-millimeter in her hand returning fire. David stared at her in wonder for a minute, then the cop kicked in, and he was firing back at the car.

It all happened so fast, there was no time for thought. David got on his radio and called in the shooting—requesting back up. He asked Dora if she was hurt. She responded with a 'no'. His next question was, "Do you have a permit for that firearm?" Dora showed him her federal firearms permit, which was good anywhere on American soil.

David handed Dora back her permit, but held on to her hand. "Dora, please let me help you. I know there is more going on here than meets the eye. Everything that has happened since you came home has all the earmarks of a big operation and somehow, you're right in the middle. I need you to let me in. I've got to get control of this situation before you get yourself killed."

Dora pitied David at that moment, but she had to make him understand. With a smile she said, "The only thing I can say for sure is you're going to need a lot of body bags. These people killed my brother and they are going to pay. For your sake, don't get in my way. I don't want anything to happen to you, so just stay out of it."

This was probably the nicest thing she had ever said to him. Unfortunately, he knew she meant every word. This lady was about things he had only seen in the movies and he wasn't sure what he should do from this point on.

The back up cars were arriving and he went to provide the details of the shooting. He omitted the part about Dora returning fire. He felt the less anyone knew about her the better. The love he had for Dora made him look the other way.

Unless she stepped outside the law, he would give her free rein to deal with whatever it was she was dealing with. He also knew it was going to get worst before it got better. Bombs attached to her car, her brother being killed, and now a drive-by shooting. This might be a little more than even he could handle.

"If you need anything, anything at all, let me know. I want to help. I know this town is about to come apart. So, the more I know, the better I can help you." David looked into the beautiful eyes of the woman he loved more than life.

"Your life has always been a mystery to me, but that hasn't stop me from loving you. I've always been there for you and for your family. Your brother being killed was like losing one of my own." David stepped back. "Yes, I am a cop. I always will be a cop, but I do understand blood for blood. I need—I need to know who the players are. I need to understand why Mark was killed, and secondly, who killed him. I can help you so much if you would just help me a little."

Dora took David's hand this time. She rubbed the back of his hand and turned it over and traced his life line.

"David, I don't know who killed my brother, but when I find out, I promise, you will be the first to know."

He was looking into her eyes and saw a softness that he had not seen in years. He believed her. She was still looking, not very sure of anything yet. At that moment, he felt closer to her then ever. It wasn't enough, but more than he'd had from her in a very long time. For that reason he decided to leave on a good note. David said, "Goodbye" and walked towards his car.

He had almost reached his car when Dora called to him. He turned and she graced him with a big smile and said, "Thank you." David shook his head, got in his car, and drove away.

Just inside the door, Regina was standing with a gun in her hand and a smile on her face. She told Dora when she came in the house, "I thought I was going to have to bail you out, but it looks like you and Prince Charming have everything under control." Dora smiled, "Don't start, he's just a friend."

"Oh I know he's just a friend, but there are friends, and then, there are friends."

They walked through the house arm in arm.

"Have you heard anything from the boat?"

Regina said, "Not yet! They should be almost there."

The two of them went down to the command center to listen in on the limo radio traffic. There were two men talking about the shipment they lost in Mexico. Seems another one was being sent to replace it. But no one mentioned its point of origination. They were calling in some big guns to guard this one and they didn't care who got killed.

One of the men asked if it was Mark's sister who had destroyed the last shipment, because she was becoming a real pain in the ass.

The other man responded, if so, it doesn't matter anymore. We sent someone to take care of that bitch once and for all.

All the girls laughed, it was obvious they hadn't gotten the word that their try had failed. The would-be assassins were now running from the police as fast as they could.

Suddenly, Dora told the girls to be quiet. There was a woman talking. Dora thought she recognized the voice. She continued to listen. There was something about the voice that was familiar. She couldn't quite put her finger on it, but decided it would come to her later. She knew so many people in town that she could be grasping at straws. The only thing Dora was sure of was there were people trying to kill her and she still didn't know why?

The lady was speaking again. "Don't play that she-devil cheap. If you don't see her on the ground, don't count her out."

"Now that's one smart lady whoever she is", thought Dora.

The other radio from the boat came in with Jodie saying, that they had reached their destination and were about to fish for the big ones. That was the code to let them know they were about to enter the waterway.

The swim was not more than a hundred yards, so it was short work for the team.

Lil' Bits and Gypsy threw out their lines and set back to enjoy the fishing.

Underwater cameras had been placed strategically nearer the pipe. Although they weren't shown on the blueprints, it was not unexpected. So the team was prepared for them. They took some underwater shots themselves of the area using a special underwater camera that allowed them to play the video back to the cameras giving the appearance that all was normal to the observers. That would allow them to continue with their job. It took Jodie only ten minutes to cut a hole in the pipe big enough for them to swim through. It was a short swim inside the pipe to a ladder where they could take off their tanks. Jodie secured the tanks to the bottom of the ladder. She took note of the remaining air in the tanks. It would not be enough to swim back to the boat underwater.

They had only brought 30-minute tanks plus a five-minute breather. They would probably need a loop to get in safely.

At the top of the ladder was a padlocked hatch, which Jodie cut. She set a bypass on the alarm. Lifting the lid a fraction, she checked out the area using a flex fiber optic camera. Once she was sure there was no one around, she pushed open the hatch. The girls scooted through in a hurry looking around for cover as they came through. They did a visual recon of the area and found no one about. They proceeded carefully towards the section in the plant that housed the computers.

They found the room without incidence. It was occupied by three men who were surrounded by computers, all in a circle. The 'sisters' donned their hoods and entered. The guys jumped to their feet. Jodie chuckled. She couldn't tell if they jumped up out of fright or if they were going to fight. One of the men stepped forward like he was the boss.

"Who are you people and how did you get in here?"

Destiny held up her gun and said, "I'm Ready."

Jodie said, "I'm Willing."

Lydia rammed a round into the chamber and said, "I'm Able."

She continued, "Now gentlemen, we're looking for some answers. You, of course, will oblige us by providing said answers. Easily, we hope. Or, you can be as stubborn as you like and suffer the consequences."

The 'boss' spoke up again. "Do you have any idea of whose property you are trespassing on? "

Lydia said, "No, but I feel you are about to tell us."

"The only thing I'm going to tell you is where the door is. I suggest you use it as quickly as possible. You're making a big mistake. There is nothing here for you to steal. This is a back-up plant for the base and the surrounding hospitals."

"In that case, you won't mind if we look around a bit," asked Lydia. She motioned for the men to move away from the computers. She was looking the terminal over when Destiny chuckled. "What's funny?" Destiny nodded her head toward a photograph of one of the men and his family. Lydia picked up the photo and studied it for a minute. She walked over to the man in the photo and asked if this was his family.

He said, "Yes."

"Do you love them?"

"Very much."

"Would you like to see them again?" And before he could answer, she said, "In this life?" The poor fellow was really sweating now. "Yes, I would." Lydia walked around with the picture in her hand. "You know, I could kill you now and them later. That way, you could all be together in the next world." He was visibly trembling.

"Why do you want to kill us? We haven't done anything to you."

Lydia, still walking around looking at everything, gave him a brief glance and said, "Oh yes you have. I'm sure you're the one." Still holding the photo, she turned to him with ice cold eyes. The message in them said, you're dead.

"Look, I'm tired of playing this game, so this is what's going to happen. You are going to tell me what all this is for," pointing to the computers. The 'boss' broke in saying, "I told you, this a back-up plant."

"We'll remember you said that when we start to shoot people."

"You don't frighten me. You really don't know who you're messing with."

"Then kind sir, why don't you enlighten us." Lydia, looking at some of the disks said, "What if I set all of these afire."

The 'boss' sneered, "That would be your second worst mistake. There would be no place on earth for you or yours to hide."

"So, what you're saying is—this place is more than a power plant?"

Lydia inserted one of the disks in the computer to scan it for a file name. It couldn't be done that way, so she nodded to Destiny for help. Destiny was delighted. She hooked up the equipment and broke through the block. She soon was on line and able to read the contents of the diskette.

"Oh wow! Lookie here! You guys won't believe what this place really is. This is an electronic bank. They are controlling all of the drug trafficking in and out of the country from here. Also, all of the money flows through here into dummy corporations all over the world."

"How much money is in the pot?" asked Jodie.

"Let's just say that starving people all over the world could be fed for a long, long time."

"Can you pull up any names?" asked Lydia.

"Nah, these folks have covered their tracks too well. They are using phony names, not that it matters. The banks they are dealing with only deal in numbers."

Lydia walked around the bank of computers. "Let me see if I understand you. Are you saying that we could move this money out of these accounts and there is nothing anyone could do about it?"

"Yup, that is what I am saying, but why would we want to move it? We certainly can't spend it. This is blood money." The 'boss' chimed in before Lydia could respond, "You better listen to your friend. There isn't a rock big enough for you to hide under, if you mess with that money."

Lydia started laughing, a deep belly laugh, "Oh ye of little faith!"

"Do you really think I would take any of this money? I was just being funny. After all that would be dishonest and I would never, ever, do anything dishonest. However, I do like that part about feeding the hungry. I would love to do something about world hunger. Now, what do we need to do, to find the accounts of all those do-good folks that feed the hungry?" Her 'sisters' started giggling and then let go some rip-snorting laughter.

"You mean electronically transfer the money to them?" said Jodie

"Yeah!" Replied Lydia. "But what I need to know is—is there a way for them to pull it all back?" Jodie thought about this for a moment or two. "I think I can fix it so a password must be used to cancel the transactions."

"Okay! Then do it kid. Go on and feed the hungry of the world. Also, make sure that they understand that they will lose the money if it is used for any other purpose than feeding the hungry."

Upon hearing this, the 'boss' became very agitated and started to protest.

"People, please, think about what you're doing. You may as well kill us now because we'll be dead anyway." Lydia knew he was telling the truth. She told Jodie to fix them up with enough to get them as far away as possible. Far enough to be out of harm's way—if possible.

Jodie was having the time of her life spending this money. She was closing out accounts, right and left. She was using a technique the IRS uses. It's known as an international loop. What this does is send a password and return it before it can be captured. This way it would always be lost and so would the money. They told the men to leave in one hour. If they were smart, they would head for the airport. The men had been given enough money to last them for the rest of their lives. Get new passports, new faces. Do it now, and do it fast. "Ciao! Gentlemen, it was nice banking with you," was Lydia's parting shot.

The 'sisters' were making their way back to the hatch when the alarm sounded. They couldn't believe their ears. Those guys had just signed their death warrant. But the man with the family was thinking that if he could prove he tried to stop the intruders by sounding the alarm, he might get to see them again. He certainly couldn't run away without them. His bosses would kill them just for fun.

The girls let the boat know that they were on the way back and would be moving fast. They each had a re-breather system that would last five minutes. They would leave the tanks behind. Lil' Bits told them to surface when they ran out of air and mark the distance with K lights. She would pick them up in the rubber raft, Seal style.

Lil' Bits told Gypsy that she would have to help by steering the boat and that she would also need her help to tie the raft to the boat. She then went to look for something she could use to pull the girls out of the water much like the Navy Seals use to pull their men aboard. She found a big fishing net with a large wire hoop. She cut away the net and broke off the handle so it wouldn't get in the way and hooked K lights to the rim so the girls would know where to hook on. Lil' Bits went below to get her gloves, as they headed out for the pick-up zone.

Gypsy was still not sure what was going to happen, but she was enjoying every minute of it.

The team broke surface and spread out about two hundred feet apart and treaded water. They saw the boat coming and got ready for the pick-up. Gypsy had been instructed to make a wide circle and then start her run straight at each girl.

Gypsy was beginning to stress out a little. She was having visions of running over the girls instead of keeping the boat in front of them. The fact that it was getting dark didn't add much to her courage. But then a chopper could be heard coming their way. Lil' Bits had secured herself to the boat with a rope. They were coming up on the first girl when the shooting started. Lil' Bits set the loop in the water. Lydia was the first to grab hold and up she flew into the boat with a mighty jerk. Next came Destiny and then Jodie. It was a 'piece of cake' and Gypsy was loving life. This was the best thing that had ever happened to her. For the first time in a long time, she felt alive and free and scared to death.

The chopper was about to make another run at the boat. Jodie picked up her weapon, saying "enough is enough" and aimed for the rotor as the chopper swept overhead. There were a lot of sparks, a big blast and the chopper veered off. It had been hit. That ended the assault on the boat.

They headed back to the boat and Santa Barbara. The girls were laughing it up—feeling good about themselves. This would be a day to remember for the rest of their lives. Lydia said, "Can you imagine the look on the faces of those people when they check out the headlines in the morning."

"WORLD HUNGER ORGANIZATIONS RECEIVE HUGE DONATIONS FROM UNKNOWN SOURCES."

The girls roared.

"I bet some of those people will jump out of windows like they did during the great depression," said Jodie.

Lydia rolled her eyes upward, and said, "Yeah! And the rest will be looking for us. I sure hope those guys used their brains and got out of town fast, but somehow I doubt it. Whoever is behind this entire operation will have them killed sure as dogs have fleas."

The ride home was fun and Gypsy really knew her way around a boat. Jodie commented on Gypsy and how well she had handled herself throughout the entire operation. "Home girl got it going on with this sea trip, but I think we had better take her back with us. You know, in case someone picked up the name of the boat. I would hate for her to be the one they catch up with. She would be dead for nothing." They agreed. When Gypsy was told of their plans, she was elated. She didn't want to be alone any longer. Besides she really enjoyed being with them.

Night was coming fast, but Gypsy had no trouble bringing the boat into its berth.

She had told them that she was the only child of a fisherman. Not being the boy her dad wanted had not stopped him from teaching her all he knew about the sea and boats. She felt she could handle a boat with the best of men and would be willing to prove it any time she was called upon. The girls felt that they had taken on another team member. This young woman was not just along for the ride. She was feeling good about herself. Very good, indeed.

They tied up the boat, disembarking at the ready. They knew that this would be a good spot for an ambush. They made it to the car without incident, but Jodi gave it a good going over before anyone climbed in. They headed for home and glad of it.

Chapter Seven

The girls were in a hurry to return home to see what kind of unrest they had caused by transferring all that beautiful blood money to legitimate hunger organizations.

Unrest was not the word. Elation. Joy. Absolute delight. Total disbelief was just a few of the adjectives that came to mind by the receiving organizations. No one knew how it came to be in their accounts. And the stipulation that the money was to be used for the 'poor only', didn't bother anyone a bit. The money was God-sent. It was a miracle and the organizations felt it was long overdue. God had said, 'go forth and feed the multitudes'. With this windfall, the organizations were going to do just that.

The news was out, and of course, the Internal Revenue Service wanted to know where all the money had come from. The agency's interest was strictly for the taxes—they said. Had any been paid on all of that lovely loot? Once the money reached the coffers of the non-profit organizations, taxes could be forgotten. But the agency needed to know its origins. An investigation could cause unrest of itself. Some of that money may have belonged to some higher ups within the agency. Anyway, it was going to be very interesting and the girls didn't want to miss any of the fun.

When the 'sisters' got home, they found Dora sitting in the kitchen looking forlorn and dejected. It was a look that few had ever seen on her face. Liz came in at the same time the girls arrived. She too, wanted to know what ailed her 'sister'.

"Hey girl, you want to talk about it? You haven't been with us since you heard that conversation from the car."

Dora looked up at Liz, "I know that voice. I know that voice and I can't believe it."

Regina walked into room as Dora was speaking. "What you're thinking is right. After those people got back in the car, I was able to see the person to whom the voice belonged." The other girls came upstairs; all of them had sad faces. Dora whispered the name, "Carrie. The voice belongs to Carrie." They all shook their heads in the affirmative. The voice was that of her friend and mentor, Lt. Col. Carolyn Marshall and their boss. Dora looked at each one of the girls. They all were thinking thoughts of their own. Not wanting to believe, but knowing it was fact.

Regina said, "That's how she knew to show up at the jail so fast. None of us called her. We didn't have to, she had inside information."

Every one took a seat. Each in their own way, they were trying to deal with the betrayal by their 'sister.' Now, they had to find out what part she played, if any, in the murder of Dora's brother.

Another problem beset Dora. What part did Capt. Anthony have in this scenario? He came to the jail ostensibly to help. Now it looks as if he may have come to hurt her or worse. What was even more baffling, why didn't he do whatever it was he came to the jail to do. She had to find out. This was the break she had been looking for since she came home. One thing for sure, if either or both Capt. Anthony and Col. Marshall were involved in the death of her brother, she would kill them. On that, you could take a bet. Dora had made up her mind to that. Anthony may be the one man on earth she was most afraid of, but if he killed Mark, she would just as surely kill him.

Downstairs the girls were whooping it up over the newscast. Some of the organizers were talking about building modern up-to-date shelters for the homeless. Others were discussing the possibility of financing people who just needed a helping hand for a short time. Elizabeth asked, "While you were being do-gooders for the world, did you give any thought to setting a little money aside for the team? You know, retirement would be a lot nicer with a little of that 'la la'." She could tell from the dumbfounded look on their faces that the thought never crossed their minds.

Elizabeth shook her head with a look of pity on her face.

"I knew there was a good reason for me to have gone with you. Now look at us, sad and broke." Everyone laughed. Dora broke in on their fun with, "Hate to break this up girls, but we had better get some sleep. Tomorrow's going to be a busy day." To herself she said, "A very busy day."

"Tracy, I want you to call your driver friend tomorrow. We need to find out where and when that new shipment is coming in. It is definitely, time to turn up the heat and make some people extremely unhappy!"

"You mean more then they will be when they find out whose money was donated," mused Jodie.

Everyone in the room was laughing as they prepared to turn in for the night.

Dora was still up long after everyone else had gone to bed. She was getting a glass of milk when she noticed Regina standing in the doorway.

"I knew you wouldn't be headed for the sack."

Dora walked around the kitchen table, shaking her head from side to side, "I can't believe this nightmare. You know how I feel about Carrie. How can she be involved with these people?"

Regina grunted, "The kind of money we found at that plant would be hard to walk away from, even for Carrie. Look at the contacts she has. The lady has clout in places we don't even know about. I just hope we don't have to take her out."

Dora, who had been exhibiting a lot of tension all evening, swung around to Regina. She said, "Money is one thing, murder is something else, especially when it's my blood. If she is anyway involved, she's dead meat." With that said she went to her room.

Sleep didn't come easy for any of the 'sisters' that night. Except Gypsy, she was sleeping like a baby. She had not been able to do that in a long time. She couldn't ever recall feeling so safe. Mark was right about his sister. He had told Gypsy that Dora would find her and take care of her, if she could. Right now, she felt like her life had taken a turn for the best—for a change.

Tracy made her call in the morning. Todd, Jr. was delighted to hear from her. He asked her to have lunch with him. "Bring your friend Maria along. I have a friend who would love to meet her." Tracy said she would, but she would meet him at the restaurant.

"Okay! But why can't I pick you up?"

" My aunt wouldn't approve of you. She still thinks I'm a little girl."

Todd, Jr. laughed, but you could tell by his voice that his ego had just got a boost. He said, "Will your friend be coming with you 'Jackie'? I want to make the reservations. Twelve-thirty okay?"

"Yeah! And don't worry, she'll be there?" Tracy hung up the phone laughing; this guy's going to be a piece of cake. Dora told her to make sure she stayed away from places that the Colonel was likely to visit. "If she sees you, it's all over. We would have to get you out of the country—and fast!"

Tracy watching the monitor, said, "Oh oh! Here comes your friendly policeman. I'm out of here."

David came visiting, not to ask about dead people, but to ask Dora to have dinner with him. She quickly agreed. She said, "I'd love to. You still owe me a dinner at the Resort." David said, "Fine. I'll pick you up at eight." As he was going down the steps, he stopped, turned to Dora and said, "Oh, by the way, did you hear about all of that money that changed hands last night? You didn't have anyth —he stopped himself—no, that's crazy." He shrugged his shoulders and continued on to his car. He was trying to convince himself that she had had nothing to do with last night's events.

Dora hated what she was doing to David. She was suffering mixed emotions about keeping him in the dark. But she felt this was the best, for his safety as well as hers and her 'sisters.'

Tracy and Sandra were headed out for their date with Todd and friend when Regina stopped them with some motherly advice. "Remember, you are going after information. This isn't a date, so keep your minds on the job. If I can't have a date, than neither can you." She was looking at them over the rim of her glasses. Tracy said, "We read you loud and clear."

Elizabeth exhaled loudly saying, "What is a date? I can't remember the last time I had a date." Lil' Bits spoke up and said, "That's because God is being kind to you. If you could remember the last one, you would still be having nightmares. That last guy you went out with was so ugly, his mother left him at the hospital when he was born." They all laughed at that, even Elizabeth. She knew that Lil' Bits was speaking the pure truth.

Tracy and Sandra were heading for Malibu and their date at the restaurant. The plan was to get the guys talking about themselves, especially Todd. He seemed to love talking about himself and his job. In this business, that was good.

Dora, on the other hand, was thinking about the Colonel. She had to find out what she was up to. She made herself a promise; she would give the Colonel an opportunity to explain. Dora called a friend at Fort Campbell and asked him to send her all the information he could gather on the Colonel. He said, "I would ask why? But I know you wouldn't be asking if you didn't have a good reason. I'll FED EX it to you overnight, okay? But you have to keep me out of this, whatever the hell it is you're doing. I would like to retire with all that is coming to me." Dora laughed, and promised him she would.

Dora had it in her mind to confront the Colonel. Regina told her she would blow everything if she did.

"First of all, she would have them go through that car with a fine tooth comb to find out how we knew she was still in town. She taught us how to do what we do. It would take no time for her to put two and two together and come up with the 'team'. You have got to get a hold on your emotions"

Dora knew that she was one hundred percent correct. She could not go off like a non-professional. She smiled. She would get the facts—and then go off.

Tracy and Sandra were waiting at the restaurant when Todd and his friend drove up. They exited the limo and walked over to them. Todd was all smiles. He apologized for being late stating that the traffic was backed up. Tracy told him that they had just arrived about five minutes ago. Todd introduced his friend Nick and suggested they go in. Nick was tall, blond and built like a Mack truck. Inside, they were escorted to their table. The conversation was light. The champagne was great. Nick seemed to like to talk about himself, too. This was good. Hopefully, one or the other of these guys might say something useful.

Dora was getting ready for her date with David. She had plenty of time so she decided a little pampering would not be out of order. She gave herself a facial and a long soak in her favorite bubble bath. Then she covered herself in a highly luminescent moisturizer. A short nap with Witch hazel pads on her eyes and she would be ready for her big date. Tonight, she would let it all hang out. She was also very interested in what Sandra and Tracy found out at their luncheon.

Tracy and Sandra were well into their meal and the boys were doing the same. It seemed that Nick was a part owner of a string of gyms called "Love Thy Body." The gyms were doing a booming business and Nick was loaded. He felt the world owed him everything and was his for the taking. The girls treated them like they were important. They say the way to a man's heart is through his stomach. Well, the way to a man's mind is through his ego. So they would stay focused and find out all they could.

Tracy was acting like the liquor was getting to her and she started to push a little.

"Todd, how is it that you, being a chauffeur and all I mean, hang out with someone rich and powerful like Nick. I mean I don't understand, it's like oil and water, they don't mix."

Todd, Jr. laughed, "Well, you do say what's on your mind."

Nick said, "I told you I had a partner. The man you call a chauffeur is also part owner of the gyms."

Todd, Jr. took up the explanation. I drive the limo because I want to. I have a driver, but sometimes we hold business meetings in the car, so its better if I drive."

Sandra said, "That's the silliest thing I have ever heard. Why would a man who doesn't have to, drive his own limousine?"

Todd, Jr. responded, "There are quite a few of us who do. Some of us use to be drivers before we made our money." Tracy said the bottle is empty and I want another drink. The guys looked at each other and Nick signaled the waiter for another bottle. He was certain this bottle would be the one that would lead him to where he most wanted to be, in bed with one or the other of these two women. He didn't know he was drinking with pros. The girls had taken a pill, which would prevent the alcohol from entering their bloodstream. The pill was especially developed for the team to take on assignment. They would drink these guys under the table. The only thing these jerks would get tonight, might be a hot cup of coffee.

Tracy and Sandra kept pushing for information. Tracy was sitting much closer to Todd on the bench seat and my man was steady running his hand up and down her thigh. She decided to let him continue as long as he didn't stop talking.

She brought him back to the subject of the limo and why anyone so rich would want to drive instead of being driven. Todd, Jr. said, "It's not unusual, one of the richest men in this town drives his own car.

"Ooh! That's hard to believe, said Tracy." Todd was beginning to look a little on the drunk side. He grabbed her by the arm and said, "Come on, I can prove to you the car is mine. He led her outside to the limo and reach into the glove compartment and pulled out the registration. "See, look right there. It says Todd Kruger, Sr. It's my car." He was having a hard time standing up. Tracy led him to the rear of the limo and put him inside. "You stay there, I'm going to get the others." She still had the registration in her hand. Once inside, she copied it.

She went over to the table and told Nick to call a taxi and take his friend home. Nick said, "That won't be necessary, there's a driver standing by." He signaled for the check. At the door, a man came forward, "Are you ready, sir?"

Nick said he was and they headed for the parking lot. Nick asked if we were going with him? He was thinking, 'to the victor goes the spoils.' He was told 'no', not this time. Tracy dropped the registration on the front seat without being seen. After a little more talk, they parted company.

Tracy and Sandra arrived home while Dora was in the midst of her pampering. Regina told them to wait until tomorrow to tell her. In the mean time, come on downstairs and let's go over everything that was said.

Dora was able to get a good rest. She felt good. To herself, she said, "I must do this more often." She stretched like a cat and went to get dressed.

She donned a long sleek black dress. Wearing nothing under it to mar the lines. It looked as if it had been painted on. The dress molded to every curve. She wore a minimum of makeup, long flashy silver earrings, silver bracelets which were narrow and petite and silver high heels with matching clutch. She had a funny looking silver ornament in hair. Not flashy, it sort of fitted to the head. She was looking good. She was admiring herself in front of the mirror when Regina walked in. She said, "Well?" All Regina could say was, "Yeah! You know, David is a pretty nice guy even if he is a cop. You could do worse. Plus it's time for you to find yourself a man. In that outfit, you surely will. There's the bell, I'll go let him in."

David watched as Dora descended the stairs, his eyes grew big as half dollars. This lady could stop a run away train with a body like that. Is she real? He was thinking, how could any one so fine, be so deadly? Then he smiled at her and said, "Oh Lord I am not worthy, but please let me be tonight." Dora laughed. She couldn't help how men looked at her, but she was very glad they did. She had not been much to look at when she was growing up, but as a woman she had made up for lost time. The only problem now was to find someone who would appreciate all that she had to offer. She would be all 'woman' with the right man. So far, the right man hadn't come along. Tonight she would find out just where David was coming from and if he could be the man he wanted her to think he was. They left for the Club and this time she let him do all the gentlemanly things he like to do. She felt like being treated like a queen tonight. She hoped all would go well this evening and that she would retain her good mood.

David's chest had swelled out about two more inches to be seen with this woman whom he thought was perfect for him. No other woman had ever affected him as she does, yet until now, he could never get her to even consider him. David was no puritan. He had been with plenty of women. Yet he could never shake what he felt for her. He doubted if he would ever be really happy with anyone else as long as this angel was walking on earth. There was nothing he wouldn't do for her, including breaking the law. They were almost to the Club and there didn't seem to be anyone following them. So far, so good.

Dora was very happy. She had been able to drop her guard for a while.

They had a lovely dinner. What made it even nicer, David didn't ask any questions?

It was as though he wanted to shut out the world for a few hours. He knew reality would set in soon enough.

Thomas Walker sent a bottle of five hundred dollar Champagne to their table. David said he couldn't accept it, but Dora did. She told him it would be impolite to refuse. The dinner was lobster and shrimp made with the special sauce that Dora loved. She told David if she could find a man that could cook like this, she would marry him in a heartbeat. David told her to be careful what she wished for. Her eyes were sparkling in the candlelight. Her smile was blinding David. He was thinking, "If this lady had any idea of what she was doing to me, she would stop." There ought to be a law against all that steamy sexuality. He couldn't ever remember being so happy, yet so afraid.

David did not know what was worse, having her near, and not being with her or being with her and not knowing for how long. She was always strong of mind. If she ever decided to make him her man, it would be forever. And she never did things halfway. He knew he would have to let her run the show. This was going to be one of the longest periods in his life. His heart would control his head. He would stay out of her way while she did what she must. Finding her brother's killer was something she must do alone until she asked him for help. But, for tonight she's mine. All mine.

David had proven to be a lot of fun and not as uptight as he could be. The guy, as they say, was good people. When he was able to come down off his high horse, he was great to be with. Dora was thinking about how far she should let this affair—that brought a smile to her face—let this affair develop. She was pretty certain it had gone as far as it was going to go, tonight. She wanted to be absolutely certain of what she wanted before she drew him in. He had been waiting a long time; he could wait a little longer. Dora knew that she liked David, very much, but she did not think that she was in love with him. They pulled up outside of her house. David had driven her home in silence, not exactly sure of what to say. He didn't want this night to end, but knew it must.

Loving this woman at a distance was going to be even harder, from this day forth.

David pulled the car up in front of the house, killed the lights and turned to Dora.

"Thanks for making me feel extremely happy this evening."

Dora smiled, "I should be thanking you, I needed this evening out."

"Yeah! So did I. Do you think we could do it again? I want so much for us to be more than friends."

"I know, but let's leave it for now, David."

David knew she wouldn't say anymore than she already had. If she ever made up her mind to be his, nothing and nobody would stop her. David got out and walked around the car to open her door. As she got out, he again caught a whiff of her perfume. It had been driving him crazy all evening. They walked to the front door. Dora turned and kissed him very gently on the cheek. Very seductively, she bid him good night and said, "Thanks once again for a wonderful evening." She opened the door and went inside.

Tracy and Sandra had stayed up to give her the good news. We found the chauffeur, Dora. The one you said looked very well 'kept' for a chauffeur. You were right. He is. As a matter of fact he can be kept anyway he wants. Tracy handed over the slip of paper bearing his name and address. Dora looked at the name on the paper. At last, something concrete. Now we can move ahead on this thing. Dora said, "Okay, let's hit the hay. First thing in the morning, we'll start looking for these guys. Between the photos that Mark left and the bits and pieces we've been picking up, we may be able to put this thing together. See ya' in the morning."

Christine was the first to arise. She was on the hook to see what had taken place during the night. There wasn't anything much being said in the first limo.

When she checked the limo that Tracy and Sandra had been in, she started laughing. The girls hearing her came over to see what was up. She said the guy is in love. He is going to take Tracy to New York to meet a ship and sail it back to California. The idea being that Tracy would be head over heals in love with him by the time they arrive back here. They all stopped laughing when they heard Todd, Jr. say, "That way I can insure the shipment gets here without incident. We'll have fifty people on the ship plus the crew. It will look very innocent. We'll just be having a "boat" load of fun. Customs has been taken care of and there won't be any problems when we land in California."

Nick wasn't convinced. He said, "We should just have the ship sail on to Mexico and drop the shipment. We can process it right away and we only have to move it once." Todd, Jr. started to reply, but Nick jumped in saying, "I know, the problem is getting it off the ship. They aren't set up with dummy fuel pumps and they won't be able to pump it off."

"That's right. Remember, the idea is to simulate having contaminated fuel on board. It's pumped off and taken into Mexico as second hand crude oil. It will be passed through by our people and we can get back on schedule."

The team was sitting there in the basement of Dora's house rubbing their hands with glee. This was the break they had been waiting for. Now all they had to decide was whether to take the shipment on land or on the sea.

There was a knock on the front door. The girls were so intent on the information being divulged, they hadn't been paying attention to the monitors. Dora looked out and saw the FED EX truck in the drive. No doubt, this was the package she had been expecting from her friend at Fort Campbell. She accepted the package from the driver. She was uncertain whether to be happy or sad. At least she would learn something about her boss and mentor.

Dora curled up in a chair in the living room and began to read the service record of one, Lt. Colonel Carolyn McKenzie Marshall. She read that the Colonel had started at the bottom and worked her way up. She was one of the very first women to be sent to Nam as supply personnel involved in a joint action with the air force. She did very well in that position and the army decided to send over more women. From her record, it seemed she was in charge of moving troops and anything else that needed to be moved. She was on duty when the VC tried to infiltrate the compound and she sounded the alarm, which saved many lives. The event that excited everyone was how many of the VC she killed herself. After it was all over, she went into shock—not certain of what had taken place. A week later, when she was to go on R and R, she declined. The first sergeant could not understand why she didn't want to go. He had noticed that something was bothering her, but whenever he asked her about it, she would shake her head and say everything was fine. One day he asked how she was doing and Carrie responded by asking if there was anyway she could join the 101st Airborne. The sergeant thought this was a funny request but he put through her papers. Nothing came of it, but she kept on asking. Soon after she was summoned to the White House. The President was awarding her the Congressional Medal of Honor—the first woman to ever be accorded such an honor. The President informed her that she could have whatever duty she wanted. She knew exactly what she wanted. She told the President that she would like to go to jump school. She wanted to be the first woman to be a part of the airborne. And if she made it, she wanted to return Nam. Permission was granted.

This was not a strange request to her buddies who knew her. She had lost her man in Viet Nam. She really seemed to get into her work after her boy friend was killed. The doctors figured that was why she was able to react to the invasion as she did. They felt she had a death wish and didn't care how it came. She would take as many with her as possible. The only problem was that they didn't get her. Now, she was one of the most decorated soldiers in history.

Carrie was sent to jump school and was able to meet all of the training requirements. Upon completion, as promised, Carrie was sent back to Nam and assigned to the 101st Airborne. She was sent back to Supply and remained there until completion of her tour.

She requested Officer's Candidate School and, once again, her wish was granted. After OCS, she formed the women's airborne and trained some of the Army's finest women for this unit.

Dora read everything and still couldn't find anything she didn't already know. To her mind, there was a lot missing from this record.

Regina came into the living room with a message from Curtis. He needed to see her ASAP. Dora went to her room to dress immediately. She left by the underground passage on her brother's motorcycle. She could not shake the feeling that there was a lot missing from Carrie's service record. She would have to wait to find out just what. She was moving along the back roads fast and sure. She felt free each time she rode the bike. She saw the car coming fast but didn't think too much about it. She believed that no one knew about the back way out of the house but the 'sister's.' When the lights on the car began to flash on and off repeatedly, she pulled over to the side of the road. Dora was thinking that this could be a setup, so she turned the bike to face the car. She was ready to go into action when she saw Regina get out of the car.

Regina rushed up and told Dora that Curtis and his little sister had been kidnapped. "This letter came just after you left. Read it and see what you think."

The car was still running and there was a lot of static coming from the radio. Regina looked at Dora and jumped on the back of the bike. Dora punched the bike and gravel flew as they drove away from the car. About a hundred yards down the road the car blew up. Dora stopped the bike and they looked at each other.

Dora said, "That was too close for comfort. It's a good thing you left the radio on. I wonder how they knew about Curtis and his family? Do you think they have found him and are now trying to use him to get to us?" That question went unanswered because a chopper was flying fast and low coming their way.

Regina asked, "Can this hog outrun that pig? If not, let's find a place to fight." They pulled off the road into some trees and parked the bike. They took cover in a ravine, weapons at the ready. The chopper made a pass over them and the girls soon realized that they were out gunned. Someone up there had a 60-caliber machine gun and they knew how to use it. The chopper made three short passes over them and then disappeared as fast as it appeared. Dora was very upset now.

First, she wanted to know how anyone else knew she would be on this back road?

Second, she must find out about Curtis. And third, she wanted to return the favor someone had just tried to extend to her.

She and Regina headed for the house. She had Elizabeth contact Curtis on his cellular phone. They all held their breath until they heard his voice. He said he was fine and that his family was out of town. Someone tried to play you guys and I bet I know whom. The only man around here that has a chopper lives up on Peak Drive. Curtis said, "I don't know him by sight, but his name is Kruger, Todd Kruger. He has the money and the clout to pull off anything. If you plan on visiting that gentleman, be prepared, he has it all. First of all, you can't get in without a three-day notice. And if you did, you probably wouldn't be able to get out. The guy is nothing to play with. He could raise the dead with the money he has."

Dora told Curtis that Todd was also the chauffeur they had been looking for. Curtis chuckled. "Now I know something is wrong with you. Why would anyone with all that money, want to drive a limousine?"

"It's a cover. That's why so few people know who he really is. Everyone thinks he's just a chauffeur."

"Umm! Yeah! I can see how that would work. But I gotta tell you," warned Curtis, "you are gonna catch hell trying to get into that place. I wish you luck, believe me, you're gonna need it. Ciao!"

Dora sent a couple of the girls to scout the house and the surrounding area.

"See if you can find a way onto the grounds and into the house."

Dora told them, "I want to know everything there is know about this dirt bag. I want to know what he eats for breakfast, lunch and dinner. I want to know his blood type and how many breaths he takes a minute. And," she said, "I want this information two days ago." The girls looked at Dora, then at each other. They knew she meant every word that she had spoken. Someone had pushed her buttons.

In this frame of mind, she was worse then Mother Nature.

The girls shoved off on their mission. Tracy was on the phone with Todd who had just invited her to come to New York and cruise back with him. She was telling him she would love to go and so would her friend. Todd informed her that Nick wasn't going but 'Maria' could still come along. He would find another date for her if she liked. Tracy quickly said, "I couldn't possibly go alone. And Maria can find her own date a lot faster." Todd told her "okay. We leave in two days time."

"Right! We'll be ready! Bye."

The rest of team sat down to brainstorm. They had to figure out how to destroy the drugs that were going to be aboard that ship and in a hurry. Christine thought they could use the same chemical they used in the truck and it travels well.

This stuff only has to be put into the tanks and it will eat its way to glory. "Why do you think they call it the blob?" Lydia asked if she could go along? She too, was getting fed up with this cat and mouse game. Regina suggested that they send as many as possible to ensure safety. The big question—will the Colonel be aboard the ship?

Elizabeth shook her head, "No, she'll be attending a conference in Washington.

So they decided they would send four members of the team. They used the computer to make the call to New York and routed it as if they were. This was done in case the agent they called to get tickets had caller ID. The idea was to make the agent think the call was being made right there in New York. They got the name of the ship and that it would sail in three days. The girls booked and packed their bags.

Lydia asked Regina for the keys to her car. "Oh! I forgot to tell you. Your car didn't make it. It blew up soon after I picked up Dora." Lydia couldn't believe what she had just heard. She looked first at Regina and then at Dora, "That was my mother's car. She is going to hit the roof. I am not going home without it."

The other girls were laughing like crazy. They all knew Lydia's mom. She loved that car. The last thing she said to Lydia was, "Don't come back if you hurt my car." Everyone was still laughing except Lydia. She was going to be in big trouble with her mom. Dora took pity on her. She went over and threw her arms around Lydia, "Don't worry. We'll buy her another just like it. Now go call Curtis. He'll give you guys a ride.

When the girls had gone, the others gathered down in the command center.

Dora looked at her 'sisters' and said, "Ladies, it is going to get very hot over the next few days. I will understand if anyone wants out. I know that not one of you needs me to say this, but I must. This is not a mission for God and country. Some of us may get killed. Personally, I would lose a lot of sleep if anything happened to any one of you. I love all of you, but if you want to leave, it's okay. I'll understand."

One of the girls spoke up. "I think I can speak for all of us here by saying 'No Way Jose'. We came to fight." After saying this, she looked around at her 'sisters' for confirmation of what she had just said. They all agreed.

"Okay my sisters, if that's the way you want it, that's the way it will be. I need each of you to do what you do best. We need to be ready to leave as soon as the others get back from their scouting trip with whatever information they've gathered. It may take them all night, but just the same be ready to move out."

One of the other girls asked, "Is the plan to take this guy out without being sure?"

"No, the plan is to learn what's going on, first. We just need to step things up a little."

Regina asked Dora if she expected David tonight. She said, "No."

"Well he's coming to the front door." Everyone looked at the monitor.

Dora didn't want to stop what she was doing, but felt she must. She went up to see what he wanted. He was smiling when she opened the door. "Sorry for showing up unannounced, but I have to ask you a question." She invited him and told him to have a seat. David had been trying to figure out, all the way to Dora's house, how to broach the subject. He was visibly uncomfortable. Dora took his hand, "Hey, what is it?"

"Do you know anything about a car on one of the old back roads that's been burned to a crisp?" Seeing how Dora was looking at him, he very quickly said, "I'll understand if you're upset by the question, but you see, I have to investigate this, because it's similar to the way Mark died. I have to find out whom the car belonged to, but the tags and ID plate had been removed. Dora was shocked to hear this, however, she maintained her cool. Neither she nor Regina had bothered to stop to remove anything from the car. It bothered her that someone would take such pains to prevent the police from identifying the owner of the car. She sat there thinking. What should she do? Should she let him on what's been happening? Then she thought about what was to come and knew he couldn't be in on something so illegal. So she told him she knew nothing. She also added, "And, I'm not angry that you asked." David said, "I have a confession to make. I don't really care if you do or if you don't, it was an excuse to come see you, that's all. I feel that my life"…. he never got to finish what he was going to say. Dora silenced him with her lips. His breathing was labored when they parted. His eyes were misty and he was shaking. His dream had come true. This was the best day of his life. He smiled and held her ever so lightly for quite a little while, not sure how to act or react. But Dora being Dora took control of the situation. "Umm, that was real nice. Now, if that's all you have to say, I'll say good-night." David saw she was serious. He got up from the couch and headed towards the door. He turned to her and said, "You won't always be in charge, you know."

Dora smiled, "I hope that's a promise." He left Dora's house walking on cloud nine. He didn't care if he lived or died. He now knew what heaven would be like. Kissing this woman had to be as close to an angel as he would ever get.

The girls were waiting for her when she went down to the command center.

"You should have finished what you started. We could feel the heat down here."

"All in good time my 'sisters'. All in good time"

Regina laughed, "Yeah! A good time is what we are talking about." Dora was happy that they were amused, but she was concerned about the car—more perplexed than ever. What in holy hell is going on?

Elizabeth said that Curtis had called. "The girls got off OK. Now all we have to do is wait for the others."

Chapter Eight

Destiny and Jodi were checking out Todd's house and they did not like what they were seeing. Curtis was right about this place. It was built like a fort. You name the security and it could be found here. Destiny was looking through a very sophisticated night scope. With it, she could see not only the men guarding the place, she could also see the tracks of dogs and of other men which gave no indication of exactly how many men were in the compound. Laser beams had also been picked up in the areas that weren't fenced off. There were smaller buildings adjacent to the main house, which could be housing just about anything.

Jodi told her she was picking up heat from one of the buildings. This had to mean that there was a chopper in there, armed to the teeth. The girls took pictures until they had the entire layout on film. It was getting close to dawn and time to move out. The suits they were wearing were beginning to get hot. They were designed to keep heat in—in case the place they were scouting had heat sensors. And looking at all the security this place had, it was a sure thing that heat sensors were at the top of the list.

The girls made their way down the hill to the car and headed for home.

The 'sisters' arrived in New York without any problems. They split up to ensure that there wouldn't be any reason to suspect they were together. After booking into the hotel, they went sightseeing. The ship would be boarded in the morning. Todd, Jr. was not scheduled to arrive until tomorrow, too. That meant Tracy and Sandra could relax for the evening.

Dora was waiting for Destiny and Jodi to return to the house. They came in the back way looking very bedraggled and whipped. She hit them with questions as soon as they showed their faces.

"Okay! Let's have it."

"You're not going to like it," Destiny warned.

"This guy has one of the best security systems we've ever seen," Jodi added.

They hooked up the Digital Camera to the computer and everyone gathered around to look at the pictures as they came up on the monitor. Regina and Elizabeth shook their heads in amazement.

"Just who the hell is this guy anyway? He has more security than the President has at the White House," said Elizabeth.

Dora, watching the pictures, groaned loudly. "We have got to penetrate that security and bug that place. We have to know what we're up against before we go tramping all over the place. You guys have got to come up with a way for us to get in there without them knowing." Then she looked at the two that had been up all night and told them to turn in and get some sleep. "You did very well. Now, its up to us to work it out." Destiny said, "Thanks, see you later."

Dora, Regina, and Liz re-ran the pictures one at a time trying to find the most likely spot to enter the grounds unseen and undetected.

One of the girls suggested that she hire out as a maid. It would get at least one of us inside. Dora pooh-poohed that idea. "With the security at this place, everyone would be checked out thoroughly—by his people—first."

They reviewed the pictures for hours—each offering an idea as to how the penetration could be accomplished. Regina looked up and spied Gypsy peeping over everyone's shoulder.

"Gypsy, how would you break into this place without being detected?

"Well—if it was me, I would go in from the sea. Liz, looking amused, "Are you nuts, girl, that's an 800 foot drop. How in the hell would you get up there?"

"Climb. How do you think?" replied Gypsy.

"Mark and I use to climb all the time. You may even find some of his gear around here. If so, I can climb from the sea to the top. I know you don't think much of me, but you're talking about something I know how to do."

Dora came over to Gypsy and putting her arm around her said, "You know she's right." She was remembering the pictures she had seen of Mark and a girl climbing mountains.

"I know I can't hold a candle to all of you, but this is something I can do and do well." She turned to face Dora, "Please, Dora, let me help you," pleaded Gypsy.

"There are a couple of problems. That is a sheer climb. And—it will have to be done in the dark. How are you going to hook into that mountain without making any noise."

Elizabeth said, "I can help you with that. You guys remember the silent charges fired from a pistol used by climbers. That's so they don't bring the mountain down on top of them, if it's kind of shaky. Well, that's all we need. They are only loud as a silencer, but you can use them to fire picks into the sides of the mountain. She can go first and hook in and we can follow."

Dora wasn't too happy about this situation. She did not want this girl to get hurt or worse—killed. She would be shot if she made one sound. Gypsy was looking at her with her big almond-shaped eyes, pleading with Dora to let her do it.

"I have to help and this is something I can do."

Truth to tell, any one of them could do it, but they weren't going to take it from her. Gypsy wanted in. Mark was her boyfriend. She wanted to help catch the people who killed him. The other members of the team were looking at Dora. Although they agreed with Gypsy, it was Dora's call.

Dora said, "Okay! But if you get killed, I am going to be very upset with you."

Lydia and Christine were already on the ship when Tracy and Sandra boarded. Tracy wasn't happy with the room arrangements. Todd, Jr. had placed her in the room with him. She had this changed. Sandra was in a room by herself so she moved in with her. Todd, Jr. came looking for her and asked why she didn't want to stay with him. Tracy admitted that she had thought about it for a while.

"Is there a reason you want to broadcast the fact that I'm here with you?" Before he could respond, she told him, she didn't like the idea of people knowing that they were together.

"I was hoping you would understand. I am sorry, but it's just the way I was brought up. If that poses a problem for you, maybe I should leave and you can call someone else."

Todd, Jr. smiled at Tracy. "Please stay, I understand—I think. It's just that all the women I know would have expected to stay with me. I just did what I normally do. You can stay in any room you wish. I can get you one of your own, if you wish."

"No! I would rather stay with my friend."

The ship was loading. People were busy going back and forth to their rooms, getting lost, laughing, having a good time before the ship even sailed.

Tracy was glad the other girls were aboard. She and Sandra were not going to be able to move around very much. The plan was to find a way to destroy the shipment. They had to find it first and they only had four days in which to complete the job.

By sharing a room with Sandra, she would be able to communicate with the other members of the team. They were each carrying a radio so they could stay in contact.

Lydia had started her search by trying to hook up with the purser of the ship. He was smiling at her when she came on board. She made sure he knew that she was interested. He had introduced himself and offered his help if she needed it. She wanted to make sure he knew that she would need it. The purser practically runs the ship so he is the best person to know. A ship like this was a floating hotel and this is the man that would make certain that it ran smoothly. Lydia hoped that she would be able to get him to talk about himself, the passengers and the cargo. All, without him knowing he was being pumped for information. Yeah!

Sandra was going after the chief engineer. Between the two, they should be able to find out what they needed to know about the ship.

The ship's horns were blowing, warning everyone that the ship was pulling out. On deck, people were waving good-by to friends and relatives who had come to wish them bon voyage. The band was playing old favorites as they pulled away from the dock. It was party-time until they reached their destination.

Meanwhile, back home, Dora was having second and third thoughts about letting Gypsy make the climb. Although she understood Gypsy's need to be involved in the operation, Dora was hoping Gypsy knew what she was doing. What bothered her most—was she wasn't sure how she, Dora, would handle it if Gypsy got herself killed. The team was used to living on the edge, it was part of the job. Gypsy, however, was an unknown quantity. They could use a four-leaf clover for this operation and all the luck it carried.

The 'sisters' had decided to hump the gear to a pick-up point using the back entrance. Dora was uneasy about going out this way. Since the chopper attack, she had to assume that someone else knew about it. Elizabeth had wired the entrance in case anyone planned on paying them an unwanted visit.

Curtis was waiting for them at the pick-up point in a road vehicle he had borrowed from his boss at the cabstand. He was a little upset that

Dora wouldn't allow him to come along. Dora explained that they needed him to make sure the coast was clear for their return. He understood, but still had protested.

The team boarded the boat and headed out to sea. They had about an hour's ride to their destination. Todd's house was the only edifice that occupied the area overlooking the sea. Dora was thinking, "This guy wasn't stupid." He knew exactly what he was doing when he built this house in that spot. He hadn't planned on anyone coming in from the sea. Actually, if it had been anyone other than the 'sisters' or a team such as themselves, he really didn't have anything to worry about.

Only some other idiots like them would even attempt such a feat.

Because of the rocks, they had to load all of the equipment onto rubber rafts.

Going in under the cover of night would give them the edge they needed. Dora was giving some last minute instructions to Gypsy on the use of night vision goggles.

"You must remove them immediately if you're hit by light. You'll be blinded if you keep them on."

There was quite a gathering of folks at the Kruger Mansion. All the people who had lost money in the transfer were gathering to see what could be done to recoup their fortunes. They were very upset, to put it mildly. Uppermost in their minds, was to find the people responsible for destroying them and kill them slowly. A slow tortuous death was what they had in mind.

They had been able to find only one of the men that was on duty that night at the plant. When they were satisfied he didn't know anything, they killed him. Some of the men gathered at the mansion had virtually their very last dime in those accounts.

They were now living off the small amounts of monies they kept in the states. One had already sold some of his property to satisfy some of his debts. Life wasn't going to be worth living if they didn't turn a profit on this shipment that would be coming in from Mexico—provided it got there, intact. But not one of those men wanted to even consider that eventuality. Most of them were almost as broke as they had been before they started their life of crime. A few were back to trying to make ends meet. None of them had ever thought that they would ever be poor again. Others had businesses that were doing very well. The trouble was, most of those businesses belonged to the organization. The guys with their names on the ownership papers were just fronts for laundering the drug money. These fellows were in big, big trouble.

Dora was standing at the bottom of the cliff, watching Gypsy ascend. It was obvious that she did know what she was doing. She used the pistol to drive in the spikes and hooked onto them as she climbed to the top. Dora was getting itchy waiting at the bottom for Gypsy to get far enough up so that she and the others could follow. She would feel better being close enough to fire at anyone who might be at the top.

Pretty soon, the entire team reached the summit, Liz whispered, "So far, so good. We had better secure some lines in the event we need to make a fast exit." Dora agreed. She sent Gypsy back to secure the boats and stay with them. This would also keep her out of harm's way. The last thing Dora needed was to be looking out for her if they had to make a fast break.

The team was able to plant their outside microphones and lipstick cameras without sounding off any alarms.

They made it back to the boat without leaving any trace that they had been there.

Dora gave Gypsy a big hug. "You did well. I am very proud of you. Mark would be proud of you, too."

Gypsy, looking at Dora with tears in her eyes, simply said, "Thanks." That was all she could manage at that moment.

The girls ran a quick check on the systems. Once satisfied that all were working as they should, headed for home.

Sandra was having the time of her life aboard the ship. She loved taking cruises even though this one was business. Sandra had teamed up with the chief engineer. She had him convinced that she was an airhead. His favorite subject seemed to be himself. Throughout dinner, he talked about the ship and how it needed his professional hands on technique to make it work. When the captain called from the bridge to say the ship was running behind and needed to make up time, he was the one who made it happen. If the ship was rocking too much, causing the passengers to become ill, he was the one who stopped it. He told her that he had been in the Navy. The one thing he had learned was that a ship on paper was much different from a ship on the sea. You had to find her spot and rub it just right. The man went on and on until Sandra wished she had the excuse of becoming seasick to get away for a breather. In the meantime, Tracy was doing her best to keep Todd entertained. Todd, Jr. had a very different meaning of entertainment. He was trying to convince her to spend the night in his cabin. Tracy was in a quandary. Either she would have to fake illness or Sandra would. But they needed to be together to make plans to stay on track. That meant not ending up in the sack with one of the guys. It would have been different if they like the guys, but they didn't, so a roll in the hay wasn't in the cards.

Tracy was cool in her responses to Todd, Jr. He sensed that she wasn't buying his 'come on.' This in itself was making Todd, Jr. a bit angry. He was rich and powerful. Nobody, but nobody, said 'no' to him. He didn't know how to handle this woman. On the other hand, he kind of liked this cat and mouse game she was playing with him. He decided to play along with her to see where it would lead. Todd, Jr. was certain that she would end up in his bed. She just couldn't be rushed. Tracy was one of the most beautiful women he had ever known and he felt she might be worth the game. To Tracy, it wasn't a game. This was business and she had better get on with it. She had to get free of Todd, Jr. so that she could help the others find and destroy the shipment.

Dora and her team made it home without incident. The girls monitored the information. They were all laughing at something being said by someone inside the house. The gist of the conversation was that if the next shipment didn't hit the streets soon, life, as they had known it would come to a halt. Dora was glad to hear that she was finally getting to the right people. Jody was taking down names as they were spoken. This was a break for the team; they had names, voices, and when the folks left this house, they would also have faces. There was a man talking now who was giving everyone there his personal guarantee.

"You won't have to worry about the next shipment. First of all, I have men on the ship that no one would believe are agents. Secondly, we have placed cameras at every possible access to the shipment. Even your men on board don't know that they are being watched. I am not taking any chances with this shipment. There is over a billion dollars in cocaine on that ship and the future of all of us in this room hangs in the balance."

Someone in the room said, "Laurence, for your sake, I hope your people can be trusted because your life depends on it." A silence fell over the room. The cold hard fact is, the persons in that room would kill anyone who came between them and their way of life. Regina was thinking about the girls on the ship. Destroying this cargo may not be as easy as they first thought. Even if they got to the shipment, they might not get out alive. They must be warned.

Todd, Jr. had introduced Tracy to his friends on board the ship. When she heard someone say "Jackie" she turned to find one of guys who came aboard with Todd. He asked her if she had seen Todd, Jr. There was a very important message for him. It was a telegram and he had to get it to him right away. Tracy offered to take it.

"I'm on my way to meet him. He should be in the main ballroom by now." The fellow said, "No. I'll find him."

"Oh, it's from another woman, I suppose," Tracy said.

Todd's friend shook his head, "No, it's not like that. It's just business, that's all."

Tracy made a face, "Yeah! Monkey business. I know how you men stick together."

"I assure you, it's not what you think. Here, take it and make sure Todd, Jr. gets it, okay?" Tracy said, "No sweat." Todd's friend was a little concerned with his decision to let Tracy take the message. He didn't want Todd, Jr. upset with him because she may have gotten the wrong impression. They all understood that this woman was special. Todd, Jr. would kill anyone who ruined his chances with this girl. On the other hand, he hoped she didn't become too inquisitive and open the telegram.

Tracy took the telegram and headed for the ballroom. En route she took out a small camera and took a picture of the message through the envelope. This particular camera could take a picture through ten pages and the first page would be perfect. She saw Lydia and managed to slip her the camera. Since it was a digital camera, there was no need to develop film. Which really was a good thing because there would be no opportunity to develop the film on board the ship. The message could be read right away.

Tracy, a beaming smile on her face after passing off the camera, found Todd.

"Jackie, where have you been? I was beginning to think you had stood me up."

"No, I just stopped to talk to your friend. He asked me to give you this telegram."

His face changed as she handed him the message. He tried to conceal his displeasure, but Tracy could tell he was upset. She also noted the relieved expression on his face when he saw that it was unopened. He excused himself and read his telegram. It was from his father. It read:

"You must make sure all is well. Trust no one. We still don't know who these people are. If they don't work for you, ask questions. We owe a lot to our people and we must stay in control. Get rid of anyone, permanently, who seems out of place or tries to get into your business."

The fourth member of the team on the boat was also receiving a message via satellite link. The message was clear. 'The team was in danger. They had to find some way to neutralize the cameras, the guards, and the drugs.' Well, at least, there were two of them who could move about the ship freely, while the other two supplied them information.

Back home, Dora was having trouble sleeping. She decided to call David and invite him over to the house. He couldn't believe she was calling him. He was pretty sure she was only after information and she was. But he didn't care. He was just happy to be setting in the same room with her. David asked after her mother and brother. Were they enjoying their vacation? David told Dora, that so much had changed, he wasn't really happy being a cop anymore.

"Nowadays, you have to fight the good, the bad, and the ugly, in order to stay alive. Seems like everyone wants what somebody else has."

Dora was looking at David. Maybe for the first time, she could see and feel his pain. She said, "And David, what do you want?" He looked at her for a long time before he replied, "To die and go to heaven in your arms." The look in his eyes was enough to convince Dora that he meant every word he spoke. Dora needed to change the subject so she asked David if he would like to go for a swim. He said, "Yes, but I don't have a suit." Dora smiled, "I guess this is the place where I'm suppose to say you won't need one. Well, I won't. We have plenty of suits at the pool."

Together they went out the back door and around the garage to the small changing rooms. Regina, the mother hen, watching all of this on the monitors said, "Go girl!" David was the first to emerge from the cabana. He dived in and swam a couple of laps. Then he heard a splash at the other end of the pool. He saw Dora swimming towards him. She swam towards him in the moonlight. He couldn't help thinking how happy he was at that moment. She swam up to him and stopped, treading water. David reached out for her with his hand, which she took.

They begin treading water in a circle. Each circle grew smaller than the first. They came closer and closer, until they were face-to-face, nose-to-nose. They both stopped and stared into each other's eyes. David didn't know whether to kiss her or say a prayer. He did know that he didn't want this moment to end. Dora knowing what was going through his mind, made it up for him. She kissed him. His arms automatically wrapped around her. It was the first time he had ever held her so close and—surprise, surprise—she was nude. David tried to speak, but she silenced him with her tongue. David felt his heart skipping beats, but he didn't care. Cardiac arrest would be a small price to pay for this moment. Dora wasn't sure she loved David. But she had a strong 'like' for this man. Dora reached past him to turn on the radio at poolside. The song that was playing was called "Super Woman." David laughed out loud. "How appropriate. Even the DJ is on your side."

Dora said, "Shut up and kiss me."

David groaned. "Lord, Dora, don't do this to me if you don't mean it. Dora's answer was to wrap her legs around him. She said, "Go for it copper." They sank below the water, came up sputtering. David pushed her against the wall and that was last coherent thought he had.

Meanwhile on board the cruise ship, the girls were having fun. The purser and the chief engineer liked to dance. And dance they did, till the break of day. The engineer was talkative. He asked the purser "how long had he been with the ship?"

The purser replied that he had been with her since she was commissioned.

"So, you've seen those pipes that don't do anything." The purser tried to shut him up by saying "you talk too much. Don't worry about what is not your concern." Lydia asked, "What's the problem with the pipes?" The engineer, in his drunken state, said he was new to the ship and he had not been able to find out exactly why they were there. There were other things about the ship that didn't make sense either. "I checked the blueprints and none of the system is recorded."

The purser intervened again. "You need to go to bed. It's not good to have diarrhea of the mouth and your toilet is running over." Lydia felt it was time to bring this conversation to an end. With a knowing look at Sandra, both girls rose and thanked the young men for a great evening. They told the guys that they'd had lots of fun and maybe they could get together later in the evening. With that, the girls retired to their cabins. They kept up the appearance that they had just met on the boat. Neither girl was sure of what they had learned but they were both certain it had something to do with the shipment of drugs. Once in their cabins they got on the two-way to map out their plans. Christine and Lydia would try to find out why the pipes didn't 'make sense' to the engineer. The girls were gone for hours, searching from one end of the ship to the other. They had donned maid's uniforms, in hopes that if seen, their appearance wouldn't be questioned.

Sandra was in her cabin when she received word about the cameras. She didn't want to pull Tracy away from Todd. And she was unable to reach either Christine or Lydia on the link. She decided she had better go look for them alone.

Unknown to Sandra, the girls' link had been broken in a fight that had taken place in the hold of the ship. The girls had been caught trying to remove the cover of a pipe. They had put up one hell of a fight, but there were just too many men for them to handle even with their training. They were finally subdued and tied up.

Sandra was still searching when she saw one of the men whom she had seen with Todd, Jr. earlier moving fast. She noted the direction he came from and backtracked him. She was being very cautious, as she moved about not being sure of where the cameras were placed. Todd, Jr. was sitting and talking with Tracy when his man came in.

"Excuse me Miss, sir—may I speak with you privately."

Todd, Jr. said, "Be right back, baby."

Whatever the man was telling Todd, Tracy could tell it was important. She watched Todd, Jr.'s face change rapidly.

"Jackie, something has come up that I have to attend to at once. Would you please excuse me for now? I'll see you later." Without waiting for her to answer, he turned and followed his man out the door.

Todd, Jr. went immediately to where the girls were being held. Sandra heard someone coming so she ducked down behind some cargo. It was Todd and his pit bull. Todd was saying something about a helicopter, but Sandra couldn't catch it all. She waited until they passed and followed. She got as close as she could after finding the first camera. She could hear the men talking and after each word there was a smack. She knew her 'sisters' were being beaten.

Todd asked, "Who are you ladies?" Another slap sounded when neither of them answered. Todd was very upset. He told them that they would talk before he finished with them. "You will not die until after I find out who you are and why you are interfering in my business. You will also tell me who else is involved. Then because you won't be good for anything else, or anybody, I will be merciful and kill you both quickly."

Todd, Jr. told his pit bull to keep working on them. "And if you kill them before they tell me what I want to know, you had better jump overboard."

Todd, Jr. went back to the ballroom feeling very happy with himself. He felt he would soon have the information needed to stop the people who were interfering with shipments. His dad would be very pleased with the way he had handled this affair.

Sandra was having a rough time. She wanted to help her 'sister.' But she had to decide whether or not to blow her cover. Something would have to be done fast because the girls were being moved.

Todd, Jr. went back to Tracy and told her he would be leaving the ship, but he would meet her in California.

One of the yachts that were following the cruise ship also carried a chopper. Todd had sent for it to take himself and the girls off the ship. Sandra only heard part of the conversation, but that was enough.

Meantime, Tracy still had no idea what was going on. She had a gut feeling that whatever it was, it concerned her 'sisters.' As soon as Todd left, she went to the cabin to find Sandra. When she couldn't find her, she tried the LINK, nothing. As she was leaving the cabin, she saw the note. It simply said, "The pyramid has eyes." Tracy's heart sank to her feet. The message was clear. Her 'sisters' were in trouble. She grabbed her LINK and tried to get them, still nothing.

Outside the chopper was landing. People were asked to stay away from the flight deck. A sixth sense told her this had something to do with her team. She went out the door, moving a little faster with each step. When she got to the flight deck, she met up with Sandra. Both headed for the plane. Sandra filling her in as they went.

"What should we do?" asked Sandra.

"We've got to help them," said Tracy. The girls were being pushed into the chopper, but not before they saw their 'sisters' coming with blood in their eyes.

Christine gave them a look to back off. She shook her head in a way they would understand. The mission was more important for the present. Tracy opened the LINK phone and took out a homing device. She stopped Sandra and ran up to the chopper. Todd was just about to climb aboard when she touched his arm. He looked back and stepped down. They had to scream at each other to be heard above the noise of the rotors. Tracy asked if she could go with him. Todd smiled and said, "No." He had to get these ladies to a hospital and there wasn't room for any more. She asked what happen to them. He said a steam pipe burst while they working in the laundry. She looked past him at the girls and got the same message. Back off. They wanted her to complete the mission. Tracy stumbled forward, grabbing Todd's arm at the same time reaching for the side of the chopper to attach the homing device. She smiled again and Todd told her to save it. He would see her soon. She stepped back out of the way. Todd climbed on board and the chopper took off. Lydia saw what she did and felt a little better. She wasn't sure if Christine had seen it or not. She would tell her the first chance she got.

Tracy and Sandra were on the hook ASAP to the rest of the team. Regina translated the message. They all hit the roof. Dora was on the back porch mooning over her wild night with David when Regina came bursting through the door with the news. All thoughts of David went out the window. Dora asked Regina if the girls had any idea where Lydia and Christine were being taken?

"No, but we should be able to track them very soon. Tracy put a homing device on the chopper."

They both went down to the command center where Regina began working her magic. "We can pinpoint them within fifty feet of where they're going."

Dora with a very determined look on her face made a promise that she intended to keep. "I'm going after the people in that house including Carrie if she happens to be there." Lil' Bits grabbed her by the arms. "Hey girl! Chill. We all feel your pain but going off half-cocked will only get them killed." Gypsy came up to her, "She's right, you know."

Dora said, "I got them into this mess and, by God, I'm going to get them out."

Regina yelled at Dora to get her attention. "Yo' girl friend, I dig what you're saying, but we have got to stay focused. Understand."

While waiting to pick up the signal from the chopper, the girls monitored the radios. Todd, Sr. and a few of his people were very happy at the present time. They had received word of the girls' capture. Todd, Sr. was saying, "we will soon know who the players are and why they are trying to put us out of business."

Dora was having 'cow niptions'. She told the girls that she would personally pull his gonads off. And then, she would feed them to his son. There was a black Jaguar with two men inside pulling into the drive way of the Todd mansion. They sat in the car for a couple of minutes before they emerged. It was none other than Senator Thomas Jackson and FBI

Director, Laurence Parker. They walked pretty fast once they got out of the car. They could be heard to say, "Now we can find the rest and get on with our business."

Dora was thinking, "Over my dead body." Regina spoke from her seat at the console. "I'm pretty certain the chopper is headed for the mansion."

"Great," said Dora. They had angered the bull, now they were going to get horned. "I'm going to push that plush house right off of that mountain." Regina was worried. Dora, taking the blame for the dilemma the girls found themselves in, could get them killed and herself, too. This was not the way for a professional to act.

She had to get through to her friend and 'sister'. She started shaking her leg as she always did when she was in a thinking mode. Dora noticed and asked, "What's the problem?" Regina took a long deep breath before she responded.

"Look kid, you have got to take a 'chill' pill. If you don't start thinking with your head instead of with your heart, we all are going to be dead. We're going to get our 'sisters' back. But we have got to do it like the soldiers we are. You are making it personal and you know that won't work. You will lose your edge and they will outthink you."

Dora knew that 'mother hen' was speaking the truth. She would have to take it as she would any other mission. So she went into a planning mode.

Back on the ship, Tracy and Sandra were trying to get all the information they could. The men that were left behind tried to make Tracy to feel at home. They felt that Todd would want them to do so. Tracy was told that Todd was one of the richest men in the world. She was told that Todd and his father were two of biggest tycoons to be found anywhere. She was advised, "You should make him your man, you won't be sorry." Tracy thought to herself, "These guys are total losers and they prove it every time they open their big mouths."

Sandra was trying to push the fellow that reminded her of a pit bull. She thought he could use a little TLC, so she was paying him a great deal of attention.

He was talking quite a bit. Saying things like he was the boss's right-hand man. While he's away, I'm in charge. She asked him, "How was it the boss had a helicopter so close?" He started to answer and stopped. "Why are you so interested in what the boss can and can't do?"

"I was just wondering how a man could have so much power. I can see he doesn't have too much to worry about with you on board. But to be able to snap a finger and have a helicopter land on the ship, that takes some clout."

Pit bull answered, "Yeah! But he also owns it. If you look behind us in the distance, you will see two ships following us. They both belong to the boss. One of them was carrying the chopper. Sandra was running her hand up and down his arm as he talked. He told her that this chopper was just short range. There were others that were larger and could fly anywhere. Those were the ones they used to fly to the islands. Tracy and one of the other men walked up to them and 'Pit Bull' stopped talking.

"Say 'Jackie', did you know you were messing around with a tycoon? He has yachts and helicopters and islands." The emphasis was on islands. Sandra was thinking that there had to be some heavy activity on the island or islands, wherever it or they are. She had to find out where. The nice thing about these guys, they didn't seem to know when they were being pumped for information. The girls felt pretty safe fishing with these two. Also strange was the enormous amount of respect everyone had for Tracy. She had everyone eating out of her hands, mostly, because the boss didn't want anyone offending his woman. She started pushing just a little harder. Looking at Sandra, she said, "Maybe we ought to go to the island and surprise our guys." She turned to the men and asked, "Just how does one get to the island." The guys laughed. Pit Bull told them that nobody ever goes to the island without an invitation and even then you would need a guide.

Sandra excused herself, pulling Tracy with her. Sandra told her that she could do whatever she wanted, but her immediate interest was in the engineer. She hadn't seen him since the night they were partying.

"That fellow knows more about this ship then anyone. If I can get him to show me around the ship, maybe I can find the best place to compromise the system and introduce the 'blob' to the shipment."

Tracy looked back over her shoulder and asked the fellows if the engineer had gone with Todd? The guys looked at each other. Pit Bull said, "I'm not sure." Tracy was more bothered by the look then she was by the answer.

She knew that they had only one more day to pull this off or they would have to follow the drugs into Mexico. Tracy felt that Sandra was on the right track. She told her to go for it.

Chapter Nine

Life for the rich and famous was not going well. The pressure of not knowing who was trying to tear down their empire, illegal as it may be, was getting to them. Parker was thinking—his people had better not fail to get this shipment of drugs in and off loaded, but just in case, he had made plans for a fast getaway. Just in case. Parker was determined that he would not be taken without a fight. He had never been a "yes" man, and he didn't intend to start now. He was one of the smart ones. He hadn't put all of his eggs in one basket like some of the others. Parker had placed his money in strategic places so that it could be moved when needed—and fast. He was feeling pretty good about now, but he would feel even better when he knew that everything had gone well with the drug drop.

The two women who were caught in the hold of the ship were on their way here. He would deal with them swiftly—and painfully, if need be. Unknown to his 'friends', Parker hid a somewhat sadistic nature. His intention to find out everything he needed to know—no matter what it took to do it, was just what he meant to do. The girls would be brought here to Todd, Sr.'s house and then transferred to the main house in Mexico, Hejo del Diablo, house of the devil. The place was built like a fortress with all the luxuries money could buy. There were hot springs and jungle all around. The Mexican government had no use for this particular area, so they leased it to people who wanted privacy. Parker was startled out of his thoughts when one of the dogs barked at him. Both men and dogs patrolled the grounds. Today, there were more then usual of both.

Regina informed Dora that the chopper was taking off from the Club. It too, seemed to be headed for Todd's mountain—top home. Regina was perplexed. She could understand why the first chopper carrying the girls went to the house on the mountain, but the second one was a mystery.

The big chopper arrived at its destination. It made a few passes over the estate before landing. Regina called to Dora that the chopper from the ship had arrived. Dora was preparing to leave for the mountaintop when they saw several people emerge from the house. The girls were off-loaded, but instead of being taken inside, they were placed aboard the larger chopper. Parker and three other men climbed in behind them and they took off. Dora became terribly agitated until she remembered that the girls were still moving on their own power, at least for now.

Back at the ship, Tracy had the pit bull talking and she planned to keep him talking as long as possible. He told her that as long as she was with Todd that she would never have to worry about anything for the rest of her life. That the boss would take good care of her. She gave him her most beautiful smile and encouraged him to tell more. The pit bull told her she would be able to live anywhere in the world. Travel all over. Have beautiful clothes, servants, and furs. She could have it all and go anywhere she wanted to go. Tracy smiled that beatific smile again and asked if that included going to the island in Mexico?

"I just want to know if I've ever been there before."

"No. As I told you before, it's private land, no one is allowed there uninvited." He stood up. "That's enough talking. I have to make rounds."

"Oh! Why do you have to make rounds on the ship?"

"The boss likes for me to keep an eye on everything. Check on the men from time to time." Tracy smiled again and said, "Okay, I understand. I'll see you later." Which, indeed, was the truth.

Sandra was deep in the bowels of the ship when she found the first camera. She had a few toys of her own that would take care of the cameras. They weren't the problem. The men who had nabbed her 'sisters' were still on the ship. They were the problem. She hoped she could find what she was looking for before she had to tangle with them.

She went to work on the first camera by placing a special digital mirror on it. This would remote link to the digital camera she was carrying. She took a picture of the area and sent the picture to the mirror. Any one monitoring the system would have the impression that all is well. She moved from one camera to the other until they were all linked. After which she could move around freely without anyone suspecting. Sandra moved as fast as she could. She had an idea that the best place to start was in the area where the girls were beaten up. As she moved along, she noticed several large containers near the bulkheads. She would need a tool of some kind to break the large nut on the pipe. Sandra wondered if she could find such a tool in the containers. She opened several of them without any luck. In the last one, Sandra found more than she was looking for—it was the remains of the chief engineer. This was the reason they had not seen him for a couple of days. It was also the reason the men had acted so strangely when she asked about him. The chief had known his business and the questions he had been asking were hitting too close to home. Since he wasn't one of them, they killed him.

Recovering from the shock of finding the body, Sandra continued her search for a wrench. She finally found one and applied it to the nut. It wouldn't budge. She tried another angle so as to use her body weight, still no luck. She was scrambling around in the container to see if she could find an extension when the wind was knocked out of her. She fell forward and at the same time tried to see who had opened the barn door. She felt as if a mule had kicked her. Actually, it was the pit bull. He had found her while making his rounds. She was thinking that there wasn't too much difference between him and the mule when he kicked her again. She fell further into the container and couldn't regain her balance. Unless she thought of a defense quickly, she would be dog meat. Just as he drew his foot back to kick her again, he went down himself. This time it was Tracy doing the kicking. She had followed the pit bull thinking he might run into Sandra. Definitely good thinking on her part. The big man rolled over and got to his feet. He had a look of disbelief on his face. This was Todd's girl, and too, she was a woman. How had she knocked him down? His time for thinking was over. Tracy was throwing kicks and punches all over the place. He was not up to this kind of fighting, but he tried hard. Because of his size, he could take a lot of punishment. He backed up the passageway until he had his back against a bulkhead. There was nowhere to go. He reached for his gun only to have it kicked out of his hand. He reached for a dogging wrench and managed to glance a blow off Tracy, which stunned her for a moment. Sandra, having regained her wind, rushed to help her 'sister.' She cold-cocked him with a piece of pipe and he dropped the wrench. She hit him again. This time he was knocked unconscious. Both girls were breathing heavily. Tracy gasped, "Go find some rope so we can tie this guy up before he comes to." Sandra tied his hands together and slung the rope over a pipe in the overhead. She and Tracy pulled him up like the pig he was. It took some doing. This was no lightweight dude, but they were able to pull him high enough then they secured his feet. He was coming around and Sandra was standing right in front of him when he regained consciousness. He was dazed, shaking his head from side to side and trying to get untied, but these girls knew how to tie up a man, the rope didn't budge. Pit bull began calling them whores, sluts and other choice names. He told them they wouldn't see nightfall.

"Look behind you, there are cameras everywhere. You're both dead." Sandra and Tracy just laughed at him and he got mad, turned very red in the face and started yelling as loud as he could. Tracy told Sandra to "gag that maggot before he wakes up our dead friend over there." Sandra was looking around for something to stick in his mouth when she began laughing again. Tracy looking at her 'sister' said, "What's with you?"

"You know, he's been trying to get into my pants for days. I'm going to grant him his wish." With that Sandra pulled off her panties and stuffed them in his mouth. Tracy laughed at her friend. This girl was out to lunch. She was going to have her checked out when they got back home.

The two of them went to work on the nut. They used the same piece of pipe Sandra had used on the pit bull to give them the leverage needed to break the seal. They looked around until they found a stick long enough and narrow enough to fit into the pipe. Sandra cut a sharp point on it, wet it down then they stuck it in the pipe.

"I feel something soft in there." She pushed the stick in further before pulling it all the way out of the pipe. The tip was covered in a white power. Tracy took out her test kit. When the color changed, she said, "Bingo!" She poured the blob into the pipe, saying in as sarcastic a voice as she could muster, "Mr. Blob meet Miss Cocaine." They poured all of the substance into the pipe and replaced the nut.

The ladies had taken their eyes off of the pit bull and he had managed to reach a blade he kept under his watchband and cut himself free. He was making for his gun when the ladies turned around. Tracy was the first to pull her weapon. She shot him in the back of the head. The front of his face came off and there was brain and tissue everywhere. Sandra said, "What do you know? He had brains." They grabbed a tarp and covered him up.

The girls made their way back to the upper decks removing the mirrors as they moved along the corridor.

Tracy told Sandra that she was having her checked out by the doc as soon as they got back to Fort Campbell. "Woman, you are sick." They were both laughing. Feeling very good. The 'blob' would destroy the drugs by the time the ship reached the docks. They would play it cool until they could get off the boat. Tracy and Sandra had decided that it was best that they not change their routine. They could only hope that everyone would stay off their backs until they tied up at the pier.

Sandra touched base with the team. The message sent was, "The pyramid is ruined. The blob is having lunch and King Tut is unaware. H.T.U.W.G.T." Simply put—"Hang Tough Until We Get There!" The girls did not want the party to start without them.

Ordinarily the news sent from ship would have made Dora and the others very happy. But they were extremely worried about the two 'sisters' who were not on their way home. Dora was like a cat on a hot tin roof. Nothing, but nothing, was going to calm her down until she knew where her friends were—exactly. David had called earlier wanting to spend a little time with her this evening, but she had declined. No way could she sit and listen to "sweet nothings" tonight. She had already checked her gear and she was ready to go make a statement.

Regina called to her. "I know where the chopper is, but from the satellite pictures, it looks like it's only beach and jungle. The place is located deep in Mexico and there doesn't seem to be any roads. They have a compound you wouldn't believe."

Dora was getting that feeling again. The back of her neck was itching.

"Something is about to happen and I don't have a clue as to where or when. I think we have covered all the bases, so what could it be." The rest of the team didn't question her feelings. Dora's itch was usually right on target. She had been right too many times for them to ignore her. The question now was how to prevent whatever it was about to happen?

Unfortunately, it was Dora's young brother who was responsible for the itch. Charlie was getting bored. He was tired of hanging out with only adults. As much as he loved his mother and aunt, he wanted to be home with his friends. Unknown to anyone, Charlie placed a call to the home of his best friend.

Director Parker couldn't have been happier. He had placed a wiretap on the young boy's phone. He knew how tight the boys were. Just like Mark and David. It was only a matter of time before he contacted him. Now that he knew where the family was, he could use them to his own advantage. Parker couldn't consider running because he would be running for the rest of life. Right off, Parker had decided that if he couldn't get out of this with a whole skin, he would serve up the kid and his mother to turn things in his favor. The people Parker did business with expected perfection. Truth of the matter was, in this business, you were only as good as your business was—for that day. Business hadn't been too good. He would like nothing better than to have all the members of the special units lying on a slab in the morgue. So far, all the licks had been on the side of the opposition. It was time to turn up the heat. His standing order was to kill anyone who asked questions they shouldn't and that included his own people. The amount of money that had been lost, so far, was unrecoverable. He would have to raise the price on everything across the board to try and recoup some of the losses.

On the other side of the coin, Todd, Sr. was certain that he had become a laughing stock in the eyes of the people who 'inhabited his world.' If he weren't careful, someone else would be running the operation. He would be disposed of without a trace.

Oh yeah! It was time to burn someone else's carcass. Parker and company had better get their act together before he stuck the lighted match to their arses. One more loss and the balloon would go up.

Regina was checking all systems when she received a strange message from Curtis. She called Dora, "You better come look at this."

"What's up?" Instead of answering, Regina handed her the message. Dora read, "Just to let you know that I'm on the inside working in the mailroom at the Cambridge Building. Haven't found out anything as yet, but will keep in touch."

Dora couldn't believe what she was reading.

"Good Lord! Has he lost his mind? What makes him think he won't be recognized? Regina, can you pinpoint his location? We may have to go in and get him out of there before he gets himself killed."

Regina said, "I'm on it."

Dora looked at the rest of the members of her team. "Let's go get 'em!"

The 'sisters' were rechecking their gear when Regina turned to them looking very puzzled. "You know—it's strange that a message would come from the mailroom of the Cambridge Building and—at this hour?"

Dora spoke up, "Now I know why the back of my neck is itching. Something is not right with this picture, guys." Another message was coming in via the computer. 'Beware of Greeks bearing gifts,' the message kept repeating over and over again. The person who sent this message must know a lot about them. This was the way they let each other know that they were walking into a trap. The question now is—who sent the message?

Regina was running a trace, but it was a loop link. The person sending it had bounced it through five different states. The party would be off the line by the time Regina found the starting point. There was no way to find out who had sent the message.

"Dora, what's going on?" said Regina. "Someone has our codes—and how do they know where we are?"

"I don't know. Do you think the girls gave us up because they couldn't stand up to the torture being inflicted on them?" Dora shook her head, "Forget I said that! I'm sure they didn't. But we need to determine if the first message is legit. We must find out if Curtis is working at that place or if he's been captured and being used for bait."

Dora decided that the Cambridge Building had to go. She explained her plans to the 'sisters'.

"The street will have to be closed off so that no innocent people will get hurt. And we'll need some street workers' clothes and everything needed to complete the job."

One of the girls asked, "Are we going to bring down the whole building?"

"Damn right," said Dora. "It's time to send a message of our own."

The 'sisters' were staring at Dora. They saw something in her eyes they had never seen before.

"I want them to know that if anything happens to our 'sisters', they will pay for it in ways they cannot imagine. I will personally dismember them one by one until I get my 'sisters' back. I want them to understand this beyond a shadow of doubt."

The girls didn't doubt her for a minute. Dora's voice had changed. It was cold and harsh. The rules had changed. No one would be the same after today. The 'sisters' would follow Dora wherever she led them. This was a mission of love to rescue the members of their team. They would fight to the last man.

Todd Sr. had sent word to 'Mister Invincible" demanding that he do something about the people who were destroying his business and do it fast.

His message read, "*You have been well paid for what you do, but so far on this project, you have dropped the ball. I need immediate results. If I do not get it, you will have to prove just how invincible you are. I will put out a contract on you and laugh when I pay it off. No man is an island and this I will prove to you unless I start to see the dead bodies of my enemies. You haven't even found out who is destroying our business. I will not take this from any man who works for me, especially one of your caliber.*"

The man to whom the message was addressed became extremely angry as he read it. He understood that out of desperation Todd, Sr. would say or do anything, but to threaten him was the worst possible thing he could do. The fool had lost his mind. He was the last person on earth his people wanted to tangle with—not even as a joke. They wanted him to turn it up, well, that's just what he would do.

The ship carrying the drugs was docking with the help of a couple of tugboats. Meanwhile, both Sandra and Tracy were hoping to get off the boat before the crew started pumping out the tanks and without running into anymore of Todd's men.

They weren't sure how long it would be before someone noticed that the drugs had been destroyed. Which would no doubt cause a search of the ship and in the process, find the bodies of two very dead men. The guys might put two and two together and come up with the two of them.

Dora's thoughts were running along the same lines. She dispatched Jody to the docks to pick up the girls.

On the dock, the crew was already preparing to pump the drugs into the tankers when Jody arrived. There was a note of anticipation on the part of men as they worked. Each man was going about his assigned task, with a minimum of confusion. People covered every inch of the dock waiting for their loved ones to disembark. As Jody picked her way through the crowd, she remembered why she had joined the Army. It was to get away from crowds. Look at me now. How in the name of God could so many people gather in one spot? She didn't have to wait for an answer, Tracy ran up to her and said, "Hey girl!"

Sandra soon joined them and they went to retrieve their bags. They kept on their toes in case their departure was prevented.

The crew had the pumps running in preparation of off loading the drugs. The dock agents were talking to the captain wanting to know the origin of the contaminated fuel. The agents' interest was the concern that other ships may have the same problem and that would be dangerous. Once they were satisfied, the paper work was completed and the agents went off on other business. Now, the ship could begin the transfer of the drugs. Dora was thinking what it was going to be like when they found out the drugs had been tampered with, yet again. She gave a nervous little whistle.

Regina straightening in her chair alerted Dora to the conversation going on in the mountain home of Todd, Sr. Carrie was speaking. The conversation had Dora stymied. To date, Carrie had denied the implication that her team was responsible for all of the killings. They all knew it was women, but that seemed to be the extent of their information. She was hoping that their luck would hold until she was able to get the girls back. The fear factor was that if Todd, Sr. and company found out what was going on, that they would take it out on the girls. In fact, Dora was sure of it. The girls would be dead before anything could be done for them.

There was another message coming in and this time, they were sure it was someone who knew them well. It was not from Curtis, but in a format that only one who had trained with them could have written. Regina was working on it while one of the other girls contacted the other members of the team. Tracy, Sandra and Jodie were on their way home.

Regina had a very cold look in her eyes as she finished decoding the message. The message alerted the team that "Christine was not doing well. She has been raped and beaten every day, but has sworn that she will die before telling them what they wanted to know." The message continued—"I have not seen or heard anything of Lydia, but feel she is holding her own. I know you're planning something, I just hope it's in time to save them."

Dora looked up, "Well, girls are we ready? It's time we sent our own message." Thumbs up all around.

"Yeah!"

"Let's get this show on the road."

"Let's go." These were just a few of the comments being tossed around.

Meanwhile, Christine was sweating it out in her little cell on the estate in Mexico. The room was small and basic. One small cot, a basin, and a commode gave testimony that others had been held here against their will. There were four cellblocks in this building set away from the main house. The American influence was prevalent in that it was clean and the toilet had a toilet seat. The door had a small window but it was one way. Someone could look in, but you couldn't see out. You couldn't hear very much either. As the message had stated, Christine was hurting, but not so badly that she couldn't think. Her body was bruised from the guys who had pinched and pulled on her during the rape. She had taken quite a beating when she started to defend herself and had thrown a couple of them across the room. From then on, no one approached her by himself. She passed out a couple of times and one of the men threw water on her to bring her to. When she had passed out yet, again, they gave up. One of the men said, "Let her digest that for awhile. She can't take much more. She will sing like a bird the next time we come back. Bet on it!"

Christine was not really out of it this time, but had decided it was best to play dead to gather her strength. Her mind was working overtime. She had made up her mind that she would not die until she could kill a couple of the pigs that had abused her. She decided to kill them in a very special way. What that way was, she didn't know right now. But she would think of something.

Christine also felt a little sorry for anyone who was in this but didn't know exactly why. If it was just for the money, they were going to work very hard to earn their pay. Knowing her team as well as she did, World War III was about to begin right here, wherever here is. She understood that it would take a little time to pull it all together, but whether she made it or not, the job would get done.

Christine made a deal with herself; life was too good to give up easily. She planned on living to die a very old woman. So—she would live.

She heard footsteps outside her door and thought it might be the pigs back to continue their abuse. She waited for the door to open holding her breath. It was only a few seconds but it seemed like minutes had passed. Still the door didn't open. Instead, a note was slipped under the door. She waited a few minutes and then went over to pick it up. She listened at the door but heard nothing so she went over to the corner of the little room that had some light. Christine opened it and read, "Hang in there, you must do all you can to stay alive. You will soon be free. You have a friend close by and help is on the way.

A similar note was slipped under door of Lydia's cell.

This was welcome news and would give them the edge they needed to stay alive. Both girls were having the same thoughts. How did the team get someone on the inside? And could they trust this person or was it a trick? They could only wait and see. The message was clear even if it was a trick. Somehow neither girl thought it was. So they'd wait.

Meanwhile back at the docks, the bodies of the two men had been found aboard the ship. The drugs were tested. Regina who had been keeping tabs on her electronic gear informed Dora what was happening. The team knew that the girls would be killed in retaliation if they didn't get to them soon.

Todd, Sr. was waiting for an answer on the test even though he was already pretty sure what the answer would be. Once it was confirmed that all the drugs had been contaminated, he sat down at his desk and at that moment, he looked very old. He did not have a clue as to what to do to keep his own people from killing him and his son. His colleagues would never accept this second destruction of drugs in silence. How in the world did these people get to the drugs and take out two men in the process?

He called the ship, "Bring me the tapes. Now."

He hoped that they would show the face of the person or persons who had caused the destruction of all that beautiful cocaine. If so, they were dead meat. He also wanted every member of his crime family at his home immediately. That order included Director Parker. He was to fly back from Mexico right away. Laurence hated being ordered about by anyone, but he knew he would have to go.

The team was finishing up the last of their preparations. Lil' Bits broke into a city lot and drove one of their trucks off the lot. She had to take out a section of fence to accomplish this feat, but that was all right. After tonight the lid would be off everything anyway. Lil' Bits had chosen the truck that was loaded with everything they needed to close off the street. Most of the explosives were at the house, so they need only make one more trip to the resort to pick up extra arsenal. Dora watched her teammates, each going about their duties, knowing exactly what needed to be done. Two hours later, preparations were complete. The only problem now, was David. He called wanting to see Dora. David had been walking on clouds ever since that night at the pool. He couldn't keep his mind on his work or anything else. He had Dora on the brain, day and night, night and day. He kept remembering that memorable night when Dora let him taste the very essence of her being.

David was transported back… They sank beneath the water. Both forgetting that they had to breathe. Fighting for air, they begin kicking for the surface. When David pulled Dora from the water, he laid her on one of the floating air mattresses by the side of the pool.

"Dora, you're so beautiful—so beautiful." He began making passionate love to her and she returned it two-fold. David nibbled on every inch of her body including her toes. When he reached the heart of her being, he nestled in the black curly hair and Dora came apart. She grasp him by the shoulders to push him away then changed her mind. Her orgasm was something to behold. His control slipped after that and he entered her in one swift motion. Dora tightened her muscles around him and his seed poured into her. Dora came again and they both were out of control. At last, hearts began to slow and breathing returned to normal.

"Wow!" was all Dora could say. David remembered that for the first time in his life, he was speechless. He pulled her to him and hung on for dear life. Later, Dora brought him to peak again, but this time she climbed on top of him and teased and licked him all over. She leaned over him so he could suck on her nipples and her ears and anywhere else he could reach. Finally, it had gotten too much for her. She lowered herself on to his rock-hard arousal and they rode the storm out together. David pulled a big fluffy white beach towel over them and they dozed for a while. David woke first. "My God," he thought, "at last I have her in my arms. Laying next to my heart." Dora awakened then, looked into his eyes and said, "I think I love you." That was enough for David. He began to kiss her hair, her eyes, her ears, her neck, and her throat. He very carefully laid her on her back and completed his worship of her body, trying to reach her soul. Before long they were both so aroused that they couldn't get close enough to each other. David tried hard to remain in control, but Dora wasn't having any. This was her night and control was not on the menu. David went very slowly at first. After that he wasn't sure what happened. It was a good thing the radio was playing a little loud, because this orgasm caused them both to holler out. What a night! And David wanted more. He became hard every time he thought about that night which meant he was in a state of almost constant arousal. He had even stopped asking questions about who and what she was. He didn't care anymore. He was trying to keep his mind off the fact that he might be in love with a killer. David was learning when to back off and give her the space she needed.

Dora was worried that he might be out and about tonight, so she was toying with the idea of inviting him over and then figuring out what to do with him. She definitely did not want him on the street tonight. Before she could say anything, David told her he had to make a run up to San Francisco.

"I'll be gone three or four days. I'll call you as soon as I return."

Dora said, "Okay! Is this business or pleasure?"

"It's business or I wouldn't go. I would much rather be with you."

"Yeah, I know. You be careful, you hear."

"I will. You do the same." There was a moment's pause, "Dora, I love you." David very quietly hung up the phone before Dora could reply.

Dora replaced the receiver, thanking the gods for getting David out of her hair.

The girls were eating when she went down to the command center. They informed her that a big pow wow was going on at Todd, Sr.'s house.

Todd, Sr. was walking around the enormous room very slowly and deliberately. He was giving a lot of thought to what he had to say before speaking.

"Gentlemen, I've called all of you together to ask a very simple question. How is it that most of you were on that ship with your fancy cameras and security systems in place, yet two men are dead and our shipment has been destroyed—again?" He stopped his pacing in front of Laurence and turned to look him in the eye. You could have heard a pin drop in a haystack at that moment. No one moved, and no one spoke. The men had their heads down. All except Laurence, that is. He wished he could do the same, but that steel glare looking him in the eyes was there for him to deal with. He found it difficult to swallow, but finally, he was able to speak.

"I believe—No, I am convinced that the person or persons responsible for all that has happened to date is a member of Mark's family." He looked around at the other men in the room and back to Todd, Sr.

"I know this may seem far-fetched to you, and I don't have anything concrete to go on, but I have gone over all of the events since Mark's death and I come up with family."

Todd, Sr. shaking his head responded by saying, "Did you, in all your infinite wisdom, figure out how two women and a boy could cause the havoc that has become a way of life for us?"

Laurence began telling Todd, Sr. of all that had been taking place. He told him about the wiretaps, and the bombs. He explained that the sister was one step ahead of everything he had done to stop her. Todd, Sr. was very upset over what he was hearing.

"It sounds to me as if you have been doing your own thing. You could be the reason for all this destruction." Todd, Sr. struck a pose like a preacher, stuck his fist in the air and yelled, "Vengeance is mind, saith the Lord!" Is that what you've done with all your shenanigans?" Todd, Sr. began his pacing again. He stopped in front of Laurence once more.

"You know, I still don't know who killed that young man—who ordered his death. Laurence, you were told to hit the others, but I don't remember requesting that you kill them all. I wonder, did you push just a little too hard? Could this be the reason for this nightmare?" He seemed to be talking to himself, but he was repeating himself to make sure that Laurence understood the position he was being pushed into.

Laurence watched the changes of expressions on Todd, Sr.'s face. Watched his eyebrows go up to make his point. Then shake his head in a very condescending manner. Laurence realized at once he was going to be the scapegoat. They needed someone to blame and he'd walked right into it. Todd, Sr. walked a short distance away from Laurence then turned back to him.

"So-o, since you have deducted that the family is the problem, what have you done about it?"

Laurence was sure, now, that he was being led to the guillotine. Knowing he could do nothing about it, he started talking. Todd, Sr. went over to sit behind his desk.

"I've figured out that the daughter, Dora, is the real problem. And I think I have figured out a way to get to her." Laurence took a seat in front of the desk. Todd said, "All right, continue with your brainstorming."

"I know where the mother and son are hiding," said Laurence. This Todd, Sr. already knew, but let the man go on. He scanned the room to determine if the others felt the same as Laurence did. Noting their agreement, he was about to ask for some feedback from them when he heard footsteps in the outer hall. Seeing that it was Carrie, he said, "Carrie dear, I have a question to ask you. I would like to know if you feel this soldier you've trained could be causing all the trouble we're having? Now be careful of your answer because I'm having a really bad day. I seem to be surrounded by some very incompetent people in this room. There is no good reason why I should be going through this maelstrom, considering the amount of money you people are being paid. So once again, I put the question to you my dear, could it be your girl that is giving me heartburn?"

Carrie looked at Todd, Sr. with all the contempt she could muster and said, "If I thought she was, she would be dead by now. There are a few things I won't put up with—one, is people messing with my money. The second is—people thinking I can't do my job. That girl couldn't whip a ninety-eight pound weakling, so how could she be causing all of this havoc? Now, if you have anything else to say, I suggest you say it and not imply it. The room was very quiet, they all knew Carrie spoke her mind and was willing to back it up.

Todd, Sr. broke into a smile. "I'm not quite sure what I was thinking. How could this girl be the old war dog you are?"

Carrie laughed, "Even I couldn't pull off what is happening to us. No, I think we are dealing with men. It could be someone who wants to take over the business." Laurence put in his two cents. "Yeah! Then how do you explain the two women we have in Mexico."

Carrie looked at him. "The last time I checked, men and women travel together. From the look of things, I'd say you were lucky to have only caught the women.

With the beating those girls put on your guys, surely, the men would have killed them all. Now if there is nothing else, I will leave you gentlemen." She left just as she entered leaving no one in doubt in her ability to take care of Carrie.

Dora and the team were listening in on this conversation. She was beginning to have mixed emotions where Carrie was concerned. Carrie had said she would kill her but at the same time emphasized that she had trained her (Dora) and knew she could not have beaten up those men. That statement in itself was very peculiar, when Carrie knew for certain, that Dora and her team could take out an entire town, because she had trained them to do just that. Very peculiar, indeed!

Dora just had to find out what this woman's motives are. Why is she trying to diffuse the situation where Dora is concerned and threaten to take her out 'if necessary' in the same breath. There had to be more to this whole mess than she knew. She hoped so. Dora really wanted to find a reason to pardon the one woman she looked up to in life other than her mother.

She brought her mind back to the present when she heard the men talking about their 'sisters'.

Todd, Sr. was saying, "Find out if any headway has been made with those two women we caught." One of guys hurried away to do his bidding.

Todd, Sr.'s voice was beginning to sound a little desperate. Looking around the room, he said, "Time has run out for us. We must find out who is trying to destroy us today."

He turned to Laurence again, "I remember you saying, and I quote, 'I bet my life they won't get this shipment'. Well sir, they did. The question now is, are you ready to give up your life or do you think you can fix this catastrophe and redeem yourself? I'll leave you to ponder this weighty matter. I'm sure you will arrive at the right decision."

Chapter Ten

Back at the house, the girls were completing their preparations for the evening's activities. Dora on the other hand, was pondering the conversation they had overheard between Todd, Sr. and Laurence Parker. She couldn't help thinking that the old man had an ulterior motive for beating up on Parker the way he did.

Actually, Todd, Sr. had been grandstanding. The fact is, he didn't trust any of them, not even Carrie. He had a lot of respect for Laurence. The man made a living at finding out things that people were trying to hide. He was very good at putting two and two together and coming up with four. If he says the daughter is responsible in some way for what had been happening to their shipments, then he, Todd, believed him. Further, in the back of his mind, he couldn't help but feel that the women Carrie trained were as dangerous as any men, maybe more so.

The men began departing and Todd, Sr. made it a point to walk Laurence out. They were outside talking where the rest of the men couldn't hear what was being said. The problem was, that neither could the girls in the command center. The gardener was working around the front of the house with an electric trimmer. The conversation concerned Dora's mother and brother. Todd instructed Laurence to send some one to pick them up. They were to be taken to Mexico. He let Laurence know that he was prepared to do whatever was necessary to pull the business back in line. One more loss and they could all say 'goodnight'.

Laurence was smiling when he and Todd, Sr. joined Carrie in the limo. Carrie was very aware of the smug look on Laurence's face, but not knowing why? acted as if nothing had happened. She knew whatever Todd, Sr. and Laurence were plotting boded no good for someone. She hoped she had allayed suspicion of Dora, at least for a little while.

Regina using the satellite photos and other information gathered through all her electronic devices was making plans for the invasion of the island in Mexico.

"We can hit them from three sides," said Regina. "Land, sea and air. But we still have to find a way to the compound itself. Everything is densely covered by foliage."

Lil' Bits spoke up then, "Don't worry. We'll get in there—and that's a fact, Jack." Everyone grinned at her bid for a bit of frivolity though no one was in a laughing mood. This was serious business. The job called for all the professionalism they could muster.

Jodie was patiently using a stone on a matching pair of pearl-handled knives that were already razor-sharp. The rest of the team was in various stages of checking and rechecking their gear. Each knew that what they did in this preliminary stage would give them a better chance of coming home from the 'war'.

Dora and Gypsy sat at the table watching Regina map out the plan.

Gypsy wasn't sure what was going on, so she took a chance and asked. Dora explained.

"We have to find a way to get our gear into Mexico. If we go by air, it would be a high-altitude jump and we would have to free-fall which would not be a problem for us, but it would be with our gear especially as we're jumping at night."

Gypsy nodded her understanding. Dora gave her shoulder a squeeze. They had all taken to Gypsy. She was 'real people' and had plenty of guts. She had earned their respect without reservation.

Regina tilted her head to one side, and began walking around the table rubbing her chin.

"Okay!" said Dora. "I see you're about to bust a gut, what's the matter?"

"You know, I bless the day my father called me a disciple of the devil, because I've been b-a-a-d ever since." The girls laughed at Regina's attempt at mimicry. Regina had them gather around and she laid it all out. She suggested they wait until she finished before digging holes in the plan.

Carrie was still upset about not knowing what plans had been hatched by Todd, Sr. and Laurence Parker. She was more convinced then ever that something was afoot when Laurence climbed into the front seat of the limo to make a phone call. That made it impossible for her to listen in on the conversation. Laurence was putting into motion his plans to kidnap Dora's mother, Hope, and her brother, Charlie. Men were on their way to the house even now. Their orders were to watch the house and find out how many people were inside. They had been told to wait for backup before attempting to enter the house.

When the other men arrived, they split up into two groups and headed up the drive. The first to arrive at the door never got to ring the bell. Kim had been watching them from the house. She and Ruthie decided to make a stand in the open. They told Charlie and his mother to stay out of sight no matter what.

Charlie made a beeline for the telephone to call Dora. Ruthie and Kim put up a good fight but there was just too many of them. Hope was horrified at the sight of these women fighting for their lives in an effort to save her and Charlie. She watched Kim go down, leaving Ruthie to continue the fight alone. In the mean time Charlie was all but screaming on the phone to Dora what was happening. One of the men gave Kim a vicious kick in the head and she was dead. Ruthie went down, too.

Hope was hanging on to Charlie the entire time he was talking to Dora. The men made their way into the house searching for them. Hope and Charlie were crouched down in a bedroom. Charlie was still on the phone when the men burst into the room. Dora was having a fit knowing that there was nothing she could do.

One of the men snatched the phone out of Charlie's hand and spoke, "Whether your family lives or dies depends on you. We want our money back and we want you." The phone went dead. The 'sisters' heard it all on the speaker. They knew that Ruthie and Kim were dead. The phone rang again. This time the voice was almost a whisper. It was Ruthie; she had managed to crawl in the house to the phone.

"Dora, they asked Hope, how was her Spanish?" Another breathy whisper—"I'm sorry sis, it was too many, too ma—n-y." Ruthie's voice faded away and the girls knew she was either dead or dying. They heard her take a last shuddering breath. It was over. After a few silent minutes, Regina looked at Dora and asked, "Are you ready to go to Mexico?"

"Oh yeah! More then ready. But first—we take out that building. They run the whole operation from there and I want it closed down. Now."

Regina argued against that. "Listen, we can do the building when we get back with your family and the girls. Right now, we need to get moving."

Jodie and Lil' Bits agreed with Regina. Dora could be so bull-headed at times. But she needed to get her head back into the ball game. They needed to be putting a much bigger machine in motion.

Dora asked if anyone was hungry? She was famished, so continued on to the kitchen without bothering to wait for a reply. Lil' Bits turned to Regina with imploring eyes which said, "Do something." The girls felt that blowing up that building before rescuing Dora's family would be the worse possible mistake they could make. No telling what the guys would do in retaliation.

Regina followed Dora to the kitchen.

"Look, I know you're ready to tear into these guys, so are we, but this is not—I repeat, this is not, the time to take down that building. We need to be heading for Mexico."

Dora watched the best friend she had in the whole world, with the exception of her mom, trying to say what had to be said without offending her.

Regina continued, "I do understand what you're going through, but you're using your heart instead of your head. The death of any of us is our choice and not one of us expects the others to feel anything but proud. You need to let it go. Taking out that building at this time will only get your family killed. We need to get the living back, first. And right now, is the perfect time.

Dora said, "Okay, why?"

"Because there is a joint training exercise taking place between Mexico and the United States in three days. It gives us an opportunity to request whatever we need and there won't be any questions at the border. But we need to touch bases with our 'brothers' and invite them to the shindig. What do ya' say?"

Dora thought over what Regina had outlined and agreed.

"You're right, as usual. I'm not thinking very well, am I?"

Dora and Regina smiled at each other and looked up to see the other girls standing in the doorway.

"Okay, let's do it!"

At the same time, Dora was praying that those clowns wouldn't do anything to her family as long as they thought they had the upper hand. Many countries held joint exercises with the USA, so this was not unusual. Their 'brothers' would help all they could once they found out the deal.

"All right what's the plan?

Regina told them that the first thing they would do is call on their Airborne 'brothers'. Then we contact the Marines and the Navy Seals.

Dora said, "Make your calls."

"Right!" As Regina ran through the door, she swiped Dora's sandwich.

The 'sisters' followed her to the command center. Recon was essential, so the first call was made to the Marine base at Camp Pendleton.

Having been alerted, they would wait for Regina to call back. They would provide the Recon team. The next call was to the naval base at Coronado to contact the Navy Seals. The commander assured Regina that they would be ready to leave at a moments notice. These guys were very anxious to meet Dora. They had heard a lot about her but had never had the pleasure. None of the guys knew her brother, either. Not that it mattered, their creed was blood for blood. They discussed their needs in armament, how to get on the island, jumping off times and other things necessary to a successful mission. A time was set for an Internet link-up on a secure line used only by the military that included their buddies at Fort Campbell, which was their third and final call. The 101st Airborne would be ready.

"Okay, you guys," said Dora, "Let's get some sleep. Tomorrow's going to be a very busy day."

Dora lay thinking instead of sleeping, her mind in overdrive. Once this mission started, it wouldn't end until the fat lady sings. She smiled to herself in the dark. The 'fat lady sings' was the password being used for this operation. She had a feeling that she had better get to her family and 'sisters' before all of this went down, otherwise, they would be in more danger than ever. In an operation such as this, timing was everything. They would not get a second chance. Dora was thinking that she had gone on several missions, but none was ever as important as the one on which they would embark day after tomorrow. She and her 'sisters' would have to be as sharp as Jodie's knives. Dora continued her musings. She and her 'sisters' would do a night jump and be there before anyone else. They could do a lot more damage unannounced. Perhaps get their people out of harms way before the main insurgence. Regina, who was also going over the plans in her own mind, was thinking the same thing.

They finally dozed off. Daybreak would come very soon and so would the reason for the itch on the back of Dora's neck just as she fell asleep.

Hope was still trying to make heads or tails of what was going on. She asked the men what they expected of her and her son. She was totally ignored. They put them in the chopper and headed for Mexico. She was extremely frightened. Charlie, holding his mother's hand, kept telling her, 'it's going to be all right.' Charlie had kicked one of the men and told him to keep his hands off of his mother. He would have been shot, but another man, whom he supposed was in charge, hollered at him.

"Leave them. You can take care of them later."

Charlie was not afraid, much, but he had heard what the man had said to his sister. He knew she was on her way to wherever this place was they were being taken. He didn't understand what the man was talking about, but he was a fast learner. He had the feeling that his sister was something more than he or his mother knew.

Mark too, had done a lot of freaky things that couldn't be explained. Seeing his sister make some of the same moves had got him to thinking. What it was, he didn't know? Whatever it was had gotten his brother killed, and he and his mother captives of some very desperate people. Charlie remembered the man saying they wanted their money back and they wanted her. It made no sense to him. He would just have to wait and see.

Back in Mexico, another note had been slid under the doors of both girls. This one read, You'll be free in one or two days. Hang in there." Bravo Six. Now, both girls were more perplexed than ever. The signature code made them aware that although the person was unknown to them, he or she knew something about them. The note made them feel a little better. It was a sure sign that the 'sisters' were on the way.

Christine was hoping that whatever happened, the guy she most wanted to kill would not get caught in the onslaught. She personally wanted that honor for herself. The dog would die in a manner worst than any dog ever had.

When morning came, Dora decided to go for a run while the girls prepared breakfast. She had not done so for awhile. She needed to clear her head for what was ahead. Dora ran like a cat and it felt good to be alive. She didn't know if she would be in another day or two, but as long as she got her mother and brother home safely, it didn't matter. Christine and Lydia were important, too, but she knew—and they knew, that they might not make it out of there. As soon as the shooting started, the girls would not be spared. That is why, she thought, they would have to go in first, at night, to give them a fighting chance.

By the time Dora returned from her run, the girls had cleaned up the kitchen. She grab a cup of coffee and a bagel and went upstairs to shower while Regina prepared for the upcoming conference call. Everything would be explained to their 'brothers'. After listening, all of the units added their input to the plans. The team would exact their pound of flesh. This would be the worst nightmare the bad guys ever had. The loss of their drugs was nothing compared to what they going to lose. Dora still wished she had time to take out the Cambridge Building. Those guys ran their businesses from there and it would definitely put a crimp in their life style for a long, long time. Unless they had a back-up hideaway somewhere else, those businesses might never be able to get up and running again.

The team gathered around the table to hear the plan. Regina was the first to speak.

"The party will begin at 0600 hours day after tomorrow. The time coincides with the beginning of the joint exercises. The folks on the island will think all of the fire is coming from the mock battle at sea. With any luck, we can be in and out long before anyone realizes that the all the gunfire is not coming from offshore."

Jodie and Lil' Bits had made a list of the stores at their disposal. Regina asked for the report. Before doing so, Jodie turned to Dora. "I would have loved to have known your brother. He could have taken on Beirut all alone."

Dora smiled, "Yeah! I guess he was a little sick. Now how about the report."

"Right! We have two 40mm machine guns and four M16s with a 203 grenade launcher attached. There are two 50 caliber sniper rifles and six Gluck 9s, also a case of HK MP5 9-mm pistols and a case of SIG sauens. All the grenades and ammo we can carry. Oh! there are night vision and infrared scopes, too."

Dora nodded her head. It certainly looked like her brother Mark had prepared for war. They wouldn't need much more.

Dora said, "Listen! We will not go in with the rest. Here's my idea. Regina, I feel that if we wait until the guys storm the beach we'll be too late. So I need you to set us up with a plane, chutes, and O2 because we will be jumping early. Our brothers in the Airborne can jump, say, 30 minutes later."

The team agreed. Their leader was back. They would do it by the numbers.

The conference call came on line and Regina informed their 'brothers' of the target and how the plan would develop. The request for the plane, chutes and oxygen was arranged. They would have everything they needed. The plane will be leaving El Toro Base at 0400 as part of the operation in Mexico anyway. It would just have a few more passengers. The supply sergeant on the plane would make sure all of their supplies were on board.

After a few more details, times and coordinates were worked out, Regina signed off. The girls were ready to go. Time was running out in more ways than one. Their leave was about up. This business had to be settled in the next couple of days or they would have to return to base and leave Dora out there all alone. It was time to push the envelope.

Dora had called on some CIA friends to take care of Kim and Ruthie. The television and news media reported a drive-by shooting in which several people had been injured and three people had been killed. Two of the victims were service women who were home on leave out on a shopping spree. This way the Army would not be looking for other reasons for their deaths. The families would get paid the small sum they had coming and any other benefits. As for them, the training exercise in Mexico would be their cover in case any of them got killed. Everything was planned to a 'T'. They were checking the gear one more time when the phone rang.

Dora answered the phone. It was Todd, Sr. "Yes! What can I do for you", she asked.

"If you ever want to see your family alive again, you will do as you're told. A plane will be landing at Oxnard Airport at 1900 hours tonight. You will bring nothing with you except our money and you will be flown to where your mother and brother are being held. Do you understand?"

"Yes, I understand. I'll be there." They both hung up. Now she understood why she had the itch at the back of her neck.

"Well, you heard. What do you think?"

"I think you're crazy if you even contemplate meeting that snake," said Jodie.

"I don't have much choice. If I don't go, they may kill mom and Charlie before we get there."

"That's true, but you don't have the money," Lola reminded her.

"I know. But I would think that they would be smart enough to realize I'm not going to bring all that money with me and just let them kill my family and me. Uh-uh, they'd have to be a lot dumber than we thought." Dora, deep in thought, shivered for some unknown reason. She said, "No, I'll have to go. But you go forward with the plans as scheduled. I'll just be there a little ahead of you."

Regina agreed. "You know, we can fix you up with a few things that they will probably miss when they search you. And they will search you thoroughly. Too bad your hair is so short, but I think we can get around that. Have a seat while I dig into my little bag of tricks." Dora sat.

Dora, who had done as Regina suggested, was oblivious to what was going on around her. It wasn't until she felt a hand on her shoulder that she realized Regina was talking to her. Dora looked up at her.

"I'm sorry. I just had the funniest feeling. It seemed like someone was trying to tell me something from far away."

The girls didn't argue with her. They had seen her like this before. Dora often seemed to be in touch with something, or someone, more often than not. It had been said that Dora had been born with a veil over her face and a hole above her left ear. The lady was clairvoyant. They were sure of it.

Regina looked at Dora and said, "Girl, you've got to stop this. If you're not up on your game, you won't make it."

"You know, Mark used to talk about how you scared everyone to death with your visions. Do you think he's trying to talk to you now," asked Gypsy. "In my country, there are people like you and we believe in them."

Dora smiled at the young woman who had come to mean so much to her and her friends. "I hope you're right kid! Maybe what I just saw will be enough to keep our people alive until we can get to them."

No one said anything for a few minutes. Then Dora spoke.

"You all know that we must get our people out of there before the shooting starts, right?" Before anyone could answer, she continued. "To help us with this mission, we are going to use a Trojan horse." She turned to Regina. "I want you to have our banking friend setup a wire transfer of some one billion dollars. That should be pretty close to what they lost. It has to appear that it is ready for transfer to one of the off—shore accounts we took it from in the first place. By the time word is given to transfer the funds, you guys have to be on the inside or we're going to be in big trouble. Understand?"

"Yeah! We understand, but you're crazy, if you think they are going to let you or anybody go who has seen their faces and I do mean Hope and Charlie. Money or no money," said Jodie.

"And what if they ask for the money before you get on the plane," queried Gypsy.

"Good question, Gypsy. Regina, can you set me up with a laptop. If they have on-line capability, and I'm sure they do, I need to be able to show them that the money is ready for transfer, but not until after my family is safe."

"You'll never get away with that. Oh, I can fix you up with the laptop, all right, but we need to give ourselves an edge. Let me think."

"Look, you need to take a camera and mike in with you, that would make it easier for us to know who all the players are. It would also let us know how many guards are around your family and the girls."

"I know, Jodie, but I'm more concerned because I can't take in a weapon. I know they will search me before letting me on the plane, guaranteed."

"Are you going to wear your boots on the plane," asked Gypsy.

"Yes I am. Why do you ask?"

"I could fit a derringer into one of the boots, if you like."

" I like, but if they have metal detectors, it would be picked up."

"Not if you have one of those two-shot plastic guns we use sometime," said Liz. She went over to her bags, and after digging around for a few seconds, she produced the gun. "Voila," and she grinned and hid her face in her hand. The other girls laughed and hollered, "thief."

As usual, Liz had not turned in the weapon as she was supposed to. They all knew she would be in big trouble if caught with this weapon. Dora just looked at her. "You know, you could be looking for a new job, if you get caught with that gun in your possession."

Liz said, "What the hell, they're not going to shoot me with it. And you know you're glad I disobeyed orders—this time."

"You're right!" Dora grabbed the gun out of Liz's hand and gave it and a boot to Gypsy. "Okay, get it done."

Time was running out and she would have to leave very soon. Gypsy asked what was she suppose to do while they were gone? Regina told her to 'hold the fort until we get back.' Then we'll talk about your future.

"I know what I want to do. I want to join the Army and serve with you guys."

Dora was glad to hear this, but admonished her to think about it while they were gone. It wasn't the easiest job in town.

A call came in from the Navy Seal team informing them that they would be embarking in an hour. The sub that was taking them in was also a part of the joint exercises. The team would be dropped about a mile off shore and they would swim in the rest of the way. They would touch bases with them again from the sub. Regina let the Seal team know that Dora was going in that night and that she had no choice in the matter. The operation was scheduled for 0600 day after tomorrow. The 'sisters' would be jumping at 0430 and the 101st Airborne at 0500. The idea was that even if they were seen, it would be close to 0600 and people would think that it was a part of the war games and not pay too much attention to them. There were innocent civilians on the peninsula and they wanted to minimize casualties among them. They worked in the fields and some also processed the drugs, but they were unaware of the all the evil doings on the estate. Security was lax except in the immediate vicinity of the estate. The local officials were well paid to mind their own business. The estate provided a livelihood for the island folk. They didn't share in the profits, but life wasn't bad for them. They were well taken care of on this peninsula. Even so, Dora made a solemn promise to burn the buildings to the ground. It was a shame, but the citizens of Diablo would just have to find a new way of life.

After signing off with the Seals, Regina contacted the other teams who would be taking part in the operation. All were ready. Date, times and places, perfectly understood. The Recon team would be going in from the woods. They felt they should get in close and dig in. They assured Dora that no one would ever know they were there. The captain informed Dora that he was only taking two teams, 24 men, which would be more than enough to get the job done. They all signed off and Liz came over to Dora and said, "We're gonna' rock and roll, kid." The 'sisters' laughed. This girl from Philadelphia loved to fight. She would fight anytime, anyplace and anybody. They were still laughing when another of those mysterious messages came in from person or persons unknown. It said, "Beware, the fortress has fifteen well-trained mercenaries camped inside the walls. Personal guards of the people who run the place. Very good at what they do. Could be a problem." The message ended without a signature. The only thing the girls knew for sure was that it was coming from the area where they were going. Regina was very upset, now. She wanted to go with Dora.

"You won't have any back-up until we get there."

"You're forgetting our two 'sisters' aren't you?" said Dora.

"I'm not forgetting them, but you don't know what kind of shape they are going to be in when you get there or even if they are still alive. You're playing with a stacked deck, this time. Be reasonable."

"I am being reasonable and you know it. If the girls are alive, I hope to have them out by the time you get there. If not—well, I'm a big girl now. Stop being such a mother hen."

Gypsy brought in the boot she had fitted out with the gun. Dora checked it out and congratulated Gypsy on doing such a good job. She beamed with joy. Gypsy loved doing things that pleased her newfound friend and sister.

Dora loaded the pistol and placed it in the boot. She then donned both her utilities and the boots.

When she had finished dressing, Jodie came to her with two small knife holders containing cameras. They fit on each collar. With any luck they would only take the knives and leave the holders. If this worked, they would be able to see exactly what Dora was seeing. They would know who the players were and determine where everyone was and the best way to get to them.

The call signs were the last to be done. The Recon teams were 'bush bunnies'; the Seal teams were 'beached whales'; the airborne was 'painted angels'; and the girls were 'Sisters Without Mercy.' Dora was 'Mother Superior.' The girls joined hands in a circle and repeated the words "Ad Mortem Fidelis", till death us do part.

Regina had one more word of warning for Dora. "If they give you a hard time about the money, tell them that half the money will be released now and the other half after your family has been released into safe hands. I've also arranged for the release of the money in five days. That'll give us a little leeway. We don't want 'em to get trigger-happy. Don't worry—they'll be able to see it on the laptop. Good Luck!"

At 6:30 that evening, a limousine pulled up to house. Dora knew it was for her although she hadn't been told she would be picked up. Without looking at her 'sisters' again, Dora picked up the laptop and left the house. They all watched as she climbed into the limo. None of them were very happy, but they at least could get the faces of the goons who picked her up. There were two men in the back. One took the laptop, looked it over and gave it back to her. Except to tell her that if she tried anything, they would kill her—there was very little conversation. It was a twenty-five minute ride to the airport. Once they were satisfied that she wasn't going to give them any trouble, the guys sat back and relaxed.

All the 'sisters' were sitting around the monitors watching—the faces of the men indelible in their minds. Not one of them would forget what they looked like. And the girls weren't too worried about Dora. She could easily take care of these two men if need be. The driver was not a factor as long as he was behind the wheel.

A small jet was waiting for them at the airport. Standing beside the jet were two more men. She was sure these guys were some of the specials they had been warned about. They had a very professional look about them. They even moved differently. One of them stopped Dora before she could climb aboard. He removed the laptop from her hands and passed it to the other guard to examine. He was smiling at her because he was going to be the one to search her. He began at the top of her head. Ran his hands all through her hair and work his way down her body, enjoying every moment of his probing. He didn't miss an inch. Dora withstood his search as stoically as she could. The goof ball was so interested in feeling her up, that he thought the collar devices were just apart of the uniform. He missed the cameras and the knives. The team was watching all of this on the monitors and breaking up. "What a turkey," said Liz. "He's a pro and let his judgment be clouded by his testosterone. What a jerk!"

When the jerk finished having his fun, he told her to get aboard. As Dora passed him to climb into the plane, he asked her "was it as good for you as it was for me?" Dora responded, "I hope I'll get the chance to show you how much."

When she entered the plane, the first person she saw was Todd, Sr. With him, were a few of the most powerful men in the country, if not the world. Todd, Sr. was very cordial in his welcome to Dora. He offered her a cocktail, which Dora refused. They settled with seat belts secured and the plane took off.

When they had reached their cruising altitude, Todd, Sr. informed Dora that they would be landing at a small Mexican airport. From there they would take a chopper. "There's not much of a road where we're going and the chopper makes it easier to get there."

"By the way, have you arranged for the transfer of the money?

Dora told him she had. "Once I've seen my family, I'll release the money."

"You know, I'm still unable to figure out how you did it. There were news broadcasts stating the money had been donated to charities, and I know you don't have that much money. So tell me, my dear, how did you do it?"

Dora smiled, "Wel-ll the plan never was to give it all away. It was an opportunity to take it away from you. I fixed it so that it would all be returned to an off—shore account in thirty days. What the charities used was the accrued interest, which you know is considerable on that amount of money. They were quite happy, I assure you."

Todd, Sr. laughed out loud. Shaking his head in disbelief, he asked, "How would you like to work for me? I am impressed. I like the way your thought processes work. The announcement shook up the banking world and it looked good in the news. Imagine someone being that benevolent. But actually, you're as big a crook as the rest of us. Now, I would like to see some proof of this transaction."

Dora asked for her laptop. The pro passed it over. "Do you have access to the Internet on the plane? If so, I can show you that it is as I say. There is one small problem. The transfer won't take place for five days. That is because the banks won't pay the interest until a full thirty days has passed. All I have to do is put in my code and it will transfer the money back to your account."

"Yes my dear, we can access the Internet from the plane, but we have started our descent. You can show me later and if I find everything is not as you say, you my dear are a dead woman. And so will your family and your friends. In fact, I have made it a standing order to kill any one of your family still living anywhere in the world, even after I'm dead and buried. Do you understand?"

Dora understood all right. This is a crazy man. The man was stark raving mad. And worse, he meant every word he said. She just hoped Regina and the bank that was working with them to pull this off, had it altogether. If not…. There would be no second chance. She knew she could kill a few, but it wouldn't save her mother and brother. This whole operation had to go like clock work, or they would all be in big trouble. Todd, Sr. and his cohorts were all lunatics.

The plane was on the ground and rolling to a stop at the far end of the runway. There were a few Mexican soldiers sitting in jeeps, but they were only there to ensure that no one bothered Todd, Sr. and his people. He stopped to pass a few words with the soldiers and they boarded the chopper.

Dora was feeling a bit emotional. This was the last leg of the trip and she would soon see her family. She was praying that all that she had been taught would come together this day. She would have to call on every bit of her training to pull this off with everyone still breathing.

This time tomorrow, the rest of team would be en route to El Toro Air Base. They wouldn't be airborne for about six hours, but they wanted time to check out the equipment brought aboard and stowed for them personally before take off.

There were a lot of people moving about at both bases, making ready to get underway. This would be a show of power, unlike anything ever seen before in Mexican waters. The movement should shield everyone connected to the operation. Regina was thinking, 'timing is everything'. The goal was to get everybody out without firing a shot. But—if they had to fight to get them out, so be it.

Christine, on the other hand, was only thinking of revenge. The notes she had received told her to hold on, help was on the way. She was doing so, barely. The toad she had learned to hate most in the world was again abusing and raping her. He had made both girls do things, which they had only read about and each time, he laughed harder than he did the last. Christine was thinking that he would not be laughing when she got through with him. He would be begging for mercy. She would have the last laugh. But right now, all she could do was wait. She prayed, "Oh God! How much longer do I have to endure this pig?"

The pig pulled his pants up, saying, "I got to go, but I'll be back." He left to go out to the landing pad. There were a number of men waiting for the chopper to land. They were finally going to see the person who had caused them so much trouble. Todd, Sr. told Dora that he really hadn't believed it was she until she accepted his invitation.

"You had my family, did you think I wouldn't come?"

"No. I knew you would, but the way you work, you're amazing. I hope we can be friends when this is over," and he reached over and patted her on the hand.

They exited the chopper as the engine slowed. Laurence was the first to come toward them. He walked toward them with a big smile on his face. "What did I tell you? I knew it was she. And that bitch of a watchdog you keep around, knew it, too." He then looked at Dora. "We have someone we want you to meet. Actually, she's an old friend of yours and she seems to think it couldn't possibly be you who was destroying our lives."

This was not news. Dora all ready knew about it. What she didn't know was why she'd said it. Once inside, Dora asked to see her mother and brother. Todd, Sr. said, "Yes, but first things first. I want to see the money." At the word 'money' Carrie drifted into the room. Dora turned at the sound of footsteps and came face to face with her. Carrie was the first to speak.

"Well, Lieutenant, I see you've managed to convince these morons that it was you who has taken them for this grand ride." With that she began to laugh, almost hysterical. Dora was starting to get angry. But still she held her peace. For the life of her, she couldn't understand why Carrie was doing what she was doing. She actually seemed to be protecting her. Not let on that it was not only possible, but also probable, that Dora had torn this outfit apart. She decided to keep an open mind until she found out what was going on. She decided to be very respectful. "Colonel, what are you doing here? I know these people can't be friends of yours."

"Well they are and they aren't," answered Carrie. "You might say we are business associates. But enough talk about me. What can you tell us about the missing money? Is it possible that I am wrong and it really was you that caused us all this grief?"

Laurence walked over to Dora. "What kind of proof do you have that our money is intact and we will get it back." Dora told him to hook up her laptop and she would show him. Todd, Sr. explained to the others in the room that it was set for a wire transfer in five days. This means that she will be our guest until then. I would like to see for myself, though."

"Laurence would you please hook the lap top up to the Internet. If all goes well, we will let you see your family and friends."

Dora turned on the unit and did as she'd been instructed by Regina. Under her breath, she said, "Thank God!" Everything was there just as Regina said it would be. It was pure magic the way that woman could work. The men were satisfied. She shut down the computer.

"The men will take you to your family, but not your friends." Dora turned to him with fire in her eyes. Todd, Sr. shrugged his shoulders. "I've got to hold on to something, just in case."

Dora took a deep breath and followed the guys through the house to the outside. They led her to a small building located inside the compound with two men on guard duty. One of the men opened the door and let her inside. She saw her mother laying on the bed looking at nothing. She seemed to have removed herself from this place in order to deal with it. Charles ran to his sister, threw his arms around her and hugged her so tight she could barely breathe.

"I knew you would come, I knew you would come."

Dora gave him another squeeze and walked over to the bed where her mother lay. She sat down on the side of the bed and placed her hand on her mother's cheek. "Mom." Hope looked at her for a long time before it finally registered that it was her daughter talking to her. Hope started to cry. She raised her arms and they embraced for a long time.

Dora was rubbing her back and her head, telling her it would soon be over. To be strong and she would soon be home tending her flowers. She leaned slightly away from her mother so they could look into each other's eyes. Holding the beautiful face of her mother in her hands, Dora said, "I promise." Hope knew this was the truth. Somehow, her daughter was going to get her away from this nightmare. Charlie came over and stood close to his mother and sister with a look of relief on his face. He knew that whatever it takes, his sister would try her damnedest to save them. The man outside the door hollered, "Times up! Let's go."

Dora looked at her family. "Mom, Charlie, don't worry. Hang tough, I'll be back for you." Hope held on to her daughter's hand, not wanting to let go. The guard opened the door, "Get a move on."

Dora turned to Charlie, "I'll be okay. Make sure she eats." Charlie shook his head, "Okay."

Back at the house Regina was watching all that was taking place via the cameras that Dora was wearing. She was very upset at the sight of Hope in those surroundings. This woman had never done anything to anyone. To see her suffer at the hands of those pigs out there really pissed her off. They were going to pay. They could not and would not get away with what they had done to the team and to Dora's family. All the grief they had caused was going to cost them plenty.

Everything was set, gear checked and rechecked. Only thing they could do now was wait. The 'sisters' weren't going to get much sleep tonight. Tomorrow night the team would sleep on the plane because it would be an early flight. Regina was thinking about the many times the team had gone off on a mission. Every time is like the first time. Never knowing how many would return, but doing it anyway. Theirs was an elite team who put it all on the line each and every time. This time, they would be breaking the laws of two governments, their own and Mexico's. However, this is probably the most important mission on which they had ever embarked. This mission was for love. Not for flag, nor for prestige. This mission was to put some things right, obliterate the wrong, and most importantly to bring home their love ones.

A lot of folks worked through the night, while others tried to get a little sleep. Though the next few days would be a game for most of the participants, for the 'sisters' it would be no game. It was for real—for keeps.

Chapter Eleven

The guards on duty were using flashlights and dogs to patrol the perimeter of the compound.

Dora was placed in a room in the main house. There were bars on the window and a guard at the door. She was brought a tray at dinnertime, but she was in no mood for food. She only hoped that her mother would have managed to eat a little of the food. Knowing Charlie, he would bully her until she gave in and least tried a few forks full. Dora was very worried about her mother. She couldn't ever remember her looking so forlorn, even when she lost husband and her son. Her mom had always seemed to find the fighting spirit to carry on. It all seemed to have hit her at once. Hope had lost her will to live. Dora knew she would have to get her mother away from here—and soon.

The door to Dora's room opened and who should waltz in but Todd, Jr. with a couple of his pals. He was quite upset with his father for not killing her right away. Todd, Jr. felt that Dora had to be taught a lesson in order for the organization to regain its respect.

"You know, I'm going to laugh while watching you slowly die for all the trouble you've caused us. I just want to know one thing," queried Todd, Jr. "How would you like to die? You do understand that someone has to pay and—you're it."

Dora looked at Todd, Jr. for a full minute before answering. "And you think that I'm the responsible for your troubles?"

"Of course, who else?"

"I don't see how you and your mighty father could think I am capable of doing all that you have accused me of doing." Dora saw something in Todd, Jr.'s eyes. The young man might not be too sure of himself, after all.

He had heard those words before and decided not to pay any attention to them. "Look woman, don't play games with me. How could you have gotten the money back if you didn't take it in the first place?"

Dora replied, "I didn't say I didn't know who did take it, I just asked, what made you people think that it was me?"

Todd grinned. "At this point it really doesn't matter, you're the one that's going to pay."

One of the guys with Todd, Jr. was the same one who searched her before she boarded the plane. He was looking at her like she was cream cheese and he was hungry. Every chance she could she looked him over from his curly head to his shiny shoes. By the time Todd, Jr. had finished talking, she was sure he would return. She was staking her life on the man's libido. Dora would have to wait and see, but she would have to find a way out of here and soon. Dora also needed to know where her 'sisters' were being held and if they were still alive. The window was open and the smell of the frangipani whispered in on a breeze. The breeze was slight but could work in the team's favor, if it was blowing in the right direction. It could keep the dogs from picking up the scent of the Recon team until they were ready to let the world know they were there.

Dora tried to count the number of guards she saw making sure the camera was picking up what she was seeing. The Recon team was also counting noses. The guys they were looking at were mercenaries. Big trouble. The guards inside the compound seem to be hired natives with no real soldier abilities. They would be in the way, but Dora didn't think they could be counted on in a knock down, drag out fight. Some would try, many would die. Dora really didn't care. All she was interested in was freeing her family and her 'sisters'. God help anyone who got in the way.

Dora heard low voices at the door. It opened and sure enough the 'pretty boy' had returned. He told the guard to take a break. "I'll be here for awhile." He gave the guard a wink.

He came in smiling. Dora smiled back.

"I knew you liked what you saw." Dora sat on the bed a smile still on her face. Pretty Boy continued to advance. He told Dora, "I can help you to stay alive. But first, you have to put out this fire you've started."

Dora spoke very softly. "There's an old saying about playing with fire, you could get burned."

He smirked, "I'll chance it."

"Come on then, big boy."

Just as he reached for her, his insides exploded from the kick she gave him in the abdomen. As he started to fall, she grabbed him and lowered him to the floor. At first she thought he had just passed out, but when she took his pulse, he was dead. The kick was hard enough to rupture his spleen. He'd bled to death internally, in minutes.

"Great—now I've got a dead man on my hands." Dora sank back on her haunches to think.

All this action was being seen on the monitors the teams were carrying. One of men said, "That woman is bad to the bone. I don't ever want to get on her wrong side."

Dora had heard her would-be lover tell the guard to take a break, but who knew how long he would be gone. She went to the door to listen. Nothing. "Now what?" Dora wanted to open the door just crack to see if anyone was outside. She went back to search the body for keys. She found a small caliber pistol and a ring of keys. She tried each one of them on the ring. None of them fit the lock on the door.

Now what was she going to do? She had to get the body out of this room or no one would ever believe she didn't do all the damage for which she had been accused. She sat on the bed, her mind in turmoil when she heard a noise at the window. Just as she turned to see what was going on, a rock popped in through the opening wrapped in paper.

She walked over to pick it up, looking out to see who had been there. It was too dark to see anyone moving about. She took the rock over to the light removing the paper at the same time. The note read, "There is a closet outside your door, put the body in there. The guard went to eat. Move fast." Dora read it again, thinking this must be a trick. Who was this person watching her back? It was just like those men in the alley, she didn't kill them and she didn't know who did.

She was trying to identify the writing when she heard someone at the door. She held her breath as doorknob turned and the door was pushed open a crack. She jumped to her feet ready to defend herself but no one came in. Finally, she went to the door to have a look. She opened the door very slowly, waited a couple of minutes and opened it still further. Dora saw the closet right away. She opened it found it large enough to hide the body. She ran to the door to check the compound, not seeing anyone around, rushed back into the room to drag out the body. He was pretty heavy, but she was strong, so it wasn't hard to do. Dora shoved the guy in as far as he would go and covered him with some old rags, blankets and paper that had been thrown in there. She shut the door and went back into her room. She also fixed the door so that she could get out when she was ready. Using one of the small knives, she removed the screws from the tumbler. Using a piece of tape from her boot, secured the tumbler back in place. Now it would appear to be locked and she could open it at will.

She lay down on the bed to think. "What is going on?" she asked herself for the umpteenth time. Dora wanted to know why the writing on the note looked familiar? Where were Christine and Lydia? And her mother—she was really worried about Hope. That note. Dora had the feeling that someone very close to her had touched it. "Oh wow! Here we go with the witchcraft stuff again." The girls would be on her if they could hear her. She smiled, stuck the note in her pocket and went to sleep.

Christine and Lydia both received a note that night stating that Dora was there and it wouldn't be much longer before they would be free. Once again the unknown person was using a code that should have only been known to the 'sisters'. Christine was thinking that the team might have put someone on the inside. This person was to stay out of sight until the right time.

Lydia was thinking that it might be Carrie. That she was taking care of them even though it appeared she was working against them.

It was evident that whoever the unknown was, he or she couldn't prevent the inhumane acts that they had been suffering at the hands of their tormentors, but the girls felt good knowing that this person was close by and that Dora was here. Both girls figured they could hang until their guardian angel sprung them. At least they were being kept informed of what was going on. This alone was worth waiting for.

Now all they had to do was stay in one piece. Both girls slept much better that night.

Morning came and there was a hustle and bustle outside. There was the sound of a chopper overhead and people were milling about as if something big was going on.

Dora waking to the sound of the chopper, was thinking she had slept too long and the shit had hit the fan and she'd missed it. What day was it? Had they started the fireworks early? Dora leaped towards the window in one stride, she looked out trying to make heads or tails of what was going on. She didn't hear any gunfire, nor was anyone moving as if his or her lives were in danger. No, something else is going on, but what?

Dora went to the door and knocked for the guard. He opened it with his gun at the ready.

"Yes," he asked, "What can I do for you?" His English wasn't perfect, but better then most she had heard talking. She asked, "What is all the commotion about?"

"Oh, the chopper. That is the boss of the bosses. When you took the money, you did not know whom you were messing with. Now, I think you find out, 'cause the main man is here." The guard laughed loudly, he thought it was very funny.

Dora was beginning to wonder, "Have I missed something here? What in the world was he talking about."? The rest of the team heard what he said and they too, wondered what this fool was talking about. Regina was also giving a lot of thought to what the man had said. She wished she could communicate with Dora, but the set was only one way. They could hear and see whatever Dora wanted them to, but they couldn't talk to her. At least, not until they were a lot closer. If Dora tried receiving a transmission now, it might be picked up and maybe pinpoint it to her.

Regina was having a royal fit because she wanted Dora to show them what was happening outside. She needed to know who this boss of bosses was.

Dora went back to the window to see if she what she see, no such luck. People were moving about as if the President of the United States had arrived. She decided that her best strategy was to get 'Mohammed' to come to her. Dora went back and knocked on the door. Again the guard opened the door at the ready.

"What d'ya want?"

Dora said, "Would you please send for Todd, Jr. I would like to talk to him."

The guard said he would. An hour passed before Todd, Jr. showed up. He was still upset with her and felt she should have been killed upon her arrival.

Todd, Jr. entered the room with a surly look on his face. "Okay, I'm here. What is so important that you have to route me out this early in the morning? Are you ready to confess to your misdeeds, so we can kill you and end this business once and for all?"

Dora looked at him very sweetly and said, "No. I feel like this room is closing in on me. Is it possible for me to walk around a bit?"

Todd, Jr. said, "Yeah! Come on. We have someone who wants to meet you anyway. He is very upset with you and with what you have done to us."

Dora didn't respond. She thought—great. I'll get to meet this person face to face. It was much better this way; she wouldn't have to sneak around trying to find out all she needed to know.

Dora went with him. Todd, Jr. asked the guard had he seen Juan lately. The guard told him not since last night. "Maybe he went to town or something."

Todd, Jr. said, "Yeah! Maybe. Juan is always looking for a new woman. If he keeps on the way he's been going, one of these days a woman is going to be the death of him."

The guard cackled at that. "Yeah! He loves himself some women. See ya' later."

Dora was thinking, "How right you are. Juan, if that was the guy's name, would never chase another woman." Dora was concerned that he would start to smell before morning.

Although this place wasn't exactly setup to smell good. There were horses, cows, pigs, chickens and who knew what else. Also, there was the man-made human waste disposal unit, which they seemed to use to fertilize what they grew on the farm. These odors should mask the dead man's odor at least for one more day—she hoped. Todd, Jr. gave her a shove and pointed in the direction of the outer door. She went peacefully but she was going to take his head off before all of this was over. He gave her another shove as they entered the main building, not because she was lagging behind, but just because he could. Inside the main house, Todd, Jr. took her into the living room. Dora stopped in her tracks.

Sitting in a big red armchair was a man she knew well, but never expected to see again.

Todd, Sr. was about to introduce them, when he spoke up, "There's no need for an introduction. Miss Moore and I have met. At least, that was the name she was using the last time I saw her.

Dora had to laugh as she thought, "Man, is this ever the boss of bosses." She hoped her team was getting all of this. This man was a sheikh from one of the Arab nations, and yes, he was considered to be the drug lord of all drug lords. This man was untouchable by order of the American Government. There was so much money and power behind him, he could only die from natural causes. Anything else would cause problems for the free world. Now, here he stood and he was upset with her. Actually, that was being a little too polite. My man was pissed. Oh yeah! The team remembered him. They knew his methods of dealing with people who crossed him. He had them beheaded, like the old cliché, quick, fast, and in a hurry. And here, standing before him, is the woman who had destroyed his drugs and took his money. He was still smiling when Dora reached where he was sitting.

The sheikh took a deep breath and spoke. "Well, young lady what have you to say for yourself? Why have you involved yourself in an operation that's larger than life? As you Americans say, you have, indeed, grabbed the bull by the horns. So, my question to you is—do you turn him loose or do you hang on? I would say that up to now, you have been very smart. I hope you can continue to impress me while I decide what to do with you. Now, I am waiting for an answer to my first question."

Dora said, "Ask your friends, they started it."

The sheikh looked around the room and said, "Would anyone like to enlighten me as to what she is talking about." No one responded.

Dora spoke up saying, "First they killed my brother, and…" The Sheikh held up his hand stopping her in mid sentence.

"What is she talking about? Who is her brother and what does he have to do with us?" His eyes were on Todd, Sr. first, than they switched to Todd, Jr. Neither wanted to answer, but Todd, Sr. tried.

"Well, it seems that someone took it upon himself to take this kid out. He had been causing us problems, but to be truthful about it, I have no idea who killed him. I have asked everyone I know, and they all deny issuing the order."

Sheikh Rajiem heard all this and turned back to Dora. This time he raised his voice.

"Are you telling me that you have caused all this havoc over the death of one man? One meaningless human being. I have lost money, lives and sleep over the death of one man." By this time, the Sheikh was standing directly in front of Dora, almost toe to toe. Only a breath separated them. It was almost a kiss between enemies. His eyes were cold and empty. He was breathing hard.

"That meaningless human being was my brother. My brother," emphasized Dora. "He meant a lot to me and my family. More then your damned money."

"The only reason you're not dead right now is my money."

"I know that," said Dora. "But you hear me good, if I don't walk with my family and my friends, I have people on the other end who can—and will—pull that money back so fast, you'll wonder if you dreamed it all. And,—before *you* can do anything about it." The Sheikh told her not to push her luck. "I'll feed you to your mother for lunch and the rest of your family and friends to the sharks. I'll get my money, even if I have to make these idiots pay it. So you see, the only thing that would make me sad–would be killing one so beautiful, before—how do you say?—I've tasted of your fruits. You do remember what we started when you were my guest. What I should do is send you to my country. Then you could repay the family of my friend you almost ruined." He turned to the others, "You see gentlemen, though I have no proof, I feel this young woman is an agent for the CIA. I know that they have said that I'm the last person they want to bring down, and that they know nothing of this woman, but I believe she is a mole. I may not have to kill you, my dear, but I may have my men make you tell me a few things I would like to know."

"With my hands and feet tied, like your men did my friend, I suppose," said Dora. "They didn't have to leave her that way, but they did."

Over in the corner, she saw one of his people with a big grin on his face. He was one of them and Dora turned toward him so that the camera would pick him up. She was sure Jodi was coming unglued right about now. She remembered this clown and had made herself a promise that she would kill him the next time she saw him. If he stuck around, she would keep her promise. Both Jodie and Regina were foaming at the mouth. Jodie because she knew the man and Regina because he had killed the girl she had brought into the service. He was another walking dead man. One or the other of the girls would take care of that gentleman when they arrived.

Todd, Jr. announced that lunch was being served. Dora requested to see her mother to ensure she was eating. The Sheik told her she could and also have lunch with her and her brother.

"How could I keep such a beautiful family apart? The smile on his face was that of a well-fed cat. The game was more important than the kill. Dora then asked if she could see her friends.

"Humm! Let me think about that. You see—I give something, than you give something. We work together here and maybe everybody goes home happy."

Dora was thinking, "Pig, I'll bury you before this is over. But she smiled and thanked him.

She was taken to see her family. On the way out of the door, Dora stopped and said, "May I ask that you find out if my friends are all right."

"If I were you," the Sheik said, "I'd be more concerned for myself." Dora was able to stick the little knife with the camera into a leaf of the plant by the door. She wasn't sure about the video because of the angle, but the team would be able to hear what was said.

Hope was very glad to see her daughter. Indeed, she looked much better to Dora than she did yesterday.

"She ate good last night," Charlie told her. "Seeing you seemed to perk her up."

Hope was lying on the bed when Dora went into the room. She raised her arms and Dora went right into them. They hugged each other a long time. Hope whispered to Dora to be careful what she said. The lady who brought her food last night put a mike behind the lamp. "She didn't think I picked up on it, but I did."

Dora squeezed her mother's hand. She smiled at Hope. They understood each other perfectly. Dora was happy that her mother was acting as sharp as ever. Dora started talking and walking close to the lamp. She took a good look, determined it was just a mike and not a camera and made conversation.

"Mom, I don't know what we are going to do. They think I'm someone I'm not. I've gone lots of places for the government, but no way could I be responsible for all of the killing they're talking about. I have their money because it was given to me to get you out." While she was talking, she was writing down what she wanted to say. When she was done she handed it to her mother. The note said, "Don't worry, help is on the way. We'll get you out safely. When the shooting starts, I just want you and Charlie to get down and stay down." Hope looked at her and smiled shaking her head that she understood. Dora took the paper, but continued talking. Everything that she said made Dora sound like a desperate woman. Charlie was busting up inside, listening to his sister come all pathetic. Dora turned to him giving him one of those sisterly looks that said, "I'm going to break your neck if you don't stop." She was smiling at the same time. They all felt better now. The team saw the look of relief on Hope's face.

Dora destroyed the paper and they ate the lunch that had been brought to them. Back at the main house they were laughing at Dora. The men were thinking they had her just where they wanted her. Laurence was uneasy. He was sure that this woman could do exactly what she had been accused of doing and more.

Carrie pushed him a little by saying, "Laurence, do you still think this pathetic woman could be the beast you think she is?"

Laurence looked at Carrie before answering, "Yes, I still think I'm right. When we lost the money, the guys said it was women who did it. On top of that, the men I sent to her house, all seasoned veterans I might add, were all killed. Ostensibly, by her. Yes, I am a firm believer that she committed everyone of the deeds of which we have accused her."

"That's true, but we didn't see who killed those guys, so that doesn't rule out men."

If looks could kill, Carrie would have dropped to the floor, dead. And Laurence wanted to kill her bad. She really pissed him off and he was fed up with her supercilious attitude. She had been rubbing him the wrong way for years and he'd had it with her and her priggishness. If he said his shoes were black, she would say they were dark gray, just to annoy him. Yeah! As far as he was concerned, Carrie had outlived her usefulness. And no, he didn't trust her. Not one jot despite the number of years she had been working with them. Time would tell.

Carrie was thinking about Laurence, too. She was going to enjoy taking him down. He didn't know it, but his days were numbered. He would either be dead or end up with a cellmate named 'Bubba'. She hoped it would be the latter. Picturing him with a 'Bubba" gave Carrie a thrill. Who better deserved it then the Director of the FBI.

The short-wave radio traffic heralded the arrival of more of the Sheikh's men. They had come down the coast by boat. There were about thirty men. The Sheik hadn't wanted to draw attention to their arrival, so he hadn't let them fly in. Too many chopper flights would invite questions. Not from the Mexican government, but because of the joint exercises, the Americans might ask questions. It was better that they maintain a low profile, at least until he got his money back in the bank.

Dora took note of these men as she was leaving the barracks where her mother and brother were being kept. She also noted that these were fighting men. All nationalities—mercenaries whose only loyalty was to whoever paid the most money. Dora made sure all this was getting on camera. She had dealt with these mercenary types before, but she wanted all of the teams to know exactly what they would be up against. With the inclusion of these fighters the stakes just went up. The teams would be fighting for their lives against these guys. No quarter given. Chances were that all the other units would run when battle got to hot, but not these guys. They would have to be killed. Quickly.

Dora was returned to her room and once again, locked in or so they thought. Todd, Jr. was still looking for Juan. He told the men to tell Juan to come to the house as soon as he returned. He left a new guard on the door. All he did was smile as she walked by him into the room. Dora noticed right away that her bed had been made; her bag was not as she had left it and the laptop was in a different position. She assumed that a camera had been placed in the room during her absence. Acting nonchalant as she moved around the room, she soon spied the camera in the same spot as the one in her mother's room.

"Great, how the hell do I get out of here now without them seeing me?" One thing in her favor, the camera was totally directional. Unless there were others in the room, she could move around freely. She found another in the bathroom. She could cover this one by hanging her robe over it. Time was fleeing, the sun going down. She would have time to take a nap before dinner. Then she thought about taking a shower and blowing the minds of those watching. On the other hand, why make them happy. She went in to run the water and at the last moment threw her robe over the camera. The men who had been watching were very disappointed. She tested the water, thought it was very good considering the place. She made short work of the shower. Donned clean clothes, and entered her bedroom to find Todd, Jr. sitting on the bed.

"How was the water," he asked.

"Adequate, I guess. What do you want?"

"I just wanted to make sure you were comfortable." Noting that she had dressed instead of putting on her robe, he asked, "Are you going out or something?"

"No, I'm not, but I was not going to give your men a free peep show. Now, if you would remove the camera, I would appreciate it. If not, I'll leave the robe hanging there."

Smiling, Todd, Jr. got up and went into the bathroom and removed the camera. But first, made an obscene gesture with a finger at the people who sat watching. Dora waited for Todd, Jr. to leave her room. He turned when he got to the door and said, "You're pretty savvy for a lady who continues to play so dumb. We'll see who has the last laugh in three days. I hope everything is as you say it is or I will personally kill you myself."

"Can you do that without your father holding your hand?

Todd, Jr. looked at Dora with malice in his eyes and in his heart. He stormed out of room muttering, "you'll find out."

Dora giggled, "I really got his goat with that one." She went into the bathroom to make sure he'd removed the camera and that there weren't anymore. Satisfied she decided to take that much needed rest.

Dora woke to the sound of a key in the lock. It was the lady bringing her dinner. She asked if the senorita wanted anything else? Dora said, "Yes, a bomb, but I don't suppose you could help me with that." The lady smiled and leaving the tray, left the room. Dora looked at the food, but found she wasn't very hungry. She was getting jumpy, time was passing and she still didn't know where her 'sisters' were. She had to find a way to get to them tonight. She was thinking about this when once again, the door opened. Now this was last person she expected to see. It was Carrie. She got to her feet and waited to hear what this was about. Carrie walked over to her. They both had a very cold look on their faces.

Carrie stopped in front of Dora. "I know you hate me, but one day you'll understand."

Dora looked her in the eye without wavering, "What can I do for you Colonel?"

Carrie said, "Just listen. I want to know what is going on? You're acting like a defeated woman. Surely, this is not the girl I trained? You seem to have given up and I want to know why?"

Carrie was gesturing and pointing up. Dora couldn't understand at first and then she spied a camera she had missed. It was attached to one of the blades on the overhead fan. She smiled to herself, had they put that one in place one day before, she would have been in big trouble.

The Colonel had heard one of the men who were watching Dora say that she had found all but one of the cameras. It also had a mike. She thought she should let Dora know. The story she used to gain access to the room was that she was going to ask Dora what she knew about the operation. That was why she was here. Carrie was still talking.

"I would like to help you, but you need to tell me what's going on. Some of that money you took is mine and I want it back."

Dora said, "Don't worry, you'll get all of your blood money back. I hope you can sleep at night after what you have done. Carrie started laughing and walking around the room.

"With the kind of money I make, sleep is never an option. You know, I can get you out of here, and make you part of the operation."

Dora looked at Carrie, wondering what the hell is going on here. "All I want is to get my family and my friends out of here to a safe place. That kind of money is not in my game plan."

Carrie asked, "You sure you wouldn't like to wine and dine some of the men here. They are all talking about you and they've already had a few talks with the other two."

"Are they all right, can I see them?" Dora asked.

"Yes, they are all right. Maybe after we get our money back, you can see them. But think about this, you can join us, if you like. I'll leave you now. Send for me if you want to talk about it some more."

She was standing by the tray of food, she picked up the meat, "I guess you don't want to eat this? Not bad," as she tasted it. She dropped a piece of paper on the tray as she put the meat back on the plate.

"I want you to understand that killing you is not part of the plan." Dora watched as Carrie exited the room. She went over and set down on the bed to think over what just happened. One thing she knew, the food was all right so she decided to eat. She noticed the note and right away, she surmised that Carrie had been the one leaving the notes all along. She picked up the paper out of sight of the overhead camera and went into the bathroom to read it. It was a map of where the girls were being kept. Carrie was trying to help. First the mike, now the note. That was a good sign. She was feeling better about everything. She went back and finished her food. After doing so, she knocked for the guard and asked if she could walk around. He told her that he would find out. She made a mental note of the map Carrie had left her. The guard came back and said she could go out with an escort.

Another guard met her at the door and she stepped out into the compound. She took in as much as she could of where everything was located. She was trying to get herself orientated as to the location of the girls. When she was pretty sure she knew where to find them, she asked the guard to take her back to her room. Now, she would wait. Soon it would be time and there would be no turning back. Dora would have to bring all her training, will power and guts into play. Tonight she would have to move like a cat if she was to save her family and friends. She peered at her watch, it was 2300. Soon, she thought, soon.

Dora turned out the light and lay down, hoping that her watchers would soon believe she had actually gone to bed and relax their vigil. In a few hours she would make a break for it. She hoped she wouldn't have to kill the guard outside her door. She didn't want to. He wasn't one of the elite force, but unless she could find something to tie him up and keep him quiet—well, she'd play it by ear.

Back at the base, the Recon teams from Pendleton were boarding the choppers. Once loaded, they took off and headed south to Mexico. Their plan was to lower themselves from the choppers at the outer perimeter of the forest. From there, they would hump it to the strike zone through terrain that was not made for man to walk through. Then they would dig in and wait. The four miles they had to cover was less than what they covered during training exercises. Even in the dark, the treacherous hike would not be a problem. Members of the Recon team were volunteers for this particular mission. They knew the score. If by chance, any of them were killed, the official notification would state, "killed in action while on maneuvers." Which makes one wonder, just how many service folk had been killed while doing their job and it was reported as a training accident. The team settled down for the hour-long flight to the drop zone. Some of the guys were thinking how good it was going to feel to kick butt. Others said prayers that begged forgiveness in case they didn't make it back. They hoped that God would accept them into His Kingdom.

All the "I's" had been dotted, all the "T's" crossed. The 'sisters' were doing what Dora was doing—waiting. The flight plan was filed and the mission was on. Each of them had gone over and over their point of entry after hitting the deck. Each knew what they had to do to pull this off without a hitch. Preflight was started and they were headed toward zero hour.

"God, why can't we ever do things the easy way," was the thought that ran across Elizabeth's mind. Having to bailout out of the plane at twenty thousand feet was giving her the heebie jeebies. What if the oxygen didn't work? They would all be dead before they reached an altitude where they could breathe. And this place looked liked the land that God forgot. Not only was it hard to get into, but hard to get out of. A perfect hideaway for the scum they were dealing with.

Christine was hoping that tonight would be the last night that she would have to put up with the savagery of the men who had used her sexually and abusively since she arrived. To keep her strength up, Christine had been eating all of her meals and doing as much exercise as she could. She wanted to be in the best shape possible when the troops landed. She intended to keep the promise she made to herself and kill the dog who had misused and abused her the most. He said he was teaching her a lesson. Chris had every intention of showing him that she had learned her lesson well. Very well, indeed.

The "Dog" made his rounds about 0300. If the note she received was right, she would be the one doing the teaching tonight.

The men who had been watching Dora via the camera finally gave up and went to bed. They thought she was asleep and there was no need for further surveillance.

The Recon team was in place and had dug in. At present they were basically in bed. These guys could call the edge of a limb home for a night or two and think nothing of it. If it really came down to it, the people involved in this were the best of the best. The guys and dolls on this venture trained night and day for something like this. They were ready! Razor-sharp. The adrenaline was flowing. Everything was go. Now, all they had to do was hurry up and wait.

At 0245, Dora was ready to make her move. She was listening at the door, but couldn't hear anyone outside. Dora was hoping the guard wasn't a very disciplined person, because if he wasn't, she just might catch him asleep. She didn't want to kill him if it could be avoided. She removed the hypodermic that is standard equipment for all airborne in case they break a limb, from her boot and very stealthily made her way to the guard's table, removed his gun and jabbed him in the neck with the hypo. He jumped, but she placed her hand over his mouth and it was all over in seconds. She returned him to his sleeping position, patted him on the head and bid him pleasant dreams.

Dora removed the ring of keys at his side and made her way to the door. She didn't see anyone about. Most people were asleep at this hour. She wanted to kill the light but feared it would be noticed if she did. There were guards about, but most of them were in a relaxed mode. They felt very safe within the walls of the compound. None of them expected the compound to be invaded. Security was lax. They would suffer for their lackadaisical error before this night was over.

Dora made her way around the building and headed for the area on the map that showed where her friends were being held. She was concerned about the open ground she had to cross. This was not the time to run into somebody that might recognize her. She moved like a cat. Soon she was outside the building. There wasn't anyone outside but inside, she saw a guard standing under a dim light.

Hum! I need to get him to come to me, thought Dora. Just as she was about to knock on the door, she heard footsteps. Dora stepped back into the shadows. She recognized the man as one she had seen a couple of times. He had made rude gestures to her but nothing more. The word was out that no one was to touch her unless they were ready to die. Todd, Sr. didn't want anything to happen to her before they got their money back. The guy called to the guard inside. This was his relief.

Dora waited in the shadows until the relieved guard had left the area. Then a thought came to her. Suppose the guard on her door was to be relieved, too. Dora hustled back to her barrack where she was being kept and just in time, too. There was a man entering through the door rather stealthily as if he had no business there. He called to the guard, muttered something under his breath about being drunk on the job and opened the door to Dora's room. He had been watching her since her arrival and liked what he saw. She was too beautiful to let get away. He made his way to the bed, but found the bed empty when he placed his hands on the covers. He then thought she might be in the bathroom and opened that door. The lights went out. Dora didn't play with this guy. She knew he was one of the specials. She kicked him in the head and down he went. When she felt for a pulse, Dora knew his fighting days was over. She picked the guy up, put him in the bed and covered him up. This would look good if anyone else looked in on her, unless they pulled back the covers.

Chapter Tweleve

Christine could hear the man she hated most in the world coming down the long hall. She could not take another night of this man. She would rather die, but if she did, he would be the winner. No, she had to deal with him until her turn came.

Dora made her way out of the building for the second time that night and was able to return to the area undetected to free her 'sisters'. She was at the door and found it locked. She began trying the keys on the ring she had taken from the guard. Finally, the fourth key opened the door. Once inside she closed the door and locked it. She looked at the map to see which way she was to go. Dora headed down the hall very quietly. As she neared the cells, she heard a man talking. Dirty talk and the voice answering him sounded very much like Chris' voice. She was telling him that one-day soon she would kill him and that she would be smiling when she did. The 'dog' laughed at her.

"You've been saying that since you got here. You know I love it when you talk dirty to me. I just live for our nights together. I was thinking about visiting your friend tonight, but you are my favorite."

"I'm glad, because I'm the one who gets to kill you, not her. This I promise you."

He laughed again. "Why are you so hostile tonight? You act like you really want to hurt me."

He was making his way to her. "Come on, how's about a little kiss between friends."

It was a mistake to ignore what Christine was saying. He was right to wonder why she was talking so much. With his back to the door, he couldn't see what Christine saw. Dora was standing in the door and Christine knew she was free. Her nightmare over, Christine let him have it with every punch and kick she knew. The man was in shock. He couldn't believe that the woman he'd had his way with all this time had just knocked him down. Trying to get up, he turned and saw Dora standing in the door.

"You," he spat. "I knew you were going to be trouble, now I'll kill you both." Christine hit him with another roundhouse as he tried to get up. Once again he went down, out for count this time. The girls hugged each other. Dora said, "Come on, we've gotta' move."

"Okay, but I've some unfinished business with this clown."

"Put it on hold, we've got more important things on our plate."

Christine looked down at the man lying at her feet. "I'm cool, but I have to come back."

Dora smiled at her friend and handed her the hypodermic. "You better give him a shot of this. It will keep him quiet for a while. A very long while. Then you can come back later."

Christine gave him the shot and she and Dora went looking for the cell where Lydia was being kept.

Lydia dreaded the sound of the door being opened. She thought it was one of the men. The smile on her face upon seeing her two 'sisters' would have illuminated the entire compound. She ran to them and again there were hugs. Dora pushed the girls inside so she could let them in on what was going down. They made their way to the main door. Dora told them that they would need to find some equipment with which to work.

"There is a shed filled with arms on the south side of the compound," said Dora. "It shouldn't be any problem getting there unnoticed."

The girls found the shed and it took but a few seconds to get the lock off the door. They slipped inside, carefully closing the door behind them. Christine broke into a big smile when she saw what was inside. She grabbed a couple of Gluck 9s, a knife and all the clips of ammo she could carry. Then she found something she just had to have. There was a roll of wire in the corner of the shed. She picked up a pair of wire cutters and cut off about twelve feet and rolled it up in a potato sack. She broke off a broom handle and tied it to her sack. She was ready. The girls were trying to figure out what she was up to.

"I'll see you when the troops land," said Chris. She headed back towards the jail.

It was almost time for the team to take to the sky. Dora wanted to make her way to the drop zone. She still wondered what Christine was up to, but she had to get on with it. One thing she did know, Christine was about to make someone very unhappy.

The 'sisters' and the rest of team were preparing to parachute into the drop zone. They were on final, checking each other chutes and oxygen tanks. De-compression of the plane had begun. Soon the doors would be opened and they would be on their way. Every mask was in place when the lights went to red.

Dora was moving fast around the compound. Luckily, up to this point she had not run into anyone. She hoped her luck would hold. In the back of her mind, she wondered what Christine was up to. The woman was on a mission and there was no changing her mind. She would hate to be the guy that Chris was angry with—he was going to be one very sorry man.

Dora checked her watch. Saw that her 'sisters' would soon be hitting the deck. She hoped the dogs wouldn't pick up their movements. Although they seem to be acting like the men who handled them—not quite sure what they are suppose to do.

The tail of the C130 was open now and the team was standing waiting for the green light to jump. It flashed and they went out the door very quietly and started their free-fall. Dora was waiting for them on the ground.

Christine was standing over the man she most wanted to kill in this world. Dog was not happy; there was nothing he could do. His hands were tied over his head with a rope thrown over a pipe and secured to a hook on the wall. Pure hate and adrenaline helped Christine to subdue him in this fashion. He was still trying to figure out how it was done and who had helped her.

Christine was toying with him—walking back and forth as he had done the first time he'd came to her cell. She asked him the same questions he had asked her. He was beginning to realize that he might be in a bit of trouble. His mind was racing trying to figure out how to get her to release him and then he would make her pay.

Chris was smiling to herself. She was thinking, 'this fool doesn't think I will kill him but he would soon find out.

He spoke, "I know things that not many people know. Interested."

"Keep talking!"

"If you will forgive me, I'll let you in on a very well kept secret."

"It depends on how good it is."

" Oh, its good."

"Well! I'm listening," said Chris. "So talk."

"Okay! Unknown to a lot a people there is another kind of business being run here."

Chris laughed. "Yeah, we know. You have a big drug operation going on here."

He said, "You're right, but there is something else going here that you and your friends know nothing about." Chris raised an eyebrow and said, "Oh! What kind of business?"

"What if I told you that there was another place on the other side of this ranch? And that it houses many people."

He had Chris' attention now. "What do you mean? More men or what."

"Yes, there are more men but not in the way you think. Doctors, nurses and technicians who work for the corporation live there. They take care of the people who are sent there until they are needed."

Chris asked, "What do you mean until they are needed?"

Dog smiled, "Before I answer that, I need to know if you are going to kill me."

"You've got my attention, so why not finish."

Dog was persistent. "Do we have a deal? You won't kill me." Chris looked him dead in the eye and shook her head. "No, I won't kill you." He breathed a little easier and continued his story.

"Well, the fact is they are using the people brought here for body parts."

"Excuse me. You did say body parts?" asked Chris.

"That's right! You see, if someone needs a heart, we find a person who fits the bill, remove the heart and send it to the person who needs it. They also harvest the rest of the body parts for future use. This is big business.

Chris could only stare at the man. She wasn't sure she heard him right. "Tell me something, how did all this get started?"

Dog responded, "We pick up people all the time just for this purpose. We started off plucking people off the street to make our pornographic movies. This was very lucrative for a while, still is as a matter of fact. But one of our good friends needed a kidney and we happened to have a perfect a match for him. The rest as they say, is history. We make so much money now; we really don't worry about the porn business anymore. We just pick up people who no one will miss and wait. Now and then we get a special pick up because the perfect donor is known but not willing to supply the part. We go get him or her. This is even bigger money."

Chris continued to look at the guy. "Wow! When you think you've heard it all …"

Standing in the open doorway, Lydia, who had been sent by Dora to check on Chris, heard every word. All she could say was, "Amen, sister, Amen." Chris looked up to see Lydia.

She turned back to Dog and asked, "Have you finished?"

He said, "Yes, that's all."

"How many people are currently being held at this house?" asked Chris.

"I'm not sure how many are there."

"Umm! Tell me this. Just where exactly is this place located on this farm?"

"Look, are you going to live up to your bargain?"

"Oh! yes, I most certainly am," said Chris. "Now answer the question. Where is this place located?" Dog gave he the directions. Lydia, who was still leaning against the doorjamb, thought to herself, "I wanted to kill this guy badly before, but after hearing that story, I want to mutilate him."

Lydia looked at Chris and shook her head. "How could anyone use people for their own personal parts farm?"

They both looked at Dog, who was again looking very scared. With fear in his eyes he begged forgiveness. He told them how sorry he was for what he had done to both of them.

Lydia spied the wire and broom handle. "What are they for?"

"They're for my friend over there."

"Oh! What were you going to do with them?" Elizabeth told Lydia what she had planned for Dog.

Now Lydia was smiling. "Are you going to follow through with it?"

"I can't," said Christine, "I promised I would not kill him if he gave me the information about the place he was talking about." Upon hearing this, Dog began to breathe a little easier; it was going to be all right. He would be free and he was thinking what he was going to do to them. He was thinking, 'what fools they are. They don't know what it takes to win it in a war'. As it turned out, he was dead wrong. The 'sisters' knew exactly what it takes to win a war. As he would soon learn.

Lydia walked across the room to stand in front of Dog. He had a smirk on his face that she was soon to wipe off. Lydia picked up the roll of wire, looked at Dog and threw one end of the wire over the pipe. He began to sweat. He hollered to Christine. "You promised you wouldn't kill me. You promised."

"You're right, I did promise, but she didn't. I can't stop her from doing whatever she plans to do."

Lydia walked over and picked up the box that Christine had put in the corner of the room, which was a part of her original plan. She went over to the bed and took out her knife and cut the pants off Dog. Then she stuck the knife in his cheek so he would raise his buttocks high enough for her to slide the box under him. Lydia strung the wire around his private parts. The man was in tears by now. He began to plead with the girls. Asking them to understand how a man thinks. That he didn't mean any harm. He thought all women had a need to be raped even if they say different. He was pleading with Christine to remember her promise. Lydia cut a hole in the mattress and stuck the broom handle through and inserted it in his rectum. He had to hold his muscles tight to keep himself from being impaled on the handle and the wire from tightening around his genitals. He begged them to kill him instead. Yelling wouldn't help him. The rooms were sound-proofed, as he had found out from visiting the girls so much and subjecting them to all kinds of sexual abuse. They were getting their own back, with a vengeance. Again, he begged them to kill him. Lydia looked back at him as she and Dora went through the door and said, "Funny, I can remember asking you to do the same thing. You laughed—thought my asking was very funny." Having said that, Lydia closed the door.

Dog's body began to shake, he knew it would soon be over—impaled on a stick and castrated. He did remember. He also remembered that the lady had said she would kill him in a way no man deserved to die. She was keeping her word. The pain was excruciating. As he relaxed, the handle tore into his bowels and wire had cut off one testicle. He would lie there and bleed to death.

Leaving Dog to his fate, Lydia and Christine made their way to the pickup point to share their new found information with Dora.

Regina was the first member of the team to hit the ground, the others landed in quick succession. They very quickly and quietly got out of their chutes and buried them. Dora hugged them all in greeting. Lydia and Christine joined them and everybody was brought up to date including the new information about the body shop. Regina told them that the images received from the satellite showed unusual activity in the area of a very large building to the north of their present position.

There is also a very high usage of energy in the same building.

"You know, I found a building that houses a couple of large generators, said Dora. "At the time I didn't think much about it, but it's a lot more power then is needed at this site. Now I understand why. We had better find this place and check it out, pronto."

"I agree," said Regina, "but what should be done once we've located it? And, what should we do with what we find? If they have body parts, it would be a shame to waste them."

"Find the doctor who is responsible for the operations and have him transport everything out," said Dora. "We will arrange for a hospital to take charge of the body parts and turn him or her or over to the authorities."

"Suppose they have people we can't move, what will we do with them?" asked Jodie.

Dora told her, "We'll bring in the medics and let them complete the cleanup.

We can't be here when they come, so all we can do is send the message and beat it.

Regina asked, "What about Hope and Charlie? And have you found out anything about the Colonel?"

"Mom and Charlie are waiting for our help to get out of here. As for Carrie, I'm not sure. She seems to be trying to help."

"Yeah! We picked up on that but couldn't you tell what's going on with her?"

"Not really. I suggest we play it by ear where Carrie's concerned. I do know that she could have had me strung up long before now if she had wanted to do so. The standing order is—no action against Carrie unless she shows her hand and it's dirty. We have to give her the benefit of the doubt for the years she has taken care of us. Carrie has been like a mother to most of us. There just has to be another reason for her being here. Regina, you take half the unit and head for the clinic. The rest of you come with me. We are going after my mother and brother. It's almost jump off time and we need to get them out of harm's way. Let's go."

Dora knew that her family would be used as a go between, if the men lost her. Dora wanted to be in control by the time the other teams landed and the firefight began. Her goal, if possible, was not to lose a single man during this operation. The only people who should die were the dogs that had caused it all.

What Dora didn't know was they had already discovered that she was gone and had found the body in the closet. At that moment, Todd, Jr. and his men were on their way to get Hope and Charlie. Todd, Jr. also sent men to the jail to kill the ladies. The three that entered the first cell got sick to their stomachs when they saw the way their compadre had been left to die. He pleaded with the men to shoot him. They did so without hesitation. The way they saw it, it was a request any man would have made in that situation.

They left him and went to the second cell and also found it empty. The men rushed back to let their boss know what had happened. They also wanted to tell the other men not to let these women take them alive. None of them would want to die as their friend had. The thought of what they had seen, gave them pain such as they had never experienced before.

Todd, Jr. was madder than a hornet. If he had his way, he would kill the mother and brother right now. "I told my father that woman was trouble. She should have been dealt with a long time ago. Now she's running around killing my men. Spread out and find her, now. Her and her friends." Todd knew that he couldn't kill Dora because his father would kill him. The sheik didn't care one way or the other. As he had said, someone was going to pay him the money he had lost. Todd, Jr. felt the only way he was going to capture Dora was through her family. He would hide them in a place that had only one door in and one door out. He was going to kill this she-devil once and for all. He couldn't remember hating any woman, or man for that matter, as much as he hated her.

Dora arrived at the place her mother had been held only to find them gone. She found a note on the pillow that spelled out what Dora already knew—her life for her mother's. She was staring at the note when Lydia walked in the room. She took it from her and after reading it, said "Don't sweat it, we'll get them, back. Then I'm going to do to Todd, Jr. what I did to that other dog." Dora smiled but knew in her heart, it was not going to be easy. As long as they had her mother, she would have to play their game, even if it meant giving up her life. She was willing to die for her family. She was thinking what to do next when Christine came in saying, "We got to get a move on. There's a welcoming party headed this way." Dora looked at her and said, "Then let's go greet them. I want them to feel right at home."

There were eight men coming towards the door. Dora told the girls to keep as quiet as possible. She wanted at least one alive. The girls filed out of the door and waited until the men filed pass them. They were standing like trees and the guys didn't' even notice them. The rest was short work. When it was over, there were two still alive. They were dragged into the shack and Lydia began questioning them. She started out by saying, "I really hope you don't answer my questions. I would love to do to you what I did to your friend." The first man's eyes got very big. The second was finding it difficult to control his body. He was shaking so badly, he could barely stand. The men were having visions of the man impaled on the stick with his member and all accessories cut off. This was enough to make them give up their own mother. They started to sing in two different languages, just to make sure they were understood.

Dora told the other girls that she was going to have to take a look at exactly what Chris and Lydia did to that man to make these guys turn green. Chris said, "Hey! It wasn't me. I told the guy he was safe and that I wasn't going to kill him. How was I to know that sister Psycho was going to do such bad things to the man." She was looking so serious, that the rest of the team started to believe her. Then she broke out into a big burst of laughter that had all of them smiling.

Meanwhile, Lydia was getting the men to talk. The first one told them that Todd, Jr. was taking the mother and son to the clinic. He is going to have them harvested then feed their bodies to the dogs. You will never get into that place. Most of us have never been in there. It is well guarded with a lot of state of the art surveillance equipment around. Lydia said, "Hah! What you don't seem to understand is we are 'state of the art,' too. Man has yet to make a system we can't penetrate."

Dora, looking at the time, stated, "we got to move. It's almost "0" hour and I need to get to Mom and Charlie."

Lydia injected both men and tied them up. The girls made their way to the clinic. Passing the shed housing the generators, Dora said, "set a timer on the power system to knock it out at 0600." They continued toward the clinic. The balloon was about to go up.

Todd, Jr. was in an argument with the doctor at the clinic who was refusing to do as he was told. He could see no reason to kill this woman and her son at this man's request. There was no need at present for their body parts and he had plenty waiting on ice. He could tell that he may have no choice. Todd, Jr. was crazy with revenge and he didn't care whom he killed to get it.

The doctor called in his nurse and told her to prepare Hope first, when he finished with her, he would do the boy.

This sorry excuse for a doctor was thinking as he scrubbed for the operation that he never really liked this job, but the money was so good, how could he not get involved? How could any doctor turn down the kind of money he was making? After all, he was doing some good, he rationalized, even though he sometimes had to take a life, he was saving lives at the same time. Wasn't he living up to his Hippocratic oath? The doctor finally admitted to himself that the taking life from perfectly healthy people such as Hope and Charlie had been bothering him for sometime, but he didn't know how to walk away from the money. He again rationalized that those two were going to die anyway and probably he with them. He best go get it done. The lady was about ready.

Regina notified Dora that her mother and brother were inside the clinic and in big trouble. That she and Liz were working on the system to get in undetected. The Recon and Seal teams were also on the move. They wanted to be inside the compound when the power went out. They had been monitoring everything so knew what was happening. Everyone in the compound was now on alert, especially at the clinic, though they still had no idea of the magnitude of what was about to happen. Dora was on the hook calling the Seal team.

"Beach Whale. Beach Whale this is Mother Superior calling, over."

"We hear you Mother Superior. We're on the move. We understand the game has changed a little. Over.

Dora knew she could count on them. She gave them the new coordinates, but before she could sign off, the Lieutenant in charge of the team informed her that they had noticed some unusual activity in the same area. They had noticed some boats leaving from a cove in the same area last night. He had a feeling that there was an underground entrance. A rough head count, he would say there were upwards of fifty men inside. Dora was happy to get this information. It would prevent them from walking into a trap.

"OK, Beach Whale, thanks for the info. Keep coming. Over."

"We're on it. Follow up on what you have and we'll see you on the dark side. Over and out."

Dora contacted the "Painted Angels" requesting a meet at the clinic, giving the new coordinates. Their response was the same, 'on the move'. She than contacted the Recon team and told them to follow the original plan. There were plenty of men in the compound that had to be dealt with.

Dora was thinking that when she got her hands on Todd, Jr., she would keep her promise to take his head off. He could not continue to walk the earth. It wasn't big enough for both of them. The more she thought about it, the more she was convinced that Todd, Jr. was responsible for her brother's death. They would all pay this day. She still hoped that Carrie wouldn't get caught in the middle of this mess. She seemed to have her own agenda, but Dora was thankful that Carrie had brought the information about her 'sisters'. Carrie had also alerted her about the hidden camera and she tried to steer Todd, Sr. and company away from her. Dora wouldn't forget that. Yes, Carrie would be given the opportunity to explain. As for the others, they had to go. Although, she rather enjoyed the picture of Laurence Parker in jail—the director of the FBI. Many inmates would be happy to have him as a cellmate. Yeah! He should live to enjoy what was in store for him.

All this and more was going through her head as the dawn begin breaking just over the horizon. Soon, very soon, the operation would begin and they would all be very busy. Dora had her team to speed it up. They had to be inside the clinic before all hell broke loose. What she didn't know was that her mother had been sedated and was being taken into the operating room located in the bowels of the structure.

Todd, Jr. had given instructions to the men guarding the clinic to kill Dora on sight. He wasn't going to take any chance with her. He would find a way to repay the money if he had to, but he had a feeling, that given the opportunity, Dora would live up to the promises she made. He, for one, did not want to be on the receiving end.

Regina figured out a way to get into the clinic. She noted that a truck went through the gate, the driver using a card to gain entrance. Regina gestured to Elizabeth.

Liz understood what mother hen was thinking and went to work. Her first chore was to put a loop on the camera at the gate then she went to work on the lock.

Todd, Jr. was as nervous as could be. He had his men checking in every ten minutes. He was also pushing the doctor to move faster. The doctor told him he wasn't going to rush just to make him happy. If he didn't do this right, he may well cut her throat and be done with it. Todd, Jr. understood what he meant and went away to check on his men.

Todd, Sr. was getting concerned. He wondered where his son was and what was he up to. After all, he was the only family he had and he didn't want anything to happen to him. Carrie thought it ironic that Todd, Sr. could be worried about his offspring. The old saying about 'a fig didn't fall far from the tree' was true. Todd, Jr. was just like his father, which was probably the reason that they never agreed about anything. The fact that the girls had gotten away gave them all the creeps. She knew something was going down, she only hoped that it would be in time to save Dora's mother and brother.

"Since you're so concerned about Todd, Jr., would you like for me to find him and see what he's doing?" asked Carrie.

"I would appreciate it, yes," said Todd, Sr.

Carrie left Todd, Sr., Laurence and the Sheik to go find Dora. It was time to bring Dora into the picture. She hopped in her jeep and was out the gate in a flash.

She had a big smile on her face. Her dreams were finally coming true. She was about to bring down the men she hated most in the world. The wait was almost over. After years of acting out a part she hated, justice was at hand. She had spent years putting together the evidence that would put them in jail in any part of the world. The only good thing to come out of it was the money she had made. She used the money to care for the families that had been torn apart and violated over the years because of the wars. She had set up a fund through a bank so that each month the families would receive a check. It was explained to the families that it was the government's way of saying thanks. There was also a stipulation that they could not report the money nor discuss it with anyone. If the silence was broken, the family would be cut off and never receive another cent. To this date, no one had broken the silence. The bank was glad to have the account. They covered her tracks well.

Carrie was feeling so good she failed to take note of what was going on around her. She did not notice that there was a man under the tarp in the back of the jeep. He had been sent by Laurence to take her out at the first opportunity. He was hoping she would come out to her car by herself. Laurence was back at the house waiting for word of a 'done deed.' He'd had enough of this woman and it was time for her to go. No one would be able to blame him because he was there in the house with the bosses. They all knew he couldn't stand her, but they would still have to back him up. He made sure he never left their sight. He only wished that he had a tape of her last breath on earth, so he could listen to it over and over again.

The sounds of gunfire and explosions cut threw the quiet. The games had started. The Airborne landed without incident and joined with their 'sisters' in converging on the clinic. Dora, Regina and Jodie had gone ahead. Dora had to get to her mother before the compound woke up to what was happening. Todd, Jr. was still checking with his men every ten minutes. He needed to get a hold of himself. His nerves were shot. His face was bathed in sweat. The men could see he was falling apart.

The doctor was ready to perform the first operation. He asked Todd, Jr. again if he wanted to through with these unnecessary operations. Todd, Jr. screamed at him. "I told you I want both of them cold before noon. That's the end of it. Do it, now! Understand." Todd, Jr. left and went topside to check on his men again. The doctor called the operating room to see if all was ready. He informed the nurse that he would be right in to begin the first operation.

Dora and her 'sisters' had worked their way through the top half of the buildin undetected. Dora signaled to Jodie that she was going to have a look see in the rooms down the hall and for the others to stand fast. She checked each room. In one, two men were making a sandwich. She made her way back and signaled there were two people in what looked like a kitchen. She would take care of them. She walked back up the hall and right on in as if she knew them.

"What's happening guys?" Both men looked up surprised and puzzled by her appearance. As the other girls filed into the room, the guys started to react. Jodie put a foot in one man's face splattering his nose and mouth all over his face. His compadre reached for his gun and Regina, standing in the doorway, shot him between the eyes. All you could hear was the 'thunk' of the bullet as it shattered his head, because of the silencer that adorned her gun. The girls put the men in a room behind the kitchen and continued their search. Dora was moving a little faster now, time was on the side of the devil. If she didn't hurry, her mother could soon be dead. Regina suggested they split up in order to cover more territory. This turned out to be a very good idea and a saving grace for Hope.

The nurse in the scrub room looked up to find Jodie standing beside her. She opened her mouth and Jodie stuck her pistol in it.

"Keep quiet and only answer the questions I ask. Do you understand?" The nurse bobbed her head.

"Where are the mother and son?"

" The boy is in the next room and mother has been taken to the O.R."

"Where is the O.R.?" The nurse indicated the direction. Then Jodi asked, "Why are they here?" She didn't like the answer. Jodie took a deep breath and punched the lady's lights out. She pulled the nurse into another room and removed her uniform, hat, gown and mask and donned them. She let Dora know where she was located and what was about to happen. Dora was a floor above. She started running. The doctor was in the O. R. ready to start the operation wondering where his nurse was? He went into the scrub room and spoke to her, but she didn't respond. He spoke to her again and as he came closer he realized that these were brown eyes looking at him not blue. He reached for her and she unleashed a couple of good rights to his head. The doctor was no fighter. He fell back. Jodie pulled off her mask. She was about to ask him a question when Todd, Jr. entered the room. He went for his gun and Jodie dived through another door just as he fired two shots.

She ran down the hall and ducked into another room. Dora and Regina heard the shots and they knew Jodie was in trouble. They talked to her as they raced to help her. She told them she was all right, but Todd, Jr., had stopped chasing her.

"Dora, he's probably gone back after your mother."

"Okay! You get to Charlie and stay with him. We'll handle Junior."

The 'sisters' heard men running in every direction and shooting as they went. The Seal team had gained entrance and had taken on the forty or so men they found in the clinic. Todd, Jr. heard all the firepower, too. He decided it was time for him to get out. He told his men to terminate the women and meet him topside. Todd headed for the front door. Carrie was pulling up into the courtyard as he came out. He stuck his gun in her face and told her to get out. With a gun pointed at her, Carrie did as she was bid. Then the man hiding in the back of the jeep threw off the tarp and got out.

Todd, Jr. asked, "Why is she still alive?"

"I was waiting for the right time," he responded.

"Oh! Well the time is now." Saying that, Todd, Jr. swung himself into the jeep and took off across the compound.

Carrie's would-be killer was all smiles. Unfortunately, he was also a fool. Instead, of just shooting Carrie and getting it over with. He decided to play macho man. Waving his gun around. Waiting for her to beg him not to kill her which only proved he knew nothing about the leader of the 101st Airborne women. Carrie noticed his red eyes and realized he had been drinking. She decided to play on his machismo.

"Are you really going to stay here to kill me while everyone else is getting away? I mean, would you like for me to turn around so that you can shoot me in the back. Or maybe you would like to use that big knife on me that you have sticking in your belt. Yeah! That might even be better than shooting me. By using your knife, you would be able to feel the flesh give away. Even better, you have a knife and I have a knife. Let's make it a fair fight. Put your gun away and let's see if you got the guts to fight me with a knife." She was goading him, and he fell for it. He pulled his knife from his belt and kissed it. Then he made the most inane statement she'd heard in awhile. He said, "You're right, a man should always treat a lady like a lady and put something in her." He started circling around her, tossing the knife back and forth, from one hand to the other. Carrie was thinking to herself, "what a fool. Why would anyone take a chance and engage in hand-to-hand combat, especially in a life and death situation when he has the upper hand. This man was about to die and he didn't have a clue. His first mistake was drinking too much, and his second was not shooting Carrie when he had the chance. What he didn't know was that this woman wrote the book on hand-to-hand combat and her use of a knife was that of a surgeon. He took a swing at her and she at him. It continued that way for a few minutes and then he got a cut on the arm. This kind of woke him up to the fact that he might be in a little over his head, but it was way too late. On her next pass, Carrie buried the ten-inch blade in his gut and twisted it to make her point.

"What a disappointment you are lover," quipped Carrie, "I thought you were going to give it to me the way I like it."

The man looked at Carrie in amazement. He was a dead man and he knew it. She held him close as she continued to twist the knife. He closed his eyes and she let him fall to the ground. She was making her way to the clinic when she noticed three more of Todd, Jr.'s men advancing on her. They had seen what she had done to their compadre and figured to even the score. She was about to go to war with these gents when she head a familiar voice behind her ask, "Would you like some help, Colonel?" It was the voice of Captain Anthony.

"Come to pay your respects, have you Captain?"

"Let's just say I'm following orders. They wish me to prove who I am. Well, I've come to do so. I cannot stand people who threaten me. I am going to teach them that I should be the one to receive the respect. You go on in. I won't be long."

Carrie entered the building in search of Dora and the rest of the team.

The men moved on Captain Anthony. It was three of them and only one of him. Capt. Anthony grinned as they came closer. Very softly, he said, "It's party time, gents." The three never knew what hit them. This was Sensei at his best. The three lay broken and maimed at his feet. Two more were heading for him, but the Airborne coming in from another direction was all over them. It was over—fast.

The Seal team was driving the remainder of the men upstairs where the Airborne and Capt. Anthony were a like a brick wall waiting for them. Dora and Regina were still fighting their way to the O.R. The last man they encountered ran into the room and pointed his weapon at Hope's head. He told Dora to back off and he'd let her live.

"If you know what's good for you, you will do it anyway."

Pressing the gun to Hope's temple, he told Dora and Regina to drop their weapons. This was against everything Dora believed in and was trained to do. She was going to make a fight of it. Regina knew there was no way Dora would do as he'd asked, so she reached out and pushed the weapon down.

"Let it go Sis, don't get your mother killed."

The man said, "You had better listen to her. She seems to be the smart one in the group." Dora let the weapon drop. "Okay, let my mother alone. I will see that no harm comes to you."

The man started to laugh. "How stupid do you think I am? I will kill you and your friend then your mother." There was movement at the door on the other side of the room and they looked in the direction of the man coming through the door.

"Man, am I glad to see you. Help me tie these two up; we may need them to get out. We'll just kill the mother. She'll only slow us down. The man advanced into the room. When he reached the table where Hope was, he grabbed the man's gun hand and shot the man in the head. Dora and Regina didn't know whether to reach for their weapons or stand still. They waited to see what this new man was going to do. The guy turned towards them but they still couldn't' see his face properly because of the hood which hid his features. Then he dropped the hood. Dora couldn't believe her eyes. Standing before her in all his handsome glory was her brother Mark. She ran to him and threw arms around him. "I knew you weren't dead. Every instinct I have was telling me that, but I just couldn't accept my vibes." She was asking questions and hugging and kissing him all the same time.

Mark was holding on to her, too. He looked over at Regina and said, "I'm her brother." Regina was dumbfounded and just shook her head in response. Things seemed to have quieted down a bit. All of them turned to the door with guns at the ready when they heard steps in the hall. It was the Colonel with the doctor in tow. She had a gun to his head and he was as pale as a corpse. Mark lowered his gun, but Dora and Regina did not. They still weren't sure what part the Colonel was playing and why? Mark saw the look in their eyes and smiled. Looking at Carrie, he said, "I hoped you would grab this piece of trash on his way out. Then he turned to Dora and Regina and said, "Put your guns away. She's with me." They didn't understand, but they would accept Mark's word.

The Colonel shoved the doctor forward towards the table. She looked at Hope, then back to doctor, "Give her something to pull her out of that deep sleep. Oh, and if she dies, you won't, but you'll wish you could." And she gave him another shove.

Next person to come through the door was Captain Anthony. Once again Dora's mouth was hanging open. Mark grinned, told her she was going to catch flies.

"Captain, what are you doing here?" The Captain held up his hand. "It's too long a story. Right now, we need to get to the main house."

The shot the doctor gave Hope brought her to consciousness. She wasn't sure what world she was in, this one or the next, but she liked the company.

The Seal corpsman came in and took charge of Hope. He told Dora not worry. He'd see that she got back to a hospital in California. Hope was looking at Mark, "I thought you said you were going to take care of me?" She smiled at all of them and Dora and Regina were completely dumbfounded, yet again. Two more Seals came in with Jodie. One was helping Charlie. He thought he was dreaming when he saw Mark. Tears of joy were streaming down his face. He had a smile on his face that would have put the sun to shame. Dora went over to hug both Charlie and Mark. She told Charlie he would have to leave, but he would be fine with the corpsmen. "I have some unfinished business here."

Dora asked another Seal to look after the good doctor. "Take very good care of him. He will be needed to testify in Court."

"Yes, mama", the team member answered, "we understand. We'll be especially careful." They all headed up and exited the building. They saw bodies everywhere.

The teams were searching those that weren't dead. In the distance, they could hear the sound of gunfire and explosions. Dora was hoping that no one had killed Todd, Jr. She wanted that pleasure for herself. Likewise, the same thought was going through Carrie's head but with a different target in mind. Carrie wanted the pleasure of killing Laurence. She had been waiting a long time. A very long time.

Chapter Thirteen

Dora's team moved as fast as they could to rejoin the fight. Dora was on the radio with the Recon leader. "We're en route. We'll muster in the court yard." He gave her a 'roger', over and out. As they got closer to the fighting, they heard women and children screaming bloody murder. This was what was holding up the cleanup. Todd, Jr. had hustled all of the women and children into the courtyard knowing that Dora and her teams would not want to kill innocent people. The Airborne was dug in and not returning much fire. Most of the shooting was coming from within the house. Dora had an idea. She asked the 'angels' to blow a hole in the south wall.

"It leads to the fields. If the people can get there, they'll be safe. We've got to get into the house before those animals get away. They know this place better than we do and probably have another way out."

How right she was. There was a planned escape route in case the Mexican government ever changed their minds and tried to run them out. The escape was by sea. Only Todd, Jr. and his father knew about it. Todd, Jr. let the others in on the plan. The boat, he told them, was tethered just below the cliffs in a cove. It had twin mercury 600 hp engines.

"If we can make it to the boat, we have a good chance of getting to the seaplane we have moored further down the coast. Once aboard, we can get back to California before anyone knows we're gone. Let's get cracking."

Meanwhile, the 'angels" set off a bangaloid torpedo which blew a hole in the wall big enough for the people to get through. Once the dust settled and they saw the way clear, no one had to tell them twice to move.

As soon as the folks had cleared the area, the teams made their assault on the compound. The nonprofessionals didn't have the guts for this kind of fighting. They were ready to surrender. Most of them followed the women and children through the opening in the wall. The main body of fighters was in the house not in the courtyard. They would make their stand in the house giving the bosses a chance to escape. Todd, Sr., the son, the sheik and all the other bosses gathered all the money and documents that had been kept at the house. Stealthily, they left the house and made for the cove. Carrie told Dora and Mark that there was an escape route, but that she didn't know where it was.

"It may only be a rumor, but I wouldn't put it pass Todd to have planned a way out."

An all out assault was made on the house and the few mercenaries that remained standing, surrendered.

A thorough search was made of the house. Todd and company was gone.

Capt. Anthony, with his trained eye for detail, spied a hundred dollar bill on the floor caught in the wall by the fireplace. He bent down to pull it out, but it was stuck. He smiled and announced, "I think I've found their way out. Now let's see if we can find the button to open it." He was looking the wall over when Carrie grabbed a 203 from one of the men.

"I think I've found a key." She fired into the fireplace. The wall crumbled. Capt. Anthony looked at Carrie and laughed, "You need to see a shrink. You're extremely hostile." This had to be the first time she had ever seen or heard him laugh.

When the dust settled, the teams made their way slowly down the stairs. This was a perfect place for an ambush so they advanced very slowly. At the foot of the stairs was a long tunnel. It had clear sides no hidden spaces, so the teams rushed right on through. As they neared the entrance, the sounds of ocean and deep-throated powerful motors could be heard.

Back in California, David found himself on the hot seat. His boss wanted an update on his investigation into the number of murders that had taken place in the past month or so. David couldn't give him an answer. Although he was sure Dora was involved up to her pretty neck, he couldn't prove it—nor did he want to. He hadn't heard from her in the last few days and he was a little upset because he couldn't find her. He had called her home numerous times and even staked out the house. Nothing. He needed to know where she was and what she was up to.

Gypsy was doing a good job of staying out of sight. She managed to go and come and so far, no one knew she was around. She was getting very worried about Dora and the rest of the team. She wished they had taken her with them.

David had been watching the house since early morning. He knew there was someone in the house. Someone had been taking in the mail and he was going to find out 'whom' it was and why he or she wouldn't answer the phone. He was not going to rest until he found Dora. He wasn't going to put her in jail; he just wanted to know she was all right. David had made up his mind sometime ago, that if Dora went to jail, it would be someone else who put her there.

Curtis was still driving the cab and keeping his eyes and ears open. He hadn't heard anything from Dora either and he too, was getting nervous. He had come to really like and respect this lady and he didn't want anything to happen to her.

David saw the mailman coming down the street so he got out of the car and got as close to the house as he could without giving himself away.

Nothing happened for about a half an hour and then a very pretty woman came to the door. David sprinted for the yard and the porch so fast; Gypsy didn't have a chance to react. She knew who he was and was trying to get back through the door, but she was a mite to slow. He grabbed her arm and pulled her back out the door. He started asking questions and then suddenly stopped—he recognized her. This was Mark's girlfriend. He grinned, shaking his head.

"Gypsy! No one knew where you were. And here you are right in the cat's mouth. She tried to pull away from him, exhibiting a tremendous amount of strength, but he held on to her. Gypsy wasn't sure whether she should be afraid or not, but she was. This man was supposed to be a friend of Dora's and she didn't think he would hurt her, but she had learned not to trust folks when it came to money and drugs. He could be the devil himself or the boss of the whole operation. Gypsy was thinking she had been watching too much television. Why should she think this was one of the men who wanted to see her dead?

She took a deep breath and asked, "What do you want?"

David pushed her inside the house. "Listen, I am not going to hurt you. I just want to know where Dora is? I need to talk to her. That is all. You can go on hiding or whatever it is you're doing. I just need to see my baby."

Gypsy was thinking that he might be telling the truth, so she told him what she knew and where Dora was. David listened carefully to all Gypsy had to say, then said, "I want to go there. She may need my help. I won't be able to rest until I know she is all right."

Gypsy snickered, "If there's one thing Dora can do and do well, is take care of Dora. And remember, she is not alone."

"I know. I just have to see her and be sure."

Unknown to David, the sheriff had been tailing him all around town. He watched David go into the house. What was David doing? The sheriff called him on the cell phone and told him to meet him at the Cambridge Building. He then called one of his other deputies who did special jobs for him. He was going to get to the bottom of this mess once and for all. Then he would act.

David told the sheriff he'd be right there. As he left, David told Gypsy to let him know if she heard from Dora. He passed her a card with his numbers on it.

Gypsy said she would. Then she said something funny, "remember the Trojan horse" and she closed the front door.

As Dora and the teams reached the bottom of the cove, the boat was heading out to sea, throttles wide open. There was no way to catch them at this point. Dora was damn mad. She grabbed the weapon out of a Reno's hand. It was a sniper rig complete with scope. She raised it to her shoulder and took aim saying, "I have to keep my promise."

Regina understood and spotted her using her shoulder as a tripod. Elizabeth shouted out distance using binoculars that gave the range. Todd, Jr. was standing beside his dad aft on the boat and both were smiling as the land fell away. Liz continued to give range. Dora allowed for windage and fired. Seconds passed, then they saw a gaping hole where Todd, Jr. s' head used to be. She had kept her promised to take his head off. His father was reaching for him as his body was falling into the sea. He was screaming at the sight of his son being beheaded. The man looked very old at that moment. His son's brain was splattered all over his face. In his heart was hatred and revenge. He looked back at the spot where the shot came from in disbelief. The driver of the boat was pushing the engines hard. He didn't want to be the next one to die. He had a job to do. About twenty minutes later as the team was returning to the house, they saw a seaplane taking off. Lights went off in their heads.

Dora said, "A seaplane. They had a seaplane stashed away and they are headed back to California." She turned to Carrie, "Colonel can you get us a taxi?

"I think that can be arranged."

She got on the horn and called her friends. "I need a ride for me and my team, ASAP."

"Righto! Colonel. Where are you?" Carrie told him. It wasn't long before a HC 46 came in over the trees and landed to pick them up. Carrie also put through a call to the locals and informed them that the beaver was gone and they could come in and clean up the mess.

Carrie turned to the rest of the troops and smiled.

"Yeah! You guessed it; it was all part of the total plan. Though some things went awry. I can see you're all wondering, what is going on? The short version is—this was a setup and it worked. It wasn't given an official operation status, just in case it didn't work. The government, however, set up the joint operation to give you a smoke screen to get you in and get you out. Less than a handful of people knew the real deal. It had to be this way because there are a lot of people on the payrolls of these men, which included the Director of the FBI. Later, you will all be invited to a debriefing. You all did your country proud, today. Thank you." Carrie looked over at the girls. "Okay ladies, shall we go fishing and finish this job?" She led them over to the chopper.

The girls climbed aboard and sat looking at each other and the Colonel. They were headed back to the States still not believing what they had been told.

Mark and Capt. Anthony climbed aboard, too.

Dora spoke, "Colonel, it was you shooting at me on that back road, wasn't it?"

"Yes, I had to push you little. It was taking you too long to make your move."

"But what about the girls that were killed? What about Kim and Ruthie?" asked Regina.

"Unfortunately, we didn't count on Charlie making that phone call. And we found out too late to do anything about it."

"But they could have killed my mother and brother," rasped Dora.

"No, we knew they had to use them to get to you. Besides Mark was there at the camp and he could have stopped it anytime he wanted. We also had people in the house that no one knew about but us.

"Was it planned to let Christine and Lydia be demoralized like they were? Was it? Do you know how many lives could have been lost, if we weren't as good as we are?"

Carrie shifted uncomfortably. "We didn't plan for any of you to be captured. They played some cards we didn't expect. We covered every one of you as much as we could."

Capt. Anthony jumped in, "Lieutenant, do you remember in the alley when those men tried to take you out?"

"Yeah! I remember."

"Like 'All State' you were in good hands." Dora just looked at him and he said, "You're welcome."

"Sis, you have got to look at this like any other operation," said Mark. "Some live, some die, but it was all for the good of mankind. You and your team have always taken on any mission thrown your way without thinking about it, this was no different. We just needed to make it a little more personal. You put your heart and soul into this mission. And that was what was needed. These men have done some things you would never believe. Others have tried to take them down and were killed for their efforts. We knew that it would take a lot more than the norm. You and your team were it. We knew you would make the difference."

Dora looked at her handsome brother. "Just wait until I get you home."

Mark looked at his sister. He was thinking to himself, wondering really. "Is she angry, or what?" He would just have to wait and see.

A call came in for Mark as the chopper was on final approach. It was his missing team player, Mike. They talked for a few minutes and Mark signed off.

"That call was from Mike. He was one of the others we had in the house. He drove the boat for the Todds. He says they are all at the Cambridge Building, so let's go wrap this thing up."

Dora was thinking about her dead friends. About the abuse and rape of her teammates. How they treated her mother and brother. Now they were going to jail and could possibly be back out on the street in ten years or so. She looked into the faces of her friends. She could tell they were thinking the same thing. Feeling the same disenchantment of a justice system that would probably let these murderers and rapists, drug lords and thieves, go free.

"How did you know every move we made?"

Mark smiled, but Regina answered, "Gypsy! She was a plant, too. You played us like puppets."

"Okay! So we've been the prize idiots of the century. So what's going to happen to those dirt bags now that their fun house has been destroyed?" asked Dora.

Carrie responded by saying, "It's like it always is, baby. We do our job and move on. It's not for us to decide what happens to them."

The chopper landed and Dora told Regina to get Gypsy on the hook and have her bring the truck to the Cambridge Building. The 'sisters' climbed into the vehicles that were waiting for them and headed downtown.

Mark got another call from Mike and this time Curtis was with him. Mark was told the rats were still in the nest. Mark told them to stay put. They were on the way. Mike also told Mark that Mr. Walker had arrived. He had just entered the building. That made the list complete.

What they didn't know was that the sheriff and a few of his friends were questioning David. They wouldn't' believe he wasn't part of the whole operation. They beat him unmercifully trying to make him talk. David looked at the sheriff and spat, "I knew you were dirty, but I just didn't realize how much." The sheriff not wanting to hear anymore, cold cocked him and it was lights out.

The men were making plans to get out of the States fast. They were transferring all their assets to the Sheikh's home. He told them that this would be the safest place for all of their monies. While the bosses were very busy making their transfers and elated because they were getting away it, the troops were gathering outside the building.

Curtis pulled up to where Dora and Regina were standing on the curb. The girls climbed in the cab so they could talk.

"Okay Dora, what's the drill?" asked Regina.

"No drill. I guess they needed the drama to pull it off because it was in the States. They couldn't trust anyone."

"I understand all that's been said, however, we lost two of our sisters. Only blood for blood rates with me. Now that's a truth even you can't deny, Dora."

"I know, but what would you have me do? Orders are orders."

"That's right!" said Regina. "And these orders are only known to a chosen few. They can't do a thing about it."

Regina looked at her friend. "Do you remember when I said I would let you know when it was time to bring down this building?" Dora shook her head in the affirmative.

"Well, it's time."

The girls sat looking into each other's eyes. Regina recognized the moment Dora had made up her mind. Dora knew that there was only one way for this business to end. The way it was originally planned and no other. She and Regina got out of the cab and Dora told Curtis to get his cab off the street.

Dora went over to the Colonel. "How do you want to play this out?"

"We'll wait for them to come out and then detain them until the police get here."

Dora went back to Regina and told her to send an E-mail to Todd, Sr. It should read: "It was nice knowing you, then again, maybe it wasn't. Checkmate!"

The bosses were still putting their plans together when Dora's message came in.

It didn't make sense to any of them, but the sheikh, a little more savvy then the others, decided that he didn't like the sound of it. His dealings with Dora in the past gave him more of an inside track to her thinking. It was time to mosey out of here.

"Sheriff, how about having your deputy there change clothes with me. I'd like to go down on the front and see if anything is going on that we should be aware of."

David had regained consciousness and was watching this tableau. He was thinking how dumb the sheriff was. This guy was about to make a run for it dressed in the deputy's clothes.

Meanwhile, out on the street, Curtis met up with Mark and Mike. "Boy! am I glad to see you two alive? But what the hell is going on?" There was a lot of backslapping and hugs between the three of them. Mark said, "I'll fill you in later. There isn't time right now."

Curtis, still looking at Mark with a stupid look on his face, said "Okay."

Gypsy pulled the truck into place and the 'sisters' were going about their job of closing off the street to keep people out.

David waited his chance and silently made his way through the door. The men weren't paying him any attention. He headed down the stairs for the street.

Dora was standing next to the Colonel watching her girls go about their work. She was having a hard time with what she was about to do. This would probably end her career in the Army. Dora also knew that there was a possibility that she could end up in prison. All the members of the team felt the same way. This was not just another mission. The reasons they had been given were fine, but the lives lost by both her sister team and Mark's team made the whole operation questionable. She took a deep breath and picked up the mike hooked to the truck's loudspeaker.

Another deep breath and she depressed the button. "Sisters, this is Mother Superior. Pull the plug. I repeat, pull the plug. All of the 'sisters' began pulling back.

Capt. Anthony looked over at Dora and spotted the detonator in her hand. He called out in a very loud voice, "Lieutenant." He was trying to reach her when they heard the police sirens and a squad car came barreling around the corner. They both looked at the car and then at each other. Then the Captain saw the smile on her face and looked up in the direction in which Dora was looking. Standing at the window with a pair of binoculars, was Todd, Sr. Dora waved to him and held up the detonator so he could see it. She formed the word, "bomb." At this time, Regina sent another E-mail. This one read: "Kiss it goodbye."

Todd, Sr. saw her lips form the word 'bomb' and started screaming. "No…No…"

Everyone in the room turned to see what he was hollering about. Dora let her eyes view the building floor by floor like a person taking inventory. Just as she pushed the button to bring the building down, she saw a figure trying to get the door open to the street. She recognized David, but she couldn't stop her finger. London Bridge was coming down. It was an implosion of an immense magnitude. Her girls knew how to set explosives.

Dora's heart stopped beating as she watched the building come down. She was screaming David's name. Mark was watching the building collapse with disbelief. He couldn't believe what his sister had done. She had disobeyed orders and killed his best friend. The same man who loved Dora and whom she discovered in that few seconds, that she loved.

Everyone was covered in dust. Dora stood with head bowed when Carrie walked over to her. "You just had to do it your way, didn't you?" Dora started to shake her head when she noticed a man coming towards her covered in dust like everybody else. As he came closer, she realized it was David, very much alive.

She smiled at the Colonel and handed her the detonator. "Sorry Colonel, I just had to 'put my heart' into it."

She ran to David. They threw their arms around each other and hugged and kissed for several minutes. "I love you. I love you." Dora kept saying it over and over.

The police came over to them to place Dora under arrest. She was handcuffed and led away. Dora didn't care. She had to do what she had to do and that, as far as she was concerned, was that.

David got his head together and pulled the officer off to the side. He told him that he would take charge of the prisoner. The officer had no problem with it and walked away.

David led Dora off to the side. "Look, the next time you want me dead, you had better do it close up. Like get a gun and shoot me"

"Oh! Is that why you're putting me in jail?"

David laughed, "You needn't think you're going to get rid of me that easy."

He turned her around and removed the cuffs. Dora reminded him that by doing so, he would probably be finished as a cop.

"Then that will make two of us without a job. Care to go slumming?"

They were standing in the middle of the street kissing when Curtis pulled up in his cab and said, "Where to?"

David and Dora climbed into the back and continued their hugging and kissing as if they didn't have an audience.

Curtis peeked in the rearview mirror. "Oh well!" he muttered, "The oath of a cab driver is—hear nothing, see nothing, and know nothing."

They both looked up from the back seat and said, "Shut up!"

As the cab went by the team, the girls snapped to attention, gave them a salute and a thumbs up. The cop, who was trying to get information from Regina, asked, "Who is that?" Regina smiled at policeman and said, "That's our sister. Our Sister Without Mercy!"

When the smoke settled around what was left of the Cambridge Building, the government, realized with the help of the Colonel that no charges could be lodged against Dora for misconduct. The entire project had been mishandled and many innocent people had lost their lives.

The Colonel, who was supposed to be on the inside of the organization did not learn of the body parts operation until it was too late to save many of the people who had been killed in the clinic. That was the catalyst that sparked the Mexico/American joint maneuvers to close down the business once and for all.

No, there was no way they could prosecute Dora for what she had done. As the Colonel pointed out, she had trained the girls to react to situations and this she had done in spades. Her mother should never have been put in danger. Once that happened, all bets were off. Both Dora and David were cleared of all charges very quietly and competently by order of the President. The fact that a Senator and the Director of the FBI were also involved was more scandal then the administration wanted to deal with. The director was reported to have had a heart attack. He had requested that his body be cremated and his ashes spread across the Potomac. The Senator resigned because of ill-health and settled at home with the threat of death hanging over his head if he ever opened his mouth during his life time and over any remaining members of his family if he ever decided to write a historic document.

After a very military style wedding, Dora and David waited out her discharge from the Army before taking off for a long overdue vacation. They were standing in line at LAX airport looking into each other's eyes as if they couldn't yet believe they were actually going off on a Hawaiian honeymoon. Like the old tree in the backyard of Dora's home, they had weathered the storm and were about to set off to enjoy themselves as Mr. and Mrs. David would have to return to work in a few weeks, but for now, they would only think about each other.

Dora was hoping the years would be good to them and that they would never have to relive the past months again. The rest of the team was seeing them off at the airport en route to their base at Fort Campbell and to whatever assignment awaited them. But first, they wanted to see their 'sister' off on the best assignment she would ever get—that of a married woman. Dora had a glow that none of them had ever seen on her face. No one, seeing her now, would ever believe that this woman could be as deadly as she was feminine and beautiful.

Regina was standing next to her friend thinking, "I hope I can find a man I can love and who loves me like David loves Dora." They were all standing around laughing and joking when Regina noticed a change come over Dora. She followed the direction of Dora's eyes, trying to pick up on what or whom Dora saw. She just continued to stare off into space. Actually, she looked as if she had seen a ghost.

Both Regina and David shook her, and asked "What's up?" Dora looked at them and forced a smile saying, "I thought I saw someone I knew."

David and Dora's plane was called and since they were flying first class, they didn't have to wait for their seat number to be called. David and Regina turned her toward the jet way with the rest of girls hollering such things as; Have a good time! Don't do any thing I wouldn't do! And a few other ribald comments. Regina watched as Dora rubbed the back of her neck and continued to look around the airport lounge. Regina had seen that look and that gesture before. Whatever or whoever Dora thought she saw was not good. Dora shook her head dismissing it as nothing.

Little did she know that she was 100 percent correct. The man she had seen was none other then the Sheikh. He had been watching her from a distance. The Sheikh had made an oath to get even with Dora someday. "Maybe I'll wait until she has children," he thought. "Then take them back to my country and make slaves of them. If they are girl children, I'll raise them in my harem and sell them to the worse dog I can find." Dora would never know peace if he had his way.

The last hugs had been given, the door to the big 747 was closed and the plane was preparing to taxi to take-off. However, Regina could not forget the look on Dora's face nor could she forget the tell-tale itch on the back of Dora's neck. Her 'sister' had seen something that was highly disturbing. She only wished she knew what it was. The Colonel along with her team made their way to the plane that would take them back to Kentucky. The Colonel was the only one who knew all of the facts regarding Dora's release from active duty. She could be called back if it ever became necessary. Unfortunately, that could happen sooner than she thought because in her pocket was a note shoved into her hand at the airport. It was from the Sheikh, warning that he would see her again, someday. Carrie knew that she would have to watch her back for the rest of her life. So would Dora and the rest of the team. They had taken a lot from this man and he would be bound and determined to get even. Carrie looked up in time to see Regina watching her.

Regina determined that Carrie had the same look on her face as Dora had. She was thinking, "Maybe this isn't over yet." The team settled down for the long flight home.

Regina stretched out her legs and sighed, "What a way to make a living!"

In the other plane, Dora and David were thinking about the years to come while toasting each other at 35,000 feet as they winged their way across the Pacific.

EPILOGUE

Two Years Later…

"Sweetheart, shouldn't you be resting while you can. Our sisters will be awake and screaming for attention pretty soon."

"I know, but Mom is here. She said that she and Charlie would take care of the twins for a while. Otherwise, she wouldn't be able to get close to them. Seems their father keeps getting in the way. I wonder who she's talking about?"

"I wonder, too," David said. "Oh, Dora, I look at you and my beautiful girls and I thank God. I must be the luckiest man in the world. This could have ended up so much different if the government hadn't decided that they had made a big mistake with that operation. Your mother was ready to climb up on every soapbox she could find to tell her story, with Charlie at her side. She threatened to go to the newspapers, go on talk shows, write her own column. I tell you, they would have had to shut her up and a lot more people, besides."

David put his arm around his beautiful wife. Pulled her close and held her to him.

"I love you, Dora, so much. You and my girls."

"I know, honey. I love you, too. You know mom wasn't going to sit still and let them place her favorite daughter in jail. Not without a fight. And she thinks that you are the cat's meow. And too, you love her favorite daughter. She thought I would never wake up and find I loved you as much as you loved me. Mom had no intention of letting her future son-in-law lose his job. And it's a good thing. You have four mouths to feed now and a dog and cat and some gold fish. It wou…"

"Wait a minute. What dog, cat and goldfish? Last time I looked, we didn't have any animals."

"I know, honey. But we have to have a dog, cat, and goldfish for the kids."

"Why? Why must we have them?"

"All kids want animals. Didn't you, when you were a kid?"

"We're not talking about me." David stopped. "Dora, how much longer do we have to wait before we can, you know?"

"Oh! Didn't I tell you? It's all right for us to snuggle up close now."

"Are you sure?"

"Yep! The doctor said, and I quote, 'You may resume your marital relations as of today' unquote. So what do you think copper? Are you up to it? Or have you just been making all those long-suffering moans and groans at night to make me think you were in pain and you actually weren't."

"Oh, I'm up to it, all right. I just don't want to hurt you. You had a difficult pregnancy. As much as I love my girls, I don't want you to suffer like that again."

"Well, don't worry about it now. Just love me."

David pulled away from Dora long enough to remove his clothes down to his briefs. He gathered Dora in his arms and lay back on the pillow with her.

"I just need to hold you, for now. Do you mind?"

"No, you can do whatever you like. You're my husband."

"Yeah! I am, aren't I?"

The End